The Mythology Builder's Toolkit

Templates, Generators & Prompts for Writers, Worldbuilders & Game Masters

Hannibal Hills

Royal Wave Media, Inc.

The Mythology Builder's Toolkit

Templates, Generators & Prompts for Writers, Worldbuilders & Game Masters

Copyright © 2026 by Hannibal Hills

This book was developed with the assistance of AI tools, which were used for research, drafting, and structural development. All content was curated, verified, and edited by the author. The mythological references, analytical frameworks, editorial voice, and creative decisions are the author's own.

Interior illustrations generated using Midjourney.

First edition.

ISBN [ebook]: 978-1-956122-91-6

ISBN [paperback]: 978-1-956122-92-3

ISBN [hardcover]: 978-1-956122-93-0

Published by Royal Wave Media, Inc.

godsandmonsters.info

Cover design by Hannibal Hills

Contents

Introduction

WHY MYTH?

Let's be honest: "myth" is a word that's been manhandled. It shows up as clickbait ("Ten Myths About Coffee That Will Blow Your Mind"), weaponized as a synonym for "lie," or mummified in textbooks until even the gods would nod off. But myth isn't a relic; it's the software that's been running in the background since language itself booted up.

Strip away the academic varnish, and myth is the original operating system for being human. Before we had charts, we had stories about why the sky makes noise and why we love, fear, fight, or build. The old tales weren't just distractions around the fire. They explained the unexplainable, gave meaning to chaos, and mapped out who we are and who we might become.

Myth, at its core, isn't about believing in the Minotaur or arguing whether Loki "really" existed. It's about making sense of a world that refuses to make itself simple. Myths let us name the monsters in the dark, whether that darkness is in the woods or inside ourselves, and then imagine ways to survive the night.

Modern life likes to think it's outgrown myth, but that's just another myth, a particularly bland one. We binge-watch hero's journeys, argue over origin stories, and spend hours online weaving new digital folklore. The hunger for myth never went away. It just put on new costumes.

This book isn't about putting myth in a museum. It's about handing you the keys to the forge and saying: go make something that matters. The world isn't finished, and neither are its stories.

WHO THIS BOOK IS FOR

If you've picked up this book, chances are you've already felt the itch, the urge to create, to make sense of the world, or maybe just to mess with it a little. Maybe you're a novelist, a game designer, a teacher trying to spark something in a restless classroom, or someone who's always been myth-curious but never found the right doorway in. Maybe you've never put "myth-maker" on a business card, but something in you knows the old stories aren't just decorations on history; they're blueprints for what comes next.

You don't need credentials to belong here. You don't have to be a classicist or a cultist, fluent in dead languages or up to your elbows in Joseph Campbell. The only requirement is a willingness to poke at the world and see what answers bubble up when you tell a new story.

This book is for the architects and the tinkerers, the epic dreamers and the meticulous worldbuilders, the skeptical and the wonder-struck alike. Whether you want to build a cosmos from scratch, breathe new life into an ancient legend, or just kick the tires of your own imagination. Welcome. The forge is open.

HOW TO USE THESE TOOLKITS

Let's get something straight: this isn't a cookbook. There's no sacred order, no required ingredients list, no "follow these ten steps and, presto!, you'll summon the gods of creativity." Real myth-making is messier than that, and frankly, more fun.

These toolkits are exactly what the word promises: a set of tools, not commandments. Take what you need. Ignore what you don't. Build from the ground up, jump to the middle, skip ahead, or circle back. There's no penalty for creative trespassing.

Each chapter opens a different door. Some readers will work through them all, constructing a living mythology brick by brick. Others might just grab what they need for a single tale or character. Game designers could treat each toolkit as a quest generator. Teachers might use them to spark curiosity in students who've never found myth especially relevant, until now. Every chapter stands on its own, but together, they give you everything you need to build a mythic world from the cosmic backdrop down to the tiniest folk legend.

Worried about "getting it right"? Don't. There is no one way to myth. The only real mistake is waiting for someone else to give you permission. Consider this your permission slip.

WHAT'S INSIDE

We're offering you nine chapters, each built as a workshop: tools, archetypes, worked examples, and a creative dare at the end of every one.

Chapter 1: Genesis Engine. How worlds begin. Creation myths, the six archetypes of cosmic origin, and the Shape of the Cosmos: how the act of making determines the architecture of what's made. If the world was torn from a giant's corpse, the underworld might be the giant's gut. If it was sung into being, there might be places where the song went flat. You'll build a creation myth and let the map grow out of it.

Chapter 2: Pantheon Builder. Gods, spirits, and the Divine Spectrum: the full continuum from the deity who made the sun to the ghost who haunts the kitchen. Most worldbuilding books separate gods, spirits, ancestors, and the hungry dead into different chapters. We're not going to do that. We're going to build them as one ecosystem, because in every living mythology, they already are.

Chapter 3: Bloodlines & Legacy. Ancestry as a political weapon. Generational curses, inherited destinies, sacred talismans, and the Adopted Line, the archetype that demolishes the assumption that blood determines belonging. The dead aren't sleeping. They're arguing about the silverware.

Chapter 4: The Hero & The Villain. Built together, not apart. The Mirror Framework: shared origin, divergent choices, complementary wounds, and a resolution that costs both sides. The villain is the truth the hero doesn't want to face, given a body and a voice and a plan.

Chapter 5: Trickster Creation Kit. The chapter that breaks its own rules. Shapeshifters, sacred fools, boundary-crossers, and the figure your mythology is afraid of. A world without tricksters is a world trapped in its own propaganda.

Chapter 6: Monster Ecologist. Creatures, undead, and the Hunger Principle: every monster worth building wants something beyond what it eats, and what it wants reveals the wound in the world that made it necessary. We'll build them as an ecology: interconnected, co-dependent, dangerous, and alive.

Chapter 7: Relics & Sanctums. Objects and places of power, built as pairs. The Pairing Principle: every relic implies a sanctum, every sanctum hungers for a relic. Excalibur needs the stone. The Grail needs the chapel. Separate them and both diminish.

Chapter 8: The Living Myth. Festivals, curses, and prophecies: the social skeleton of a mythology, the part that shows up on the calendar and changes what people eat, who they marry, and which roads they won't walk after dark. This is where myth stops being backstory and starts being daily life.

Chapter 9: Quest & Apocalypse. How the journey and the ending are the same story at different scales. The Scale Shift: every quest is a small apocalypse, every apocalypse is someone's quest. This is the chapter that closes the circle.

THE LOOM

One more thing. Across this book, we're going to build a mythology from scratch.

It starts in Chapter 1: a weaver, a grief, a song that becomes a world, and it accumulates chapter by chapter, growing more complicated, more contradictory, and more alive as each new toolkit adds a layer. By the time you reach Chapter 9, you'll have watched a complete myth cycle take shape: creation, gods, bloodlines, heroes, tricksters, monsters, relics, prophecy, quest, and apocalypse. It's called the Loom, and it appears at the end of every chapter in a register that's different from the instructional voice: mythic, spare, and strange.

Think of it as the book practicing what it preaches. And if you want to build alongside it, starting your own myth from scratch, adding a layer with each chapter, the invitation is open.

WHY THIS APPROACH?

The world's great myths weren't written by committees or polished by editors in search of a market. They were thrown together by people with questions and a bit of nerve, people who weren't afraid to mash up the sacred and the profane, mix borrowed stories with homegrown fears, or twist the rules for the sheer pleasure of seeing what happened next. If they'd waited for permission, we'd still be sitting in the dark.

This book is built on the stubborn belief that myth-making should be hands-on, playful, and gloriously idiosyncratic. It's a deliberate rebellion against the two camps that dominate the field: the academic, which suffocates you with footnotes and theory until your eyes glaze over, and the formulaic, which promises a shortcut to greatness if you just color inside the lines. Neither feels much like creative freedom.

You won't find pages of "correct" myths to memorize. There's no masterclass in dissecting ancient epics, and no formula that promises to do the hard work for you. What you will find is a set of tools, sometimes messy, sometimes sharp, that only work if you pick them up and use them. This isn't a substitute for your imagination, and it won't do the heavy lifting for you. It won't protect you from creative risk, or guarantee that what you make will matter to anyone but yourself. That's the point.

The mythic tradition doesn't need another rulebook. It needs a thousand new sparks. Here's your invitation to light your own.

WHAT MYTH-MAKING OFFERS YOU

It's easy to shrug off stories as entertainment, as if myth is just a luxury for bored minds. But anyone who's ever lost themselves in a tale, or built a world from scratch, knows it runs deeper than that. Myth is the original technology for transformation. It's how we make sense of joy and suffering, order and chaos, the private and the cosmic. When you create myth, you're not just killing time; you're tuning yourself to the oldest frequencies in the human mind.

There's a reason every culture, everywhere, has spun stories about creation and destruction, monsters and tricksters, gods and ghosts. Myths are blueprints for handling the rough stuff: fear, longing, exile, the urge to build or burn. They let us play out our deepest dilemmas in safe territory, inventing heroes who get back up after a fall and villains who reveal something uncomfortable about ourselves.

For writers and worldbuilders, myth is the master key. It lets you create stories that stick: characters with gravity, worlds with depth, conflicts that matter. But the gift goes further. Myth-making trains you to ask better questions, to spot patterns in the noise, and to look at the mess of real life and see meaning hiding in the shadows.

Myth isn't just for stories about far-off gods or dragons. It's for anyone trying to make sense of this world: its chaos, its cruelty, its flickers of beauty and hope. It offers a way to connect with the past, but also to invent futures. It lets you make a world that isn't only inherited, but imagined.

Maybe you want to entertain, to provoke, to heal, or just to amuse yourself. Good. Myth is flexible. It grows with its maker. The world has enough algorithms and automated answers. What it needs now are new stories: new ways to dream, to argue, to wonder. Making myth isn't just a hobby. It's a way of staying alive, and helping the world stay alive with you.

So, grab your tools. Stoke the fire. The forge is hot, the toolkit's open, and the old rules are yours to keep or discard. Whatever you make here, make it boldly. Question everything. Mix the sacred and the profane, the old and the brand new. The world's never been finished, and the stories that matter most are still waiting to be written.

Let's get to work.

Chapter 1: Genesis Engine

Origins, Cosmology, and the Shape of Worlds

I. Opening Manifesto

Every world begins in darkness, or, more accurately, in confusion. The first lie any god tells is, *"I made this on purpose."* That's the grubby truth behind every creation myth, whether scratched onto bone, mumbled over a campfire, or hammered out in the mind of a midnight novelist: we crave beginnings that make sense, even when sense is the last thing the cosmos ever had.

Creation myths are the bones beneath your story's skin. They're why your readers believe your world exists, and why it hurts when it breaks. Too many builders settle for borrowed myths or limp Tolkien-knockoffs, a vague god, a vague darkness, a vague explosion of light that reads like someone photocopied Genesis with the serial numbers filed off. You can do better. You *must* do better, because the shape of your creation determines the shape of everything that follows: the gods that wake inside it, the monsters lurking at its edges, and the places where reality starts to fray.

Here's your blueprint. You'll learn how real-world cosmogonies work, why they contradict themselves, and how to invent something only you could write. We'll move from *how the world was made* to *what shape the making gave it*, because a creation myth that doesn't produce a cosmos isn't finished. It's wallpaper. Stick around. I'll build a myth live, no safety net, and dare you to write the one your world is afraid to speak aloud.

II. WHAT IS A CREATION MYTH?

A creation myth explains how the world, its laws, and its monsters came to be.

That's the textbook answer. Here's the real one: a creation myth is the story a culture tells itself about why anything exists at all, and it always, *always*, reveals more about the tellers than the told. It's not history. It's a narrative weapon: explanation, justification, warning, and sometimes cosmic joke, all braided together. Get it right, and every other story you tell inside that world resonates with a strange authority. Get it wrong, and your world is a theme park.

Every culture on Earth has one. Most are stranger, sadder, or funnier than you remember from school. In the Kono creation story of Guinea, the old man Sa, who is also Death, builds a muddy hut on a river of slime, and his guest Alatangana improves the place by solidifying the earth and planting trees. The world gets better, and the price is that Sa can now claim anyone's children whenever he chooses. In the Heliopolitan myth of Egypt, the god Atum pulls himself into being from an infinite dark ocean, then sneezes out the god of air and spits out the goddess of moisture, creation by bodily function, the cosmos as a magnificent accident of phlegm. In the Ainu tradition of northern Japan, the creator deity Kamui sends a confused little wagtail to stomp mud into solid ground, and the bird flutters and stamps and beats its tail until the islands appear, the world shaped by a creature too small to understand what it was making.

These stories aren't quaint. They're engines. Each one generates an entire worldview: who made us, what we owe, what went wrong, and whether anything can be fixed. Your creation myth will do the same for your fictional world, whether you write it into the text or bury it beneath the surface where only you and the world itself can feel it humming.

III. Core Archetypes: How the Cosmos Gets Made

Every creation story is a remix of a few key moves. Here's your menu, not a checklist, but a palette. Mix them. Break them. Let two archetypes collide and see what crawls out of the wreckage.

1. The Personal God

A singular, willful creator speaks, thinks, or commands the world into being. The defining feature: *intention*. Someone meant for this to happen. In Genesis, God speaks and the universe obeys. In Yoruba tradition, Obatala descends from the sky on a golden chain, scatters sand over the primordial waters, and lets a five-toed hen scratch it into continents. The Memphite theology of Egypt gives us Ptah, who conceives the world in his heart and speaks it into existence, creation as an act of divine rhetoric.

The gift of this archetype: purpose. The world exists because someone wanted it to. The trap: if your creator is too perfect, too intentional, then suffering becomes a design flaw and your myth has to answer for it. The most interesting Personal God myths leave room for regret, surprise, or the creator walking away from the mess they've made.

2. The Corpse World

A primeval being is slain, or dies, or is dismembered, and the body becomes the raw material of the cosmos. In Norse mythology, the gods kill the frost giant Ymir and build the world from his remains: his flesh becomes the earth, his blood the seas, his skull the vault of the sky. The Chinese tradition of Pangu tells of a cosmic giant who dies after holding sky and earth apart for eighteen thousand years, his body dissolving into the landscape, his breath becoming wind, his voice thunder, his left eye the sun and his right the moon. The Aztec creation myth describes the gods tearing the monstrous earth-crocodile Cipactli in half to fashion the ground beneath and the heavens above.

This is creation as violence, sacrifice, or entropy. The gift: the world is made of something that was once alive, and that aliveness never entirely leaves. Every mountain is a knuckle. Every river is a vein. Landscapes can ache. The trap: the Corpse World encodes suffering into the bedrock. The world began in death, so death belongs here, and beauty is just the shimmer on a corpse. If you're not careful, your whole mythology becomes a dirge.

3. The Cosmic Craftsman

The world is shaped, forged, or built, often from raw chaos, by a figure who is less a god and more an artisan. In Dogon tradition from Mali, the blacksmith god Amma shapes the earth like a potter working clay, and the world carries the marks of his hands. The Greek Prometheus molds humans from river mud. The Finnish Kalevala gives us Ilmarinen, the eternal hammerer, who forges the dome of the sky and pins the stars in place.

The gift: skill, labor, and the implication that the world can be *understood* because it was *designed*. A crafted world can have seams and flaws the maker didn't intend. It also implies tools, and tools can be stolen, lost, or wielded by someone who shouldn't have them. The trap: if the world was built, then somewhere the blueprints might still exist, and someone is going to go looking for them.

4. THE BIRTHER

The universe is born, hatched, or grown, painful, messy, alive. Greek myth gives us Gaia, the earth herself, who springs from Chaos and then gives birth to the sky, the mountains, and the sea without needing a partner. In Māori tradition, Ranginui the Sky Father and Papatuanuku the Earth Mother lie locked in a tight embrace, their many children trapped in the darkness between them until the god Tane forces his parents apart with his legs, creation as a family argument that reshapes the cosmos, and the rain that falls is Ranginui's grief. World Egg myths appear across Hindu, Orphic Greek, Finnish, and Chinese traditions: a cosmic egg cracks open to release the raw material of existence.

The gift: intimacy. Creation carries the weight of parenthood, the world was made in pain, the makers love what they made, and separation is the price of growth. It's the archetype that most naturally encodes grief, because birth always means something that was whole is now divided. The trap: the Birther archetype can slide into sentimentality. If the cosmic parents are *too* sympathetic, you risk a world that feels coddled rather than wild. The best Birther myths, like the Māori, let the family argument be genuinely violent.

5. THE ACCIDENTAL

No one meant for this to happen. Creation by overflow, dream, blunder, or cosmic glitch, the world as an unintended consequence. The Kuba people of Central Africa tell of Mbombo, a white giant alone in primordial darkness, who vomits the sun, moon, and stars out of sheer stomach pain, and the heat of the sun dries the waters, and the dry land appears, and none of it was planned. Australian Aboriginal Dreaming traditions describe an eternal time when ancestral beings moved across a formless land, and the landscape arose not from intention but from their actions, their journeys, their songs, creation as a side effect of *being*. (A caveat: the Dreaming is a living, continuous cosmology far richer than any single archetype can contain. It sits here as the closest fit, not a tidy one.)

The gift: liberation. There is no Grand Plan. There might not even be a Planner. The world just *happened*, which means your characters are truly on their own, and any meaning they find, they'll have to make for themselves. The trap: a world without intentional creation can feel adrift. If nothing was meant, then nothing is sacred, and a world where nothing is sacred can be hard to care about. The trick is giving the accident *consequences* that feel as weighty as purpose.

6. THE UNLIKELY / THE SMALL

The world is shaped by something modest, overlooked, or absurd. In the Ainu myth, it's a wagtail, a tiny bird sent by the deity Kamui to stomp mud into islands, fluttering and stamping without understanding what it's making. In many Native American earth-diver traditions, it's a muskrat or a beetle who dives into the primordial waters to bring up a pawful of mud that becomes the continent. In the Kalevala, the creation of the world hinges on a bird landing on the knee of Ilmatar as she floats in an endless ocean, and the egg it lays, when it rolls off her knee and shatters, becomes the earth, sky, sun, and moon.

The gift: wonder. The biggest things can come from the smallest causes. The confused little bird flapping over the mud might be the most important creature in the universe, and it doesn't even know it. The trap: "small" can become "twee." If your unlikely creator is too cute, the myth loses its weight. The best Unlikely myths carry a note of cosmic indifference, the wagtail doesn't know it's building a world, and the world doesn't care.

Author's Hack: Don't settle for "water and darkness" as your primordial state. Let your world's origin be a taste, a rumor, a regret, or the sound of a god's first curse. Try creation by music gone wrong. Try a world that exists because someone forgot to stop dreaming. Try a cosmos that's actually a wound. Strange is memorable, and memorable is what keeps readers believing.

IV. THE SHAPE OF THE COSMOS

No world is truly mythic until its edges fray, until the road splits, the river vanishes, and somewhere out there, logic breaks.

A creation myth doesn't just explain *how*, it produces a *where*. The act of making determines the architecture of what's made. If your world was hatched from an egg, then maybe it's round, enclosed, layered in shell and membrane. If it was torn from a corpse, maybe every landscape echoes the anatomy it was carved from. If it was woven, well, we'll get to weaving.

This is where creation and cartography merge. The most resonant mythic worlds don't just have maps, they have *structures* that are direct consequences of how they came to be. Here are the places that creation leaves behind.

THE UNDERWORLD

Every mythic cosmos has a place for its dead, and the nature of the underworld reveals what the culture fears about endings. Greek Hades is a bureaucracy of shade and forgetting. The Maya Xibalba is a sadistic obstacle course run by death gods who find suffering hilarious. The Egyptian Duat is a twelve-hour night journey through which the dead must navigate with spells and maps, because even in death, the Egyptians believed in being prepared. Norse Hel is cold, gray, and mostly just boring, which might be the most terrifying underworld of all.

The gift: death becomes a *place*, which means it can be visited, mapped, and broken into. The trap: if getting in is easy and getting out is unremarkable, you've built a subway station, not a mythic threshold. The best underworlds cost something to enter and something worse to leave.

THE SPIRIT ROAD

Paths, rivers, trees, and bridges that link the realms. Yggdrasil, the Norse World Tree, connects nine worlds through its roots and branches, and even the gods must travel its length to reach each other. The River Styx divides the Greek living world from the dead, and crossing it costs a coin. In Yoruba cosmology, the crossroads is where the living world (Aiye) and the spirit realm (Orun) intersect, watched over by the orisha Eshu, who controls passage and demands respect.

The gift: borders imply gatekeepers, gatekeepers imply prices, prices imply negotiations, tricks, bargains, and betrayals. Every threshold crossing is a scene waiting to happen. The trap: if your spirit roads are always open and always safe, they stop being thresholds and become highways.

THE FAERIE REALM / PARALLEL WORLD

A place of altered time, reversed logic, or living metaphor that exists alongside the main world. In Irish tradition, the sidhe live under the hills, and their time runs differently, a night's feasting might be a century in the mortal world. The Shinto concept of Takamagahara places the heavenly realm above, home of the kami, while the terrestrial and underworld realms each operate by different laws.

The gift: a parallel world lets you run two sets of rules simultaneously and generate story from the friction between them. Characters who cross over carry the wrong assumptions; characters who return find their world has moved on without them. The trap: parallel worlds that are too internally consistent become merely *alternate* worlds, interesting, but not mythic. Their logic should feel dreamlike: coherent in the moment, impossible to explain afterward.

THE DREAMSCAPE

Worlds made of thought, memory, or dream, fluid, dangerous, revelatory. Australian Aboriginal traditions describe the Dreaming not as a distant past but as an ongoing reality: a layer of existence where ancestral beings still move, and the land itself is a living record of their journeys. The Tibetan Buddhist concept of the Bardo describes an intermediate state between death and rebirth where the dead encounter visions shaped by their own consciousness, the afterlife as a mirror, not a destination.

The gift: the dreamscape is the most flexible cosmic structure because its rules are subjective. What one character sees, another doesn't. For worldbuilders, the dreamscape is where the world's repressed truths surface, the things the waking world can't or won't acknowledge. The trap: total subjectivity is total chaos. A dreamscape with no rules at all becomes a narrative free-for-all where nothing matters. Establish *some* logic, dream-logic, yes, but logic, and let characters discover what it is.

THE FORBIDDEN ZONE

Haunted ruins, plague zones, wild borders, cosmic voids, the places that creation left unfinished or that have been ruined since. Every great mythic world has a place where you *cannot go*, or more precisely, where you *should not go* but someone always does. The Blasted Heath, the Bermuda Triangle, Chernobyl's exclusion zone: these are the places where the rules of the world visibly fail, and the failure itself becomes a landmark.

The gift: forbidden zones are your world's mystery engines. They generate rumors, expeditions, heretics, and the kind of characters who can't leave a closed door alone. They also provide a pressure valve, a place where the tensions of your creation myth are physically manifest. If the world was made by violence, the forbidden zone is the wound. If made by song, it's where the song went silent. The trap: a forbidden zone that everyone avoids and no one visits is scenery, not story. Someone has to go there. Something has to come back out.

THE CELESTIAL COURT

Sky kingdoms, heavenly bureaucracies, and houses of the gods. Mount Olympus. The Jade Emperor's Court in Chinese tradition. The divine assembly in Mesopotamian myth where the gods meet to argue over the fate of humans. These are the places where cosmic politics happen, and cosmic politics, like all politics, are petty, vindictive, and absurdly human.

The gift: a celestial court makes your gods accountable to each other, with hierarchies, rivalries, and resentments that generate story. Divine authority becomes negotiated, not absolute. The trap: celestial courts that are too orderly become dull. The best are magnificent messes, gorgeous, dysfunctional, and one bad day away from civil war.

The key principle: your creation myth should *produce* your cosmic structure as a natural consequence. If the world was torn from a giant's corpse, the underworld might be the giant's gut. If it was woven on a loom, the edges might fray into a realm of unraveling. If it was sung into being, there might be places where the song went flat, dissonant zones where reality warps.

Don't build your map and then bolt a creation story onto it. Build your creation story and let the map *grow out of it.*

V. THE GENESIS ENGINE: WORKSHOP

This isn't a quiz. It's a build. We're going to construct a creation myth from the ground up, and along the way, we'll make the world it produces. Grab a notebook. Work fast. Let the contradictions in.

STEP 1: START WITH NOTHING

Before the world, there was __________.

Not darkness. Not water. Not unless you mean it. What is the texture of your void? The Kalevala starts with a lonely goddess floating on an endless sea. The Kono myth starts with Sa and his family adrift in a murky, lightless slime. The Norse begin with Ginnungagap, a gap between fire and ice that's not emptiness but *potential*, the collision point where opposites will meet.

Your "nothing" is your world's first aesthetic choice. It will color everything that follows. If the void was silence, then sound is sacred. If the void was hunger, then abundance is a miracle and famine is a return to the original state. In the Sour Note example later in this chapter, the void is a chord, total harmony, with no variation. That one choice made the entire world a story about music, dissonance, and the terror of perfect silence.

Write it down. One sentence. What came before everything.

STEP 2: CHOOSE YOUR PRIME MOVER

Who or what made the world? A god, a monster, a child, a force, an accident? Are they conscious? Wounded? Proud? Bored? Did they mean to do this, or did the world happen *to* them?

Here's the move most beginners miss: your creator doesn't have to be sympathetic or comprehensible. The Gnostic traditions give us a *flawed* creator, a god who botched the job, and the world's suffering is the evidence. That's a creation myth that generates an entire theology of resistance. In the Sour Note, there is no maker at all, the chord breaks on its own, and the "prime mover" is a frequency that drifted. The heretics call it the First Freedom. The priests call it the original sin.

Name your maker. One sentence. What are they, and did they mean to do this?

STEP 3: DEFINE THE ACT

Is the world spoken, sung, hammered, bled, excreted, birthed, broken, woven, dreamed, or stolen? The verb matters more than you think. In Hindu tradition, Brahma's self-division produces the cosmos, creation as a fracturing of the self. In the Popol Vuh of the K'iche' Maya, the gods attempt creation multiple times and keep failing, they make people from mud (too soft), then wood (too empty), before finally getting it right with maize. That's creation as *iteration*, and it means the world carries the memory of its own drafts.

The act of creation determines the world's material. A spoken world is made of language. A bled world is made of sacrifice. A woven world is made of thread, and thread can be cut.

Name the act. One verb. How did the making happen?

STEP 4: WHAT WENT WRONG?

This is the step most worldbuilders skip, and it's the one that makes the difference between a myth and a Wikipedia entry. Something in the creation was incomplete, unwanted, or broken. Monsters came from the leftover scraps. Death entered through a bargain no one should have struck. The light reached everywhere except one place, and that place became a wound. In the Sour Note, the "wrong" is the shattering itself, the break that made the world possible also made the world imperfect. Every fragment carries a partial tone. Nothing is whole. And somewhere, the original sour note is still missing.

A too-tidy creation is a dead one. Leave something unfinished. Leave something *dangerous.*

Name the flaw. What was broken, missing, or left behind?

STEP 5: MAP THE AFTERMATH

Now let the creation produce the world it implies. This is where you shift from origin story to cosmic architecture.

Walk through the consequences: If the world was torn apart, where are the seams? If it was sung, where did the song go flat? Think about the structures from Section IV. Does your world have an underworld? What made it? Who guards the borders between realms, and what does passage cost? Is there a forbidden zone, a wound in the landscape where the rules visibly fail? Where do the dead go, and who decided?

In the Sour Note, the creation produced four structures: the Fundamental (the center no one can reach), the Overtone (the half-real dreamscape above), the Silence (the terrifying below), and the Dissonant Lands (the edges where reality warps). None were "designed", they all grew from a single premise: a shattering chord.

Draw the map. What places did your creation leave behind? Name at least two: one above or beyond the world, and one below or beneath it.

STEP 6: WHO TELLS THIS STORY?

A creation myth is never neutral. It's told by someone, for someone, with an agenda. The priests tell one version to justify the throne. The outcasts whisper another in the dark. The heretics have a third that could get you killed.

Who in your world controls the creation story? Who doubts it? What happens when myths clash? In the Sour Note, the priests maintain a four-hundred-year choir because they believe silence will end the world. The heretics think the sour note was freedom, not sin. Children with perfect pitch are watched by the authorities. These aren't background details, they're the engine of the world's politics.

Name the tellers. Who tells this myth, who doubts it, and what do they each have to gain?

VI. QUICK MENU FOR INSPIRATION

Stuck? Pick one from each column and see what collides.

Primordial Texture: Silence - Hunger - A chord - Static - Regret - Fever - Endless water - The smell of iron - A single sustained scream - Boredom

Prime Mover: A god who forgot - A corpse - A child - An animal too small - A force with no name - Two enemies - An absence - A machine - A wound - No one

The Act: Spoken - Bled - Hammered - Woven - Vomited - Split - Dreamed - Stolen - Grown - Sung off-key

What Went Wrong: The maker died - Something was left out - A second maker interfered - The material fought back - The world remembers its void - Nothing went wrong (and that's the problem) - The creation is still happening - A piece was stolen - The making couldn't stop - Someone lied about how it happened

The Shape It Left: Layers - A wound - Echoes - A maze - A prison - Concentric rings - A body - Fraying edges - A silence at the center - A road with no end

VII. Worked Examples

The Classic Model

"In the beginning, there was only darkness and endless water. The first god, exhausted by loneliness, spit into the void, her spit became land, her sigh became wind, and her regret became the first shadow. But she was tired, and she could not finish. The southern coast trails off into fog because she fell asleep before she got there. The mountains in the north are too tall because she was angry and her hands shook. And the shadow, the first shadow, made from the first regret, crept into the place where she rested and made a home there, and it has been there ever since, whispering to anyone who sleeps too long."

This is the safe version, clean, archetypal, effective. It uses the Personal God and the Accidental archetypes together. Notice that even the "Classic Model" has a flaw (the unfinished south, the angry mountains) and an unresolved threat (the living shadow). Without those, it's a bedtime story. With them, it's a world.

The Sour Note (Showcase)

Before the world, there was a chord.

Not silence, silence came later, and was afraid. The chord had no beginning because it had never needed one. It simply was: a sound so complete that the concept of "music" didn't apply. Music implies variation. The chord was everything, and everything was enough.

Until it wasn't.

The break started small. A single frequency, the texts disagree on which, began to vibrate at a slightly different rate. Not much. A quarter-tone's difference, less than a hair's width in the architecture of sound. But in a system built on absolute harmony, a quarter-tone is a cataclysm.

The frequency fought to return to the chord. The chord fought to absorb it. Neither won. The struggle produced heat, and the heat produced light, and the light illuminated what the chord had never needed to see: that it had an inside and an outside. That it had edges. That it was, despite its wholeness, a thing among potential things.

The sour note, for that is what the devout call it, and what the heretics call the First Freedom, could not be reabsorbed. It shattered outward, and every fragment that broke from the chord carried its own partial tone: land from the bass notes, sky from the treble, water from the middle registers where sound feels like touch. The living things came from the overtones, the ghost-frequencies that exist inside every sound but are never quite heard. This is why, the philosophers say, all living things seem to be searching for something they can almost remember but never name.

The world the shattering made has a structure the scholars call the Resonance. At its center is the Fundamental, a place no one can reach but everyone can hear in rare moments of total silence. It hums beneath the ground, beneath the ocean floor, beneath the roots of the oldest trees. The priests say it is the last remnant of the original chord. The heretics say it is the sour note, still singing, still free, still refusing to harmonize.

Above the world stretches the Overtone, a shimmering, half-real realm that exists in the spaces between sounds. Dreamers visit it. Musicians stumble into it during performances they cannot afterward remember. The dead are said to dissolve into it, their individual frequencies slowly merging back into the ambient hum of the cosmos.

Below the world is the Silence, and it is feared. The Silence is what exists where the chord does not reach: the places where creation's reverberations have faded to nothing. Things live in the Silence, but they are not things that were made. They are what was left when making stopped. They are holes in the music shaped like hunger.

At the borders of the world, where the last echoes of creation grow faint, the sound distorts. These are the Dissonant Lands, places where the original frequencies collided and never resolved. Time stutters. Geography contradicts itself. The trees grow sideways and the rivers run in circles. Travelers who enter the Dissonant Lands report hearing music that makes them weep without knowing why. Some come back changed. Some come back singing a note that no one in the known world has ever heard before.

And at the heart of the world's greatest temple, the priesthood maintains a single sustained tone, a choir that has not stopped singing in four hundred years. They believe that if the tone ever ceases, the world will notice the silence, and the Silence will notice the world.

The sour note has never been found. But every child born with perfect pitch is watched carefully by the authorities. And every musician knows the rule: you may play in any key, in any mode, in any rhythm you choose. But there is one interval that is forbidden. The priests call it the Dissonance. The musicians call it the god-gap. And late at night, when the choir shifts and the sustained tone wavers for just a heartbeat, some say they can hear it, the original break, the first imperfection, the sound that made the world possible by making the chord imperfect.

They say it sounds like laughter.

Notice what happened: the creation myth (a chord shatters) produced the cosmic structure (the Fundamental, the Overtone, the Silence, the Dissonant Lands). The unfinished element (the missing sour note) generates ongoing tension. The rival interpretations create political conflict. The forbidden interval gives every musician a secret to keep. That's what a Genesis Engine does. It doesn't just explain how the world began, it generates the world's ongoing problems.

VIII. Pitfalls, Traps, and Common Mistakes

The Borrowed Myth Trap. Your creation myth reads like Tolkien's with the names swapped, or like Norse mythology with a coat of paint. Influence is inevitable and fine. Pastiche is death. If a well-read friend could name your source in one guess, start over.

Too Neat, Too Safe. You answered every question your myth raises. There are no gaps, no contradictions, no loose threads. Congratulations, you've written a Wikipedia entry, not a myth. Real creation stories contradict themselves. They leave gaps. They sometimes offer two incompatible explanations and shrug. Let your myth contain the mess.

No Consequences. Your creation myth is a pretty story that has no bearing on your world's politics, geography, religion, or daily life. It's decoration. A good creation myth is a load-bearing wall: pull it out and the world falls down. If your myth doesn't explain at least one thing about why your world works the way it does, it isn't working hard enough.

Explaining the Monster Away. You left nothing unfinished, nothing unexplained, nothing that could crawl out of the dark and surprise anyone, including you. The power of a creation story comes from what it *doesn't* resolve. What's still loose? What was never explained? What question does the myth raise that it refuses to answer?

The Static Map. Your cosmos never shifts, your borders never migrate, your forbidden zones stay politely forbidden. If no one is tempted to cross, if nothing bleeds through the walls between realms, you're missing the story. The best mythic worlds have places that move and rules that occasionally crack.

IX. Worldbuilding Hooks

Who tells this myth in your world? Who doubts it? Is it the official story, or the underground one?

Does the creation myth justify the current rulers, or is it the rallying cry of outcasts and revolutionaries?

How do daily rituals, festivals, or taboos reflect the creation story? If the world was spoken into being, is there a festival of silence? If it was torn from a body, are there rites of mending?

Do rival cultures tell the story differently? What happens when two creation myths collide, politically, theologically, violently?

What place in your world is a direct scar from the creation, a landscape that still bears the wound? Who profits from passage between worlds, who forbids it, and who risks everything to cross?

X. Annotated Reading List

Primary Myths:

Theogony (Hesiod) - Blood, ambition, castration, and cosmic family feuds. The original dysfunctional divine family, and still one of the most viscerally physical creation accounts ever written.

Enuma Elish (Babylonian) - The world built from the corpse of a slain chaos goddess. Cosmic violence as civic engineering. If you want to understand the Corpse World archetype, start here.

Popol Vuh (K'iche' Maya) - Creation by trial, error, and divine mischief. The gods try three times to make humans and fail twice. The myth that teaches you the power of iteration and imperfection.

Prose Edda (Snorri Sturluson) - Recycled giants, corpse worlds, a gap between fire and ice, and gods who know they're doomed. Norse creation encodes its own apocalypse from the first line.

The Kalevala (Elias Lonnrot) - A goddess floating on an endless sea, a bird, an egg, and a world born from breakage. Finnish creation myth as poetry, ecology, and enchantment.

Analysis & Craft:

Creation Myths of the World (David Leeming) - Encyclopedic, global, and wonderfully odd. The single best reference for surveying how different cultures solve the same impossible question.

Primal Myths (Barbara Sproul) - A primary-source anthology that lets the myths speak for themselves. Pairs well with Leeming: he maps the territory, she hands you the originals.

Wonderbook (Jeff VanderMeer) - Not a mythology book, but one of the most brain-bending creative toolkits ever assembled. If you want to think about worldbuilding as an act of imagination rather than a set of forms, this is the place.

Modern & Speculative:

Annihilation (Jeff VanderMeer) - The unknowable border. The landscape that watches you. A modern myth about what happens when the map stops making sense.

His Dark Materials (Philip Pullman) - Multiple worlds, thresholds, and a cosmos that is also a theological argument. The best modern example of creation-as-story-engine.

XI. CREATIVE DARE: THE RULEBREAKER'S CHALLENGE

Write a creation myth your world is afraid to tell, the kind that could topple its gods, kings, or even its author. Let your characters discover it, bit by trembling bit. Whoever controls the myth controls the future.

When you're done, ask yourself:

What was left unfinished? What does your world still fear in the dark? And what shape did the making leave behind?

Go break something beautiful. Then build something that lasts, wrong, glorious, and unmistakably yours.

THE LOOM, PART 1: THE FIRST THREAD

The Weaver sits in nothing.

Not darkness, nothing has no color yet. There is no "before" because before requires time, and time is a thread that has not been spun. There is no space because space is a pattern, and the pattern has not been started. There is only the Weaver, and the Weaver is only a pair of hands with no body, a voice with no mouth, a grief with no name.

She does not decide to sing.

Later, the theologians will argue about this. The Bright Needle's priests will say she chose to create, that the song was an act of divine will, proof that the world was wanted. The followers of the Fraying Edge will counter that she was compelled, that grief, once large enough, becomes indistinguishable from creation, that the universe is what happens when sorrow has nowhere else to go. The Shuttle's wandering scholars will claim it doesn't matter, that the distinction between choosing and being compelled is a luxury only beings who live inside time can afford.

What is not disputed: the song begins.

It is not beautiful. It is not anything yet, beauty requires a listener, and there is no one listening. The sound moves outward into the nothing, and where it touches, nothing gains a quality. A texture. A direction. The first difference: here and there. The second: now and then. The nothing does not resist. It has no opinion about being made into something. But it holds a shape reluctantly, the way wet cloth holds a fold, present but impermanent, waiting to relax back into formlessness.

The Weaver sings, and as she sings, thread appears. Not from her hands, her hands are not yet relevant. The thread comes from the song itself, from the vibration of grief given a frequency and a direction. The first thread is silver-gray, and it hums with a note that will later be called sorrow. The second is the color of absence made visible. The third has no name in any language that will ever be spoken, because it is the thread of before, the memory of nothing, woven into the pattern so the world will never forget what it replaced.

She weaves. The pattern forms. It is not a plan, the Weaver has no blueprint, no grand design, no purpose beyond the unbearable need to make the silence into something that is not silence. The pattern grows the way a wound scabs: organically, imperfectly, the body of the world knitting itself together around a hurt that will never fully heal.

The first flaw appears seven threads in.

It is not a mistake. Or it is, but "mistake" implies an intention that was missed, and the Weaver's intention is nothing more specific than continuation. The seventh thread catches on the fourth. The pattern knots. And in the knot, something stirs.

Not yet alive. Not yet a god. But present, a density in the weave, a snarl where the pattern loops back on itself and generates a tiny, furious complexity. The Weaver could undo it. She doesn't. Later, the theologians will argue about this too.

She keeps weaving. The knots multiply. Where the pattern is smooth, there is stone, water, silence, law. Where the pattern knots, there is something else, something that squirms and whispers and wants. The Weaver does not name these knots. She does not need to. They will name themselves, in time.

And the first thread, the silver-gray one, the grief-thread, runs through everything. It is the warp on which the world is strung. Pull it, and the pattern unravels. Cut it, and the world falls still. It cannot be removed because it was there first, because the world is built on it, because the Weaver's grief is not an accident of creation but its foundation.

The pattern grows. The knots awaken. The Weaver keeps weaving.

She has not stopped.

Next: The Weaver's stitches slip, and the knots learn to speak.

Chapter 2: Pantheon Builder

Gods, Spirits, and Divine Disorder

I. Opening Manifesto

Pantheons are the nervous systems of imaginary worlds; but here's what nobody tells you: the nervous system doesn't end at the gods. It runs all the way down through the spirits crouching in the river, the dead grandmother whose opinion still matters at the dinner table, and the thing that lives behind the stove and steals your socks when you forget to leave it bread. A world with gods but no spirits is a mansion with electricity but no plumbing. Everything looks impressive from the outside, and nothing actually works.

Too many builders treat their supernatural inhabitants like separate departments: gods in the throne room, spirits in the forest, ancestors in the crypt, no overlap, no mess. That's not how myth works. In Yoruba tradition, the orishas interact constantly with ancestral spirits and nature forces; Obatala shapes human bodies in the womb while the Egungun masquerades bring the collective dead dancing through the streets. In Shinto, the eight million kami include everything from Amaterasu the sun goddess down to the spirit of a particular oddly shaped rock. In Slavic tradition, the domovoi household spirit is the ancestor who refused to leave, inhabiting the space behind the stove and making your livestock sick if you insult his memory. The supernatural is an ecosystem, not an org chart.

This chapter gives you the whole ecosystem. We'll move from the throne room to the threshold to the crawlspace, from the god who made the world to the hungry ghost who can't leave it. You'll build a pantheon that breathes, and when you're done, the gods in your world won't just have names and domains. They'll have neighbors, rivals, tenants, and pests. They'll have a food chain. And somewhere at the bottom of that food chain, something small and angry will be waiting for someone to forget its offering.

II. What Is a Pantheon? (And What Lives Below It)

A pantheon is a society of supernatural beings, linked by kinship, rivalry, duty, or accident, whose relationships explain the world and give it tension. That's the short version.

Here's the real one: a pantheon is a political ecosystem masquerading as a theology. Every divine hierarchy encodes who has power, who lost it, who's trying to get it back, and what happens to the mortals caught in the middle. The Greek gods hold a family reunion on Olympus where Zeus maintains order through a combination of thunderbolts and barely contained adultery. The Yoruba orishas form courts and guilds, each deity governing a domain but answerable to the supreme Olodumare in ways that look suspiciously like the political structure of a Yoruba city-state. The Japanese kami number in the uncountable millions: the phrase *yaoyorozu no kami* literally means "eight million gods," an idiom for "more than anyone could ever list", squabbling over everything from thunder to the proper way mold should grow on rice.

But every pantheon is also a map of the invisible world, and that world doesn't stop at the divine court. Below the gods sit the nature spirits who personify particular places: rivers, mountains, forests, crossroads. Below them, or beside them, or tangled up with them, sit the ancestral dead, who never fully leave and whose opinions on how the living should behave are rarely polite. Below *them* wander the hungry and the lost: spirits too angry, too sad, or too hungry to rest, who persist because something went wrong in the dying or the remembering.

I call this the **Divine Spectrum**: the full continuum from the god who made the sun to the ghost who haunts the kitchen. Most worldbuilding books separate these into different chapters, different toolkits, different problems. We're not going to do that. We're going to build them as one system; because in every living mythology, they already are.

III. The Divine Spectrum: A Supernatural Ecology

The spectrum isn't a hierarchy, though hierarchies appear inside it. It's an ecosystem. Think of it the way an ecologist thinks about a forest: the canopy trees are the most visible, but they depend on the fungal networks underground, and both depend on the insects nobody notices until something goes wrong. Remove the canopy and the understory burns. Remove the understory and the canopy starves.

Here's how the spectrum works, from the top of the canopy to the things that crawl beneath the roots.

1. The High Gods (The Canopy)

The big ones. Creator-figures, cosmic rulers, the deities whose domains span the entire world. In Yoruba tradition, Obatala, whose very name breaks down into *Oba* (king) and *ala* (white cloth, purity, boundary), is the eldest of the orishas, the sculptor of human bodies, the founder and king of Ile-Ife. He was given the task of creating the Earth, got drunk on palm wine, and left the job half-finished for Oduduwa to complete. That single story: a creator who failed through his own excess and was punished by being reassigned to shape human bodies, generates an entire theology of imperfection, disability as divine mark, and the complicated relationship between authority and competence. In Norse mythology, Odin gave up an eye for wisdom and hanged himself from Yggdrasil for nine days, the All-Father earning his knowledge through self-mutilation and something that looks uncomfortably like suicide.

Cultural examples: Obatala (Yoruba), Zeus (Greek), Odin (Norse), Amaterasu (Shinto), Vishnu (Hindu).

The Gift: High gods provide cosmic stakes. When they argue, continents crack. When they grieve, the seasons change. They make your world feel *consequential*. Actions have divine witnesses, and those witnesses have opinions.

The Trap: The tyranny of omnipotence. If your high god can do anything, nothing is at risk. The most interesting high gods are the ones who are powerful but constrained, by their own promises, their own flaws, or the inconvenient existence of other gods who disagree with them. Zeus can throw thunderbolts, but he can't make Hera forgive him. Obatala sculpts humanity, but the bodies he shaped while drunk came out different from what he intended. And he became their protector. The flaw is the feature.

2. THE SPECIALIST GODS (THE UNDERSTORY)

Gods of specific domains: war, love, death, harvest, the sea, the forge. These are the workhorses of a pantheon, the deities mortals actually interact with on a daily basis. You don't pray to the supreme creator when your crops are failing. You pray to the god of rain and hope they're not currently feuding with the god of drought.

Specialist gods derive their power from a narrower domain, but that narrowness gives them depth. Osanyin, the Yoruba orisha of herbs and healing, knows every plant in the forest and what it cures. The story goes that his brother Orunmila tasked him with clearing weeds from a field, and Osanyin wept; because he couldn't find a single plant that didn't have a purpose, a medicine hidden inside it. He refused to pull a single stem. That's a nurturer archetype built on obsessive knowledge, not gentle kindness, a healer who would rather let the garden grow wild than destroy a single remedy.

Cultural examples: Ares/Mars (Greek/Roman, war), Brigid (Irish, healing/smithcraft/poetry), Osanyin (Yoruba, herbs and medicine), Thor (Norse, thunder), Saraswati (Hindu, knowledge and arts).

The Gift: Specialist gods give your world texture. They're the reason a blacksmith prays differently than a sailor. They create professional rivalries, guild structures, and the wonderful problem of what happens when two gods' domains overlap. (Who governs the battlefield medic, the god of war or the god of healing?)

The Trap: The job-description god. If your deity is nothing but their domain. God of war who only does war things, god of love who only does love things, they're a signpost, not a character. Real mythological gods contradict their own portfolios constantly. Aphrodite instigates wars. Ares has a tender side. Give your specialist gods at least one obsession that has nothing to do with their domain.

3. THE PSYCHOPOMP (THE BRIDGE)

The guide between worlds. Not quite a specialist god, not quite a spirit, the psychopomp is the figure who stands at the threshold between life and death, sacred and profane, known and unknown, and charges a toll. In Haitian Vodou, Baron Samedi is the loa of death who digs the graves, meets the rising souls, and guides them to the afterlife; but he's also a healer, a comedian, and an obscene trickster who shows up in a top hat and skull-painted face, smoking cigars, drinking rum, and making jokes so filthy they'd make a sailor blush. He can refuse to dig your grave and thereby prevent your death. He embodies the uncomfortable truth that the boundary between life and death is not a wall but a negotiation.

In Greek tradition, Hermes guides the dead to the underworld but also presides over commerce, thieves, and travelers. Anubis weighs hearts against a feather. The psychopomp's power isn't destruction or creation: it's *access*. They hold the keys.

Cultural examples: Baron Samedi (Haitian Vodou), Anubis (Egyptian), Hermes/Mercury (Greek/Roman), Xolotl (Aztec), Valkyries (Norse).

The Gift: The psychopomp generates the richest narrative crossroads in any mythology. Every death scene, every journey to the underworld, every threshold crossing runs through them. They're the reason your world's funerals matter and your quests to the land of the dead have rules.

The Trap: Reducing the psychopomp to a grim ferryman. The most resonant guides of the dead are also deeply connected to life: Baron Samedi is a fertility figure as much as a death figure, and Hermes is the god of newborns as well as the escort of the dead. If your psychopomp only shows up at funerals, you're wasting half their potential.

4. The Nature Spirit / Genius Loci (The Root Network)

Spirits bound to specific places, forces, or living things. This is where the divine spectrum begins to dissolve the line between "god" and "something else." Japanese kami inhabit rivers, mountains, ancient trees, and rocks of unusual shape, and the greatest of these, like Amaterasu, are worshipped as gods, while the smallest are honored with a roadside shrine and a prayer. In Greek tradition, naiads personified springs and rivers while dryads inhabited individual trees; kill the tree, kill the dryad. In many Indigenous Australian traditions, the ancestral beings who shaped the land during the Dreaming are inseparable from the landscape itself: the mountain *is* the ancestor, resting.

The key insight: nature spirits turn your geography into a cast of characters. A river isn't just water. It has a personality, a mood, a temper. It can be offended. It can be bribed.

Cultural examples: Kami (Shinto), naiads and dryads (Greek), river and mountain spirits across West African traditions, the Dreaming beings of Aboriginal Australian cosmology, vaettir (Norse).

The Gift: Genius loci make the landscape *alive*. Every place in your world can have a voice, a grudge, a story. The forest the villagers won't enter isn't just dark; it's angry, and it remembers what the villagers' great-grandparents did to it.

The Trap: The pretty sprite problem. Nature spirits reduced to whimsical forest fairies lose their teeth. In genuine traditions, nature spirits are often dangerous, capricious, and alien: the kami can be terrifying, the river spirit can drown you for a slight, and the forest spirit doesn't share your values. If your nature spirits are too nice, your landscape is Disneyland.

5. The Household Spirit (The Fungi)

Invisible, essential, underappreciated until they're gone. The Slavic domovoi is the household guardian, a small, hairy, bearded creature that resembles the family's deceased patriarch and dwells behind the stove. He protects the family, watches over the children and livestock, and foretells the future through groans or laughter. But if the family is lazy, uses foul language at meals, or lets the house fall into disrepair, the domovoi turns vindictive: milk curdles, objects vanish, something sits on your chest at night and you can't breathe. In Roman tradition, the Lares were household gods honored at a family shrine, and the Penates guarded the pantry. In Korean tradition, the *Seongju* is the house guardian spirit associated with the main roof beam.

The household spirit is where the divine spectrum gets domestic; and domestic is where myth becomes daily life.

Cultural examples: Domovoi (Slavic), Lares and Penates (Roman), *Seongju* (Korean), *cofgodas* (Anglo-Saxon), brownies (Scottish).

The Gift: Household spirits embed the supernatural into the ordinary. They give your world rituals that happen at the dinner table, not just the temple. They create a mythology of chores: sweep the floor to please the spirit, leave bread by the stove, don't curse in the kitchen. This is where religion becomes habit, and habit becomes culture.

The Trap: Making them cute. A domovoi is not a garden gnome. It's the spirit of your dead grandfather who will strangle you in your sleep if you disrespect his memory. Household spirits carry the weight of ancestral obligation, and that obligation has teeth.

6. The Ancestral Shade (The Soil)

The dead who are not gone. In Yoruba tradition, the Egungun masquerade is one of the most powerful expressions of ancestor veneration in any world mythology. During the annual festival, masked performers wearing elaborate layered costumes of richly brocaded fabric move through the community. They are not *representing* the ancestors, according to belief, through drumming, dance, and ritual, the masked performer *becomes* the ancestor, who has temporarily returned from Orun (the spirit realm) to bless, discipline, and cleanse the living community. The Egungun expose the strengths and weaknesses of the community, give warnings, and dispense blessings. Their whips are both punishment and benediction. Touch the ancestor's costume without permission, and you may be struck. Be struck, and you have been noticed by the dead, which is, depending on your behavior, either a gift or a reckoning.

This is the divine spectrum's most political layer. Ancestral shades are not neutral. They have opinions. They have favorites. They can be manipulated, offended, or weaponized by the living.

Cultural examples: Egungun (Yoruba), *manes* (Roman), ancestral spirits in Chinese folk religion, *pitrs* (Hindu).

The Gift: Ancestral shades make your world's past *present tense*. The dead are not historical; they're stakeholders. They attend family meetings. They vote. A culture that venerates its ancestors is a culture where the past has literal power over the present, and that creates story at every level: inheritance disputes, contested memories, the question of whose ancestor gets honored and whose gets erased.

The Trap: The benevolent grandparent. Not all ancestors are wise. Not all ancestors are good. Some ancestors are the reason the family is cursed in the first place. If your ancestral shades are uniformly helpful, you've lost the best part: the dead who won't forgive, the dead who demand something terrible, the dead who were wrong about everything and still won't shut up.

7. THE HUNGRY / THE LOST (THE PARASITES)

Spirits defined by what they lack. The Buddhist concept of the *preta*, the hungry ghost, originates in ancient Indian tradition and became one of the six realms of rebirth in Buddhist cosmology. Pretas are depicted with enormous, bloated bellies and throats too narrow to swallow: beings of insatiable desire who can never consume enough to ease their suffering. They are the karmic consequence of greed, possessiveness, and jealousy in a previous life, condemned to a state where craving persists but satisfaction is anatomically impossible.

In Chinese folk tradition, hungry ghosts are the dead whose living relatives failed to make proper offerings; they wander, starving, because no one remembered to feed them. The Japanese *gaki* must eat excrement or devour human corpses. In Irish tradition, the banshee wails before a death not from malice but from grief she cannot discharge.

This is the ecosystem's bottom; but "bottom" doesn't mean unimportant. Hungry spirits are the divine spectrum's warning system. They exist because something went wrong: a bad death, a forgotten offering, a life lived in the grip of a desire that consumed everything else. They are the cost of the system failing.

Cultural examples: Preta/hungry ghosts (Buddhist/Hindu/Taoist/Chinese folk religion), banshees (Irish), *gaki* (Japanese), unquiet dead across virtually every tradition.

The Gift: The Hunger Principle. Hungry spirits embody the idea that need doesn't end at death; and that the living have obligations to the dead that, if broken, produce consequences. They're your world's guilt made visible, its neglect made audible, its unfinished business given a body and a voice.

The Trap: The generic ghost. A hungry spirit that's just "scary" is wasted. The power of the *preta* isn't the bloated belly: it's the *why*. Every hungry ghost is a story about what went wrong: what was the greed, who did the forgetting, what offering was never made. If you don't know what your ghost is hungry *for*, you don't have a spirit. You have a special effect.

The Spectrum Principle: These layers don't stay in their lanes. High gods meddle with household affairs. Ancestral shades challenge the authority of nature spirits. Hungry ghosts haunt the temples of the high gods. The most interesting mythologies are the ones where the layers interact, contradict, and compete; where the river spirit and the village ancestors are in a territorial dispute, where the household guardian picks fights with the hungry ghost trying to get in through the kitchen window, where the high god's decree is being quietly ignored by every local spirit in the district.

Build your spectrum as a single system, and the stories will generate themselves.

IV. Core Divine Archetypes: The Recurring Cast

Within the spectrum, certain roles keep appearing across traditions. Here are the seven that matter most; not as a checklist, but as a recurring cast whose interactions generate story.

The Creator

Often absent, aloof, or retired. Brahma created the universe and is barely worshipped. Odin made the world and then went looking for more interesting problems. The creator's departure creates a power vacuum that generates the rest of the pantheon's drama.

The Ruler

Maintains cosmic order; or tries to. Obatala, the "King of White Cloth," was the eldest orisha, creator of human beings, the judge who sits silent at the trial. Zeus on Olympus. Amaterasu in the heavenly court. The ruler's authority is never total, always contested, and usually exhausting.

The Trickster

Disrupts, mocks, and accidentally saves the world by breaking it. A full chapter is coming (Chapter 5), but the trickster's role in the pantheon is structural: they prevent the system from calcifying. Eshu at the crossroads. Loki in Asgard. The trickster is the immune system: destructive, necessary, hated by everyone who benefits from them.

THE WARRIOR

Patron of necessary violence. Not evil; but not safe. Kali dances on corpses. Thor protects Asgard but breaks everything he touches. Huitzilopochtli demanded hearts to keep the sun moving. The warrior archetype asks: what is the cost of survival?

THE NURTURER

Sustains, heals, feeds, protects. But the nurturer is never passive; Osanyin refuses to pull weeds because he sees medicine in every plant; Isis resurrects Osiris through magical cunning, not gentle sympathy; Brigid presides over healing, smithcraft, and poetry simultaneously, because the Celts understood that making things whole is a form of making things. The nurturer's power is preservation, and preservation is a fight.

THE OUTSIDER

Not quite a god, not quite a monster. Set in the Egyptian pantheon: the god of the desert, of storms, of foreigners, who murdered his own brother and yet was necessary; because someone had to guard the sun-barque against the chaos serpent Apophis during its nightly passage through the underworld. Fenrir in Norse myth, chained by the gods who knew they'd need his destruction to trigger Ragnarok. The outsider tests the system's boundaries and asks: who decides who belongs?

THE DIVINE ANCESTOR

The god who becomes a bloodline. This is where the divine spectrum bridges into Chapter 3. Gilgamesh was two-thirds divine and one-third human, a lineage claim that gave Uruk's rulers cosmic authority. The Japanese imperial line traces its descent from Amaterasu. In many traditions, the founding ancestor *was* a god, or married one, or stole something from one, and the family has been dealing with the consequences ever since.

V. THE PANTHEON BUILDER: WORKSHOP

This is a build. We're going to construct a pantheon from the spectrum up; not a list of gods, but a living ecosystem of divine, spiritual, and spectral beings that generates conflict on its own. Work fast. Let the contradictions in. They're features, not bugs.

STEP 1: HOW DID THE DIVINE GET HERE?

Your creation myth (Chapter 1) already gave your world an origin. Now: how did the gods emerge from it? Were they born from the creation? Did they *cause* it? Are they side effects: knots in the fabric, overtones in the chord, cracks in the egg? Or did they arrive later, finding a world already in motion and claiming it?

In the Loom (the through-line myth we're building), the gods are accidents, flaws in the Weaver's pattern that learned to speak. That origin determines everything about how they relate to each other: with suspicion, with rivalry, with the nagging question of whether any of them were *meant* to exist.

Write it down. One sentence: Where did the gods in your world come from, and were they wanted?

STEP 2: BUILD THE TOP OF THE SPECTRUM

Start with two or three high gods. Not a full roster; just the ones at the top. Give each one a domain, a flaw, and a grudge. The domain is what they rule. The flaw is what undermines them. The grudge is who they blame for the flaw. In the worked example later in this chapter, the Ash Pantheon starts with three: the Kiln-Mother (creation, but she can't stop making things), the Quiet King (order, but he's afraid of his own authority), and the Red Tongue (destruction, but she loves what she destroys).

Now make them disagree about something fundamental. Not a petty squabble: a genuine, irreconcilable disagreement about how the world should work. That disagreement is the engine of your pantheon's drama.

Name your top gods. For each: one domain, one flaw, one grudge. Then name the disagreement that will never be resolved.

STEP 3: FILL THE SPECTRUM DOWN

This is the step most worldbuilders skip, and it's the one that makes the difference between a pantheon and a filing cabinet. Work downward through the spectrum:

Nature spirits: What places in your world are alive? What rivers have moods? What forests have memories? Pick at least one landscape feature and give it a spirit with an agenda that conflicts with someone higher up the spectrum. The river spirit who refuses to flow where the Ruler-god directed it. The mountain spirit who remembers the world before the gods arrived.

Household spirits: What supernatural presence lives in the homes of ordinary people? What do they want? What offends them? In the Ash Pantheon worked example, every kiln has a *cinder-imp*, a tiny spirit born from the first firing, who protects the household's creative work but destroys anything made without passion.

Ancestral shades: How do the dead participate in the living world? Are they consulted?

Are they feared? Do they show up uninvited?

Hungry ghosts: What produces the lost and the starving in your world? What kind of death, what kind of life, what kind of forgetting turns a soul into something that wanders and wants?

For each layer: one sentence naming the spirit and one sentence describing what it wants that the gods can't or won't provide.

STEP 4: THE DIVINE FOOD CHAIN

Now connect the layers. Who serves whom? Who feeds on whom? Who competes? In every real-world mythology, the layers of the divine spectrum interact constantly. The orishas depend on human worship. The Egungun ancestors mediate between the living and the divine. The kami at the bottom of the Japanese spectrum are tended by the same priesthood that serves the highest gods.

Ask: What flows upward in your spectrum? (Worship? Sacrifice? Memory? Fear?) What flows downward? (Power? Blessing? Punishment? Neglect?) What happens when the flow is interrupted; when mortals stop worshipping, when the gods stop paying attention, when the dead are forgotten?

Draw the connections. What does each layer need from the layers above and below it? What happens when it doesn't get it?

STEP 5: THE CRACKS

Every ecosystem has its failure modes. Where does your divine spectrum break down? Where are the dead ends, the abandoned temples, the gods who lost their worshippers, the spirits no one tends? In Pratchett's *Small Gods*, a deity without believers becomes a tortoise. In Gaiman's *American Gods*, the old gods fade as the new gods of media and technology rise. Miyazaki's *Spirited Away* populates its bathhouse with spirits adapting, sometimes desperately, to a world that has moved on without them.

These cracks are where the best stories live. A forgotten god trying to claw their way back. A household spirit whose family emigrated and left it alone in an empty apartment. An ancestral shade whose descendants converted to a new religion and stopped making offerings.

Name one crack in your spectrum. Who was forgotten, and what are they going to do about it?

STEP 6: WHO TELLS THIS STORY?

Just as your creation myth has tellers and doubters, your divine spectrum has competing theologies. The priests tell one version of who the gods are and what they want. The village wise-woman tells another. The heretics say the gods are parasites, or that the ancestral shades are the *real* power, or that the hungry ghosts are the gods' abandoned children.

Name two competing accounts of how the divine spectrum works in your world. Who benefits from each version?

VI. QUICK MENU FOR INSPIRATION

Stuck? Pick one from each row and see what collides.

Divine Origin: Born from the creation; Arrived after; Side effects of something else; Always existed; Rose from mortal worship; Stole divinity from someone older

High God Flaw: Drunk on power; Absent without explanation; Broke a promise they can't take back; Forgot something vital; Afraid of their own worshippers; In love with a mortal; Dying slowly

Spirit of Place: The river that remembers; The mountain that migrates; The crossroads that bargains; The tree that judges; The ruin that rebuilds itself; The bog that swallows liars

Household Presence: A bearded thing behind the stove; A sound in the rafters; A handprint that appears on cold glass; The chair that no one sits in; The fire that won't go out; Something that braids the children's hair at night

Ancestral Mood: Proud and interfering; Ashamed and hiding; Angry and specific; Forgiving but conditional; Silent and watchful; Demanding and never satisfied

Hungry Ghost Hunger: For a name; For an offering; For an apology; For a body; For the truth about how they died; For one more look at the sun

VII. WORKED EXAMPLES

THE CLASSIC MODEL

"Three gods share one sky: the Lawgiver, who set the stars in their tracks and forbids them to wander; the Lamplighter, who carries the sun across the heavens and weeps because she is not allowed to rest; and the Thief, who steals moments from the day to give to the night and is punished for it every dawn. Beneath them, a thousand unnamed spirits tend the rivers and the grain, and each household keeps a stone in the hearth that holds the family's first ancestor. The stone must be fed with oil on the new moon, or the ancestor grows restless, and restless ancestors attract the Hollow Ones, the dead who were never named, who drift between the stones and steal warmth from the living."

This is the safe version: clean, efficient, archetypal. Notice that even this sketch has all seven layers of the spectrum in miniature: high gods (the three), nature spirits (the unnamed thousands), household spirits (the hearthstone ancestor), and hungry ghosts (the Hollow Ones). The system connects: the household ritual (feeding the stone) keeps the hungry ghosts away, which means domestic neglect has supernatural consequences. That's a pantheon working as an ecosystem.

THE ASH PANTHEON (SHOWCASE)

In the world called Pyre, everything burns.

Not with fire; or not only with fire. The scholars of the Ash Quarter, who spend their lives debating such things, use the word "kindling" to describe the process by which all matter in Pyre slowly, inevitably consumes itself. Wood kindles fastest. Stone kindles slowest. A mountain might take ten thousand years to become ash, but it will become ash. This is not entropy. Entropy is passive. Kindling is an act; the world is not winding down, it is burning up, and there is a difference, because burning means someone lit the match.

The someone, according to the Ashwright priests, was the Kiln-Mother.

She did not mean to set the world on fire. She meant to make it. The Kiln-Mother is the eldest god: a vast, faceless presence whose domain is creation, ceramics, and the terrible compulsion to keep making things even when the raw material runs out. She shaped the first land from her own body's heat, and the land was beautiful, and it began to smolder immediately. This is the Kiln-Mother's flaw: she cannot make anything that doesn't eventually burn. Her creations are gorgeous and temporary, and she loves them desperately and makes more to replace them, and the replacements burn too, and the ash accumulates, and the Ash Quarter scholars have calculated that the world gains sixteen inches of ash per century and will eventually be buried in the residue of its own beauty.

The Quiet King arrived second. He is the god of order, patience, and the desperate hope that things will stop changing. He does not create; he preserves. His priests maintain the Firebreaks, great trenches dug into the landscape and filled with water and salt, which slow the kindling process in the surrounding land. The Quiet King's domain is everything the Kiln-Mother has already made: he inherits her creations and tries, with increasing exhaustion, to keep them from turning to ash. His flaw is fear. He is afraid that if he exerts his full power, if he truly stopped the kindling, the Kiln-Mother would cease to exist, because her existence is inseparable from the act of making, and making in Pyre means burning. He loves her. He will not save the world if it means destroying her. The Ashwright priests consider this a noble sacrifice. The Firebreak monks consider it a dereliction of cosmic duty.

The Red Tongue is the third high god, and she is the most dangerous, because she is the god of destruction who loves what she destroys. Her domain is fire, endings, and the ecstatic moment when something beautiful becomes something gone. She does not hate the Kiln-Mother's creations. She adores them, the way a gourmand adores a meal. She savors them as they burn. Her priests, the Ember-Eaters, consume a fragment of ash before every meal and claim that in it they can taste the beauty of whatever was destroyed: the sweetness of a burned orchard, the salt of a collapsed bridge, the strange mineral tang of a mountain that has finally finished kindling. The Red Tongue's flaw is love. She cannot bring herself to destroy anything she does not love first, which means she is the gentlest of the three gods; right up until the moment she isn't.

The fundamental disagreement: the Kiln-Mother will not stop making. The Quiet King will not stop preserving. The Red Tongue will not stop destroying. Each believes the other two are the source of the world's suffering, and each is correct.

But the high gods are only the canopy.

Below them, the cinder-imps tend every kiln, forge, and hearthfire in the world. A cinder-imp is born from the first fire ever lit in a new hearth, and it lives as long as the fire is maintained. It protects the household's craft: the potter's glaze, the blacksmith's temper, the baker's crust, but it despises carelessness. A cinder-imp whose family makes shoddy work will sabotage their tools, crack their pots, and spoil their bread until they remember that creation, in Pyre, is sacred even when it's small. Every household leaves a pinch of the finest ash in a dish by the hearth. The imps eat it the way we eat chocolate: with guilty, trembling pleasure.

Deeper still, the Char Walkers move through the landscape, vast, slow spirits that inhabit the ash-fields where the kindling has finished. They are the ghosts of places: the memory of a forest that burned, the echo of a city that turned to powder. They do not speak. They do not want. They simply walk, endlessly, through the remains of what they were, and anyone who walks with them too long begins to forget their own name, their own face, their own fire.

And at the very bottom of the spectrum are the Unkinds, the hungry ghosts of Pyre. These are the souls of the dead who were cremated improperly. In Pyre, cremation is the holiest rite: a body given to fire kindles clean and releases the soul to join the Kiln-Mother's next creation. But a body buried, or drowned, or left to rot; that soul kindles slowly, agonizingly, without release. The Unkinds wander the edges of settlements, drawn to heat, trying to press their cold hands against hearthfires they can feel but cannot reach. The cinder-imps fight them off. The Ember-Eaters perform a rite called the Second Burning to release them. But there are always more, because there are always bodies that are lost, forgotten, or denied the fire.

The Ashwright priests say the Kiln-Mother grieves for the Unkinds. The Firebreak monks say the Quiet King refuses to look at them. The Ember-Eaters say the Red Tongue weeps when she sees them, because they are the one thing in the world she cannot bring herself to love.

The Ash Pantheon's central mystery: every century, the ash-level rises, and every century, the world buries a little more of itself. The Ashwrights call this the Long Smothering. Their prophecy is simple: one day, the ash will cover everything, and the Kiln-Mother will have nothing left to make, and the Quiet King will have nothing left to keep, and the Red Tongue will have nothing left to love. On that day, the three gods will finally agree on something.

Nobody wants to know what.

Notice what happened: the creation principle (the Kiln-Mother's compulsive making) produced the cosmic problem (everything kindles). The divine disagreement (make / preserve / destroy) generates political factions. The spectrum runs from high gods through household spirits (cinder-imps) to nature spirits (Char Walkers) to hungry ghosts (the Unkinds). The system connects: improper cremation produces Unkinds; cinder-imps guard against them; the Ember-Eaters perform rites to release them; and the whole thing is driven by the same principle: fire, that powers the cosmos. That's a pantheon working as an ecology. Every layer depends on the others, and removing any one layer collapses the system.

VIII. PITFALLS, TRAPS, AND COMMON MISTAKES

The Org Chart Pantheon. Your gods have domains, titles, and a neat hierarchy, but they never interact with anything below them. The high gods float in a vacuum while the spirits and ghosts are handled by a separate department. Mythology doesn't have departments. Let the gods get their hands dirty. Let the household spirit talk back to the war god. Let the hungry ghost show up at the divine assembly and embarrass everyone.

Monotheism in Disguise. You say your world has a pantheon, but one god is clearly in charge and the others are glorified middle management. If the other gods never meaningfully disagree with, disobey, or outwit the top god, you don't have a pantheon. You have a monarchy with courtiers.

The Flawless Divine. Your gods don't drink too much, lust after mortals, hold petty grudges, or make catastrophic mistakes. Congratulations. You've built a stained-glass window, not a mythology. Real gods are magnificent disasters. Obatala got drunk and shaped humans imperfectly. Odin sacrificed his own eye and still didn't get all the answers. Baron Samedi guards the dead while being the most obscene figure in his entire tradition. Flaws aren't imperfections in your pantheon. They *are* your pantheon.

The Empty Spectrum. You have high gods and nothing below them. No spirits, no shades, no hungry dead. Your world's supernatural population consists entirely of management with no workers, no retirees, and no vagrants. Fill the spectrum. The divine ecosystem needs every layer.

The One-Note Spirit. Every ghost is scary. Every nature spirit is whimsical. Every ancestor is wise. You've built a world where the supernatural has exactly one emotion per category. Let your ghosts be sad, or furious, or confused. Let your nature spirits be territorial, or lonely, or bored. Let your ancestors be wrong.

IX. WORLDBUILDING HOOKS

Who in your world speaks for the gods? Are they appointed, chosen, self-proclaimed, or possessed?

What happens when a god loses all their worshippers? Do they weaken, change, go mad, or simply forget what they were?

How do the different layers of the spectrum interact in daily life? Does the household spirit warn you when the hungry ghosts are near? Does the nature spirit demand a different offering than the high god?

Can mortals ascend to divinity? Can gods fall to mortality? What's the process, and who controls it?

What's the most dangerous job in your world's religious hierarchy: the person who tends the gods, the person who tends the dead, or the person who tends the spirits that don't fit into either category?

If the divine spectrum is an ecosystem, what's the invasive species? What new god, spirit, or practice is disrupting the old order?

X. ANNOTATED READING LIST

PRIMARY MYTHS:

The Iliad (Homer); Gods as schemers, meddlers, and sore losers. The original case study in what happens when divine egos collide with human wars. Nobody comes out looking good.

Yoruba Mythology (Abimbola, Drewal, et al.); Rival courts, political deities, and a spirit ecology that runs from Olodumare at the top to the Egungun masquerades that bring the dead back dancing. The richest polytheistic system you've never studied.

Kojiki / Nihon Shoki; The chronicles of Japan's divine origins: kami succession, cosmic rivalry, and the idea that eight million spirits can inhabit everything from the sun to a stone. The diversity here will break your assumptions.

Popol Vuh (K'iche' Maya); Gods who compete, fail, cheat, and accidentally create the world through serial incompetence. The best argument in any mythology for why divine flaws are features, not bugs.

ANALYSIS:

Myth and Reality (Mircea Eliade); How societies encode their dreams and terrors into gods. Dense, brilliant, and the reason you'll never look at a ritual the same way again.

MODERN & SPECULATIVE:

Small Gods (Terry Pratchett); A god reduced to a tortoise because no one believes in him anymore. The funniest and most theologically serious fantasy novel ever written about power, belief, and the cost of heresy.

American Gods (Neil Gaiman); Old gods fading, new gods rising, and the uncomfortable question of what divinity means when the culture that sustained it moves on. Required reading for anyone building a pantheon in a changing world.

Spirited Away (Hayao Miyazaki, film); A bathhouse full of spirits adapting to modernity. The most beautiful depiction of an urban spirit ecology ever made, and the best argument for why the divine spectrum doesn't end at the temple door.

XI. CREATIVE DARE: THE HERETIC'S CHALLENGE

Design a god your world's establishment would suppress: a deity so dangerous, so inconvenient, or so embarrassing that the official priesthood pretends it doesn't exist. Then design the cult that worships it anyway: in secret, in basements, in code.

Now push further. Give that god a household spirit that's been quietly protecting the cult for generations. Give it a hungry ghost that *is* the cult's founding martyr, still starving for the justice they were denied in life. Fill the spectrum from top to bottom, and ask yourself:

What does your world most fear to worship? What does it worship anyway? And what's the cost of pretending the forbidden god isn't real when everyone can feel it breathing under the floorboards?

Go cause divine trouble. Then fill the crawlspace with something worse.

THE LOOM, PART 2: THE GODS WHO WERE NOT MEANT

The knots are speaking.

Not words. Not yet. What comes out of them is closer to static, to the sound a fire makes when it argues with the wind. The Weaver does not pause. Her hands move through the pattern, and where her attention falls the weave runs smooth: stone, water, silence, law. But behind her, always behind her, where her eyes cannot reach, the knots pulse and twist and begin to take on qualities that the original thread was never meant to carry.

The first to speak is the one that will later call itself the Bright Needle.

It wakes as a density in the pattern: a place where the threads are pulled so tight they hum. It does not yet have a shape, but it has an opinion: things should be straight. Threads should run parallel. The pattern should make sense. The Bright Needle looks at the Weaver's work and sees chaos: gorgeous, grief-born chaos, and it is offended. It begins to pull.

Where the Bright Needle pulls, the weave tightens. Loose threads snap into alignment. Colors sort themselves. The pattern in its vicinity becomes precise, geometric, beautiful in a way that is also, somehow, a little frightening. The Weaver feels the resistance but says nothing. Later, the scholars of the Needle's own priesthood will call this the First Ordering, and they will claim that the world's laws, gravity, time, cause and effect, are the Bright Needle's gift, imposed on the Weaver's raw chaos to make existence survivable.

They are not entirely wrong.

The second to speak is the Fraying Edge.

It wakes where the Bright Needle's order meets the Weaver's unregulated pattern, at the border between the geometric and the wild. It does not pull. It picks. Where the Needle tightens, the Fraying Edge loosens; not undoing the order, exactly, but testing it, worrying at its margins, tugging at the corners where the precision isn't quite perfect. A thread comes free. Then another. The Fraying Edge does not want disorder. It wants to know what happens when order is stressed. It is the first question the pattern ever asked itself, and the question is: what are you made of?

The followers of the Fraying Edge, who are not numerous, and not welcome in most temples, will later claim that death, change, erosion, and entropy are their god's gifts: the forces that prevent the world from becoming a crystal, perfect and dead. The Bright Needle's priests call the Fraying Edge a vandal. The Fraying Edge's followers call the Needle a tyrant. Both are correct. Both are incomplete.

The third to speak is the Shuttle.

It does not wake in one place. It wakes in the movement between places: in the passage of thread from one side of the pattern to the other. The Shuttle is not a knot at all. It is the space between knots, the tension in the thread as it crosses the loom. It carries the warp through the weft and the weft through the warp, and it belongs to neither. It is the first traveler, the first messenger, the first thing in the world that is defined not by where it is but by where it is going.

The Shuttle looks at the Bright Needle and the Fraying Edge and says: You are both the *pattern. I am the thread.*

They argue, of course. They argue immediately and have not stopped. The Bright Needle insists it was first; that order preceded chaos, that the Weaver's intention was always to make something structured, and the Needle is merely the fulfillment of that intention. The Fraying Edge insists it was first; that the original knot, the first flaw, the place where the pattern caught on itself, was an act of unraveling, not ordering, and that the Needle is a parasite that mistook its host for its creation. The Shuttle insists that the question is meaningless, that "first" is a concept that belongs to beings who live inside time, and all three of them woke in the same moment.

They look to the Weaver for an answer.

She does not turn. Her hands continue to move. The thread passes from shuttle to loom to pattern, and the pattern grows, and the gods, for that is what they are now, gods, flaws in the fabric that learned to speak and argue and want; watch her work and wonder what they are for.

The Bright Needle begins to organize its portion of the weave. The Fraying Edge tests the edges. The Shuttle moves between them, carrying thread that is starting to smell like something new: like kinship, like inheritance, like the weight of a name passed from one generation to the next.

The gods do not notice the smell. They will, soon.

The Weaver does not stop.

Next: The gods make echoes, and the echoes begin to look like families.

Chapter 3: Bloodlines & Legacy

Ancestry, Inheritance, and the Weight of the Past

I. Opening Manifesto

The dead are not sleeping. They are arguing, about land, about money, about who married whom and which branch of the family deserves the good silverware. A world without ancestors is a world with amnesia, yes, but more dangerously, it's a world without politics. Because ancestry is never just biology. It's a claim. A weapon. A verdict delivered by people who are no longer around to be cross-examined, and therefore impossible to overrule.

Too many builders treat lineage as decoration, a noble house name here, a prophecy about a chosen bloodline there, a tragic curse that mostly serves to make the protagonist brood attractively. That's wallpaper. Real mythic ancestry is a system of power: who inherits the throne, who controls the story of the founding, who gets written out of the family record and why, and what happens when someone from the erased branch comes back with proof. The dead don't haunt because they're sad. They haunt because they have unfinished *business*, legal, financial, political, and deeply personal.

Here's what this chapter will give you: the tools to build families that drive your world's conflicts, not just decorate them. We'll move from the god who became a bloodline to the bastard who rewrote the family history, from the inherited curse that shapes law for centuries to the adopted stranger who earns a name that blood couldn't buy. By the end, your ancestors will be politicians, litigants, and revolutionaries, not museum pieces collecting dust in a genealogy scroll nobody reads.

II. WHAT IS AN ANCESTOR MYTH?

An ancestor myth is a story about who your people *were* that determines who they're *allowed to be.*

That's the functional definition. Here's the honest one: an ancestor myth is a power structure disguised as a bedtime story. Every culture that venerates its dead is also, consciously or not, making an argument about inheritance, legitimacy, and control. The family that controls the founding story controls the present; because if your great-great-grandmother was the one who slew the dragon, then your family gets the dragon's hoard, and everyone else can argue about it until the dragon comes back.

The House of Atreus is the Western tradition's most famous case study in ancestral devastation. Tantalus, a son of Zeus, tests the gods by butchering his own son Pelops and serving him at a divine banquet. The gods, horrified, condemn Tantalus to eternal torment, hunger and thirst in the presence of food and water forever out of reach. But the curse doesn't stop with him. Pelops, restored to life, wins his bride through a rigged chariot race and murders his co-conspirator, earning another curse. His sons Atreus and Thyestes murder their half-brother Chrysippus, then turn on each other, Atreus slaughtering Thyestes' children and serving them to their father at dinner, an atrocity that echoes Tantalus's original crime like a verse returning to its chorus. Agamemnon, Atreus's son, sacrifices his daughter Iphigenia for favorable winds. His wife Clytemnestra murders him in return. Their son Orestes kills Clytemnestra and is hunted by the Furies until, at last, Athena convenes a court and breaks the cycle. Five generations. Every crime answered by a worse one. The defining feature: each act of violence felt *justified* to the person committing it, and the curse endured because self-righteousness ran in the blood as surely as the violence did.

In the Mande epic of Sundiata, ancestry operates differently; as destiny earned through suffering rather than guilt inherited through crime. Sundiata, born to the ugly, hunchbacked Sogolon after a prophecy tells his father the king that an ungainly bride will produce a mighty heir, spends his childhood unable to walk. He is mocked by his half-brother's mother, exiled, written off. But the Mande tradition holds that lineage alone isn't enough: you prove your blood through action. Sundiata's transformation, rising to walk, to fight, to unite the Mandinka clans and defeat the sorcerer-king Sumanguru, is not just a hero's journey. It's a vindication of his mother's line, proof that the prophecy was right, and the founding act of an empire whose ruling families (the Keitas, the Kondes, the Konnates) still carry those names today. The jelis, the griots, preserve these genealogies as sacred oral history, because to know a family's story is to know its claim to power.

In the Mabinogion, the Four Branches of Welsh myth trace the fortunes of Pryderi, born to Pwyll, lord of Dyfed, and the semi-divine Rhiannon, stolen as an infant, raised by a foster father who doesn't know his parentage, eventually returned to his rightful parents. But the cycle doesn't end with reunion. Pryderi inherits his father's supernatural alliances and his father's enemies. A grudge against Pwyll from a humiliated rival, Gwawl, echoes forward through magical retribution: Dyfed itself is cursed into a wasteland, and Pryderi is eventually killed in a conflict that traces back to his father's generation. Ancestry in Welsh myth isn't just about bloodlines; it's about debts that follow the name.

These stories aren't just about families. They're about the gravitational pull of the past on the present, and the question every mythic descendant must eventually answer: *Do I carry this forward, or do I try to put it down?*

III. CORE ARCHETYPES: THE MYTHIC BLOODLINE

Every ancestral story is built on one of these patterns, or, in the best cases, on the collision between two or three of them at once.

1. THE DEMI-GOD FOUNDER

A family claims descent from a god, a hero, or a supernatural being, and the claim shapes everything. In the Khitan tradition, the founding myth of the Liao Dynasty holds that a sacred man riding a white horse floated down the Laoha River and met a heavenly woman riding a cart drawn by a grey ox on the Xar Moron River; where the rivers converged, they mated and produced eight sons, who became the ancestors of the eight Khitan tribes. The Keita dynasty of the Mali Empire traced its lineage through Sundiata back to Bilali Bounama, a companion of the Prophet Muhammad, braiding political and spiritual legitimacy into a single genealogical thread. Herakles, son of Zeus, founded bloodlines across the Greek world, and the Heracleidae, his descendants, used that descent to justify the Dorian invasions.

The Gift: Divine descent gives a bloodline cosmic authorization. Laws, territories, rituals, all of it can be anchored to the ancestor who walked with the gods. It's the most powerful legitimating story in any world's toolkit.

The Trap: The "chosen one" problem. If the founder was divine, what does that make the descendants? Too special to challenge, too sacred to fail, too destined to be interesting. The best demi-god founder myths build in a flaw: Herakles' divine strength came with madness. Sundiata's prophesied greatness came with years of paralysis and mockery. The founder's divinity should be a burden as much as a badge.

2. THE ANCESTRAL CURSE

An old crime, a broken promise, a violated taboo, and the family pays for it across generations. The House of Atreus is the definitive example, but curses come in many registers. In Maori tradition, the violation of *tapu* (sacred restrictions) can bring down consequences that persist through a lineage. Norse sagas are thick with families bound by oaths that prove ruinous three generations later.

The Gift: A curse is a story engine. It generates conflict at every generational turn: Who inherits the punishment? Can it be broken? What happens to the family member who tries to break it and fails? A curse gives a bloodline a ticking clock and a moral question that can never be cleanly answered.

The Trap: The passive curse. If the descendants merely *suffer* the curse without agency, without the opportunity to confront, negotiate, resist, or accidentally make it worse, it's not mythic. It's just bad luck with a pedigree. The Atreid curse is devastating because every generation *chooses* the violence that perpetuates it. They could stop. They don't.

3. THE SACRED TALISMAN

An object, mark, or practice passed down through a lineage, a sword, a birthmark, a song, a scar, a secret. Excalibur belongs to the rightful king of Britain, and its loss matters as much as its possession. In many West African traditions, the objects carried by the founding ancestor, a staff, a drum, a mask, are themselves repositories of *nyama* (spiritual power) that the family is obligated to maintain.

The Gift: A talisman makes inheritance *physical*. It can be stolen, broken, hidden, or forged. It gives your family saga a material stake, not just "who inherits the name" but "who possesses the thing that proves the name."

The Trap: The magic sword and nothing else. A talisman that only grants power is a video game item. A talisman that demands something, a sacrifice, a secret, a behavioral code, a terrible knowledge; is a story.

4. THE FORGOTTEN BRANCH

The lost heir, the erased sibling, the exiled line, the family secret buried so deep that discovering it reshapes the entire political landscape. Every royal family in every mythology has at least one: the bastard child, the defeated branch, the line that was supposed to die out and didn't. In the Norse sagas, Sigurd's descendants splinter into competing claims and hidden identities. In Chinese dynastic history, lost branches and secret heirs are so common they constitute their own genre.

The Gift: A forgotten branch is a loaded gun on the mantelpiece. The moment it resurfaces, every existing power structure is threatened. Legitimacy, inheritance law, marriage alliances, all of it is suddenly in question. The forgotten branch doesn't need to be powerful. It just needs to *exist*.

The Trap: The soap opera reveal. "You're actually the true heir!" is only interesting if it costs something. What does the forgotten branch *want*? What have they become in their exile? Do they even want the inheritance, or has their erasure turned them into something the main family can't recognize, or can't survive?

5. THE INHERITED DESTINY

A fate, prophecy, or role that the family cannot escape, only fulfill, resist, or reinterpret. In Hindu tradition, the concept of *dharma* encompasses duties that flow from birth, family, and station: the warrior's child inherits the warrior's obligation. In many indigenous traditions, certain families carry specific ceremonial responsibilities, not by choice but by descent, and shirking these responsibilities endangers not just the family but the community.

The Gift: Inherited destiny raises the question every mythic descendant must confront: *Am I this name, or am I something else?* It generates rebels, conformists, tragic inheritors, and the occasional revolutionary who transforms the destiny by fulfilling it wrong.

The Trap: Fate without friction. If the destiny is inevitable and the descendant simply complies, you've written a conveyor belt, not a story. The best inherited destinies include a cost, a paradox, or a choice that makes fulfillment and rebellion equally devastating.

6. THE ADOPTED LINE

This is the archetype the "blood is destiny" model never sees coming: ancestry by choice, by ritual, by law, or by theft.

In ancient Rome, adoption wasn't a consolation prize; it was a political technology. Julius Caesar adopted his great-nephew Octavian, who became Augustus, Rome's first emperor. The Five Good Emperors, Nerva, Trajan, Hadrian, Antoninus Pius, and Marcus Aurelius, each adopted their successor rather than passing power to a biological son, and Roman law made adoption legally equivalent to blood kinship. The experiment ended when Marcus Aurelius chose his biological son Commodus; Commodus's disastrous reign is often marked as the beginning of Rome's decline. The lesson: the chosen child may outperform the born one.

In Hawaiian tradition, *hanai* means "to feed" or "to nourish," tying kinship to the act of care rather than the accident of birth. In pre-contact Hawai'i, grandparents traditionally had claims on firstborn children. Hanai children maintained connections with their biological families while being fully integrated into their adoptive households; the family didn't shrink, it expanded. Queen Lili'uokalani herself was a hanai child.

In medieval Ireland, fosterage was governed by the Brehon Laws and considered among the most sacred bonds in the social order, the affection between foster-child and foster-parent often exceeded that between blood relations. Children were placed in allied households from age seven, educated according to rank, and owed their foster-family support in old age. It was alliance, education, and obligation wrapped in the language of family, and in wartime, the foster-bond could prove more reliable than blood.

The Gift: The Adopted Line demolishes the assumption that blood determines belonging. It opens up found families, political dynasties, ritual kinship, and the radical idea that you can *earn* an ancestry, or that an ancestry can choose *you*. For worldbuilders, it creates a second track of inheritance that runs parallel to (and often conflicts with) biological descent. Who has the stronger claim: the blood heir who was absent, or the adopted child who was raised in the house and knows every secret?

The Trap: Romanticizing adoption while ignoring its politics. Real adopted lineages are as tangled with power, obligation, and resentment as biological ones. The Roman adoption system worked brilliantly; until it was convenient to stop using it. Hawaiian hanai expanded the family beautifully; and missionaries tried to dismantle it as uncivilized. Celtic fosterage built alliances; and also created potential hostages. The Adopted Line isn't a utopian alternative to blood. It's another form of family, with all the mess that entails.

IV. WORKSHOP: BUILD A FAMILY THAT MATTERS

This isn't a questionnaire; it's a build. By the end, you'll have a bloodline with a founding act, a wound that won't heal, branches that don't speak to each other, and at least one descendant whose very existence is a political crisis.

STEP 1: THE FOUNDING CRIME (OR MIRACLE)

Every family begins with a story that gives them power, and that story is almost never clean. Tantalus butchered his son. Sundiata's mother was mocked and exiled before she was vindicated. Romulus killed Remus. The Keita dynasty's founder overcame paralysis, exile, and sorcery. What happened at the root of your family that gave them their name, their land, their authority, and what was the cost?

In the worked example below, the Ashenmoor family's founding act was a betrayal: the first Ashenmoor swore an oath to a dying river spirit, promising to guard its waters forever in exchange for the power to make barren land bloom. She kept the oath for exactly one generation before her son dammed the river to irrigate his fields. *What's your family's founding act? Was it heroic, criminal, or both? Who paid the price? Write it down, one paragraph, no more.*

STEP 2: THE SIGNATURE TRAIT

What mark, gift, flaw, or inheritance runs in the blood; or is said to? This can be physical (the golden eyes of the Giltmorrow, the Atreid streak of violence), cultural (the Keita family's claim to the lion's name, the griot's obligation to preserve their genealogy), or supernatural (the ancestral spirit that visits every third-born daughter).

The Ashenmoors carry green-stained hands, a discoloration that appears at puberty and never fades, said to be the river spirit's mark. Some branches display it prominently as proof of lineage. Others wear gloves. *What does your family carry that they can't hide, can't fake, and can't quite explain? Write it.*

STEP 3: THE GENERATIONAL WOUND

The founding crime leaves a wound that the family transmits along with its name. Not a curse, a *tendency*. The Atreids' wound was self-righteous violence: every generation believed they were justified. The Ashenmoors' wound is broken promises: the first betrayal set a pattern, and now every branch of the family has a reputation for oaths that bend. Some Ashenmoors fight this reputation. Others have learned to use it.

What behavioral pattern does your family carry? Not a magical curse (too easy), a psychological or social inheritance that shapes how the family makes decisions. Name it.

STEP 4: THE SPLINTERED BRANCHES

No family stays unified. Disagreements about the founding story, the inheritance, the signature trait, or the generational wound will fracture any bloodline given enough time. The Ashenmoors split three ways: the Greenthorns, who honor the original oath and tend the river's remnants; the Fieldholders, who built an agricultural empire on the dammed land and consider the oath sentimental nonsense; and the Ashenmoor-in-Exile, a single line descended from the founder's second child, who refused the river bargain entirely and left.

Draw your family's fracture. What caused it? What does each branch believe about the founding story? Do they still speak to each other? Write the split, and the grudge.

STEP 5: THE LIVING CONSEQUENCES

Ancestry only matters if it shapes the present. The Ashenmoor split affects everything: the Greenthorns control the temple districts and claim spiritual authority; the Fieldholders control the economy; the Exiles are rumored to have allied with the river spirit's surviving kin. Inheritance law in the region is a mess because the three branches can't agree on whether the founder's oath was binding on all descendants or only on the eldest line. Marriages between branches are politically explosive. And the river, what's left of it, is dying.

How does your family's past shape the present-day world? Who has power? Who wants it? What would happen if the founding story turned out to be wrong? Write the consequences.

V. QUICK MENU FOR INSPIRATION

Roll, pick, or collide. No combination is wrong; the stranger the pairing, the more interesting the family.

Founder: God's lover | Exile | Monster-slayer | Oath-breaker | Adopted stranger | Trickster | Failed hero | Conqueror | Refugee | Prophet who was wrong

Signature Trait: Birthmark | Unusual eye color | Immunity to something | A voice that compels | Green thumb / cursed crops | Dreams of the founder | Second sight on the solstice | A talent for languages | Ambidexterity | Can't cross running water

Wound: Broken oaths | Fratricide | Stolen inheritance | Cowardice in a crucial moment | A forbidden marriage | A truth no one will speak | Collaboration with an enemy | A child sold for power | Abandonment of a sacred duty

Talisman: A sword that rusts near liars | A songbook written in blood | A map to nowhere | A sealed letter from the founder | A lock of divine hair | A debt-ledger | A ring that fits no descendant | A recipe | A key to a door no one has found

Branch Type: The Loyalists (who guard the story) | The Revisionists (who rewrote it) | The Exiles (who reject it) | The Pretenders (who claim it falsely) | The Adopted (who earned their place) | The Forgotten (who were erased)

Destiny: Guard the seal until it breaks | Produce the prophesied child | Maintain the alliance at any cost | Atone for the founding crime | Keep the secret | Destroy what the founder built

VI. WORKED EXAMPLES

SHOWCASE: THE ASHENMOOR BLOODLINE

Three generations of an oath broken, a river dying, and a family that can't agree on what it owes.

The first Ashenmoor was a woman named Vael who walked into a drought-stricken valley and found a river spirit dying in its own silted bed. The spirit, a serpentine thing of mud and green fire, barely more than a voice by the time Vael found it, offered a bargain: tend my waters, keep my channel clean, and I will make your soil remember what it was before the drought burned it. The power Vael received was modest but real. Where she planted, things grew. Not miraculously, not overnight, but with the stubborn, impossible persistence of something that should have died and didn't. She swore the oath. Her hands turned green at the wrists, as if the river had stained them from the inside.

Vael kept her word. Her settlement grew around the river, which recovered, slowly, into a deep, cold current that ran green-brown through a valley that had been dust. She died old, respected, and slightly feared, because the people who lived on her land noticed that when Vael was angry, the river rose, and when she was grieving, the wells tasted of salt.

Her son, Torvald Ashenmoor, inherited the green-stained hands and the responsibility. He also inherited ambition. The river was powerful, but it was also wild, flooding in spring, drying to a trickle in high summer. Torvald built a dam. Not to destroy the river, he said, but to *manage* it, to make its gifts predictable, to expand the fertile land, to feed a growing population that couldn't survive on the river's unpredictable generosity. The dam held. The fields expanded. The river, confined to its new channel, stopped flooding. It also stopped singing, though only the old women who remembered Vael's time noticed this, and no one listened to them.

The river spirit did not die. But it diminished. Its voice, once audible at the riverbank on quiet nights, could now only be heard in the deepest cisterns. Torvald's hands were still green. His children's hands were still green. But the shade was paler; less river, more bruise.

Torvald's three children split the Ashenmoor line. Eris, the eldest, was horrified by what her father had done. She dismantled a section of the dam on the family's western holdings, restored a stretch of natural riverbed, and declared her branch the true keepers of Vael's oath. Her descendants, the Greenthorns, became temple-builders and water-priests, and they have a habit of drowning on calm days, which they consider a mark of the river spirit's attention. Maren, the middle child, expanded the dam system and founded the agricultural settlements that eventually became the region's economic backbone. Her descendants, the Fieldholders, consider the oath outdated sentimentality and the green-stained hands an embarrassment to be covered with gloves at formal occasions. And Lias, the youngest, who heard the river spirit weeping in a cistern when she was nine and never recovered from the sound, walked east into the marshlands and was not seen again for fifteen years. When she returned, she had a child whose hands were not green but blue, and she would not say who the father was. Her descendants, the Ashenmoor-in-Exile, live in the marshes, and the things they know about water make the Greenthorns uneasy and the Fieldholders nervous.

Three generations later, the river is failing. The dam holds, but the water behind it has turned brackish. The Greenthorns say the oath must be honored in full; the dam must come down. The Fieldholders say the dam is the only thing keeping the valley alive and the Greenthorns are fanatics. The Exiles have been seen at the river's source, doing something with blue fire that neither branch can identify. And in the capital, someone has found a document, old, fragile, possibly forged, suggesting that Vael's oath included a clause no one mentions: that if the river died, the Ashenmoor line would end with it.

Analytical note: The Ashenmoor bloodline demonstrates how a single founding act (the oath) generates consequences that compound across generations, political, spiritual, and personal. Each branch represents a different relationship to the ancestral inheritance: the Greenthorns embrace it, the Fieldholders reject it, and the Exiles have transformed it into something the founder wouldn't recognize. The unresolved question, what does the family actually owe?, is the engine that drives every conflict. Notice that no branch is entirely right. The Greenthorns are sincere but rigid. The Fieldholders are pragmatic but in denial. The Exiles know things but won't share them. This is how mythic families generate story: not through clear heroes and villains, but through irreconcilable positions that all have a legitimate claim on the truth.

CLASSIC MODEL: THE IRONVOW COMPACT

In the frozen northern reaches, three clans, the Ironvows, the Ashfells, and the Driftkin, trace their alliance not to blood but to a shared ordeal. Six hundred years ago, their founders survived a winter so brutal it killed every other settlement in the region. They swore a compact: their children would be raised communally, each child spending three years with each clan, so that no Ironvow, Ashfell, or Driftkin would ever be a stranger to the others. The compact has held, more or less. But the Ironvows have grown wealthy. The Ashfells have grown militant. And the Driftkin, who were always the smallest, have begun refusing to return the children, claiming that the compact makes every child equally theirs. The question tearing the alliance apart: does shared upbringing create shared ancestry, or is it just a treaty dressed in the language of family?

VII. PITFALLS

The Genealogy Dump. Your family tree is not your story. If you find yourself listing names and dates across generations without establishing what each generation *did differently* with their inheritance, you've written a census, not a myth. Every generation that appears should make a choice that changes the family's trajectory.

The Clean Curse. If your ancestral curse works like a machine, predictable, automatic, impersonal, it's not mythic. It's a malfunction. The Atreid curse is devastating because the family *participates* in it. Every generation could have stopped. They didn't, because stopping would have meant surrendering the pride that was also the family's defining strength.

Blood Essentialism. The assumption that blood determines character is lazy and, frankly, dangerous. The most interesting mythic bloodlines include adopted members, bastard lines, and individuals who inherit the name but not the nature, and the tension between "what the blood says" and "who the person actually is" generates far richer story than "the bloodline breeds true."

The Fossil Family. If your ancestral lineage was established in the founding era and nothing has changed since, you don't have a mythic family, you have a monument. Families evolve. They fracture, merge, decline, reinvent. The Ashenmoors look nothing like Vael intended, and that's the point.

VIII. WORLDBUILDING HOOKS

Who controls the family story, and what happens when someone challenges it? In your world, are genealogies maintained by priests, bards, state archivists, or the families themselves? What happens when two families claim the same founder?

How does ancestry shape law? Can a member of a cursed line hold public office? Are there inheritance laws that distinguish between blood heirs and adopted heirs? Does a bastard child inherit the family's obligations as well as its property, or just the obligations?

What are the politics of marriage between branches? When the Greenthorns marry a Fieldholder, whose interpretation of the oath wins? When a family with divine descent marries into a family of adopted lineage, does the divine blood "outrank" the earned name?

Can you leave a bloodline? In a world where ancestry carries spiritual weight; where the dead can literally haunt you, where the founding curse is real and verifiable, what does it mean to renounce your family? Is it possible? Is it survivable? Or does the lineage follow you regardless, like a debt you didn't sign for but must pay?

What happens when the founding story turns out to be a lie? Every family mythology is, at some level, propaganda. What if the divine ancestor was actually a refugee? What if the founding miracle was a con? What if the great betrayal was actually self-defense, and the family has been atoning for a crime that was never committed?

IX. Annotated Reading List

Primary Myths:

The House of Atreus (Greek myth cycle, esp. Aeschylus's *Oresteia*), Five generations of self-righteous murder, the most complete generational curse in Western mythology, and the radical idea that a court of law might break what blood could not.

The Mabinogion (trans. Sioned Davies), Welsh myth where ancestry is a live wire: Pryderi inherits his father's supernatural alliances and his enemies, and the debts of one generation reshape the landscape for the next.

The Epic of Sundiata (trans. D.T. Niane or J.W. Johnson), The Mande tradition's foundational epic, where lineage is prophecy, disability is a test, and the griot's recitation of genealogy is itself an act of political power.

West African oral traditions, Ancestor veneration not as passive remembrance but as active negotiation. The dead participate. They have demands. Start with the Yoruba Egungun tradition if you need a single entry point.

Modern & Speculative:

One Hundred Years of Solitude (Gabriel Garcia Marquez), The Buendia family repeats its names, its mistakes, and its obsessions across a century until the repetition devours them. The definitive novel about what happens when a family can't outrun its own mythology.

Kindred (Octavia Butler), Ancestry as literal haunting. A modern Black woman pulled back in time to save the white slaveholder she descends from. The most unflinching exploration of what "inherited legacy" actually costs.

The Song of Achilles (Madeline Miller), Lineage as fate, love as the thing that almost breaks fate's hold, and the devastating weight of being someone's son in a world where divine blood demands divine sacrifice.

X. Creative Dare: The Reckoning

Build a family with a secret so old that no living member knows it, but whose consequences are shaping every conflict in your world right now. Then put a descendant in a room with the proof. Not the "chosen one" descendant. The one who never wanted the name. The one who has been quietly building a life that has nothing to do with the bloodline.

Now ask: What do they do with the truth? And what does the family, every branch, every grudge, every ghost, do about them?

Write the moment the past catches up.

THE LOOM, PART 3: THE ECHO IN THE BLOOD

The gods do not have children. Not in the way the mortals will; not through the body's slow and tender labor. The gods have echoes.

Wherever the Bright Needle's story is told, a mortal family begins to build. Not because the Needle wills it, the Needle is too busy stitching the sky to notice, but because a story told often enough leaves a mark on the teller. The Needle's people do not know they are the Needle's people. They only know that their eldest child always has steady hands. That their houses are built with walls so straight they seem to reproach the wind. That their laws, once written, are not revised; because revision implies the first draft was flawed, and the Needle's people do not draft. They declare.

The first family of the Needle calls itself the Lineborn. They build their city at the place where two rivers meet at a perfect right angle, the only such junction in the world, and they consider this proof that the world was designed for them. Their laws are carved into the foundation stones of their houses, and to move house means to carry the stone. Their inheritance passes to the child whose hands are steadiest, determined by a test involving a needle, a thread, and a flame. The child who threads the needle without the thread touching the flame inherits the family name. The child who fails is given a different name and a different house and is loved, but not trusted with sharp things.

The Fraying Edge's people are harder to find. They do not build cities. They do not write laws. Every third generation, one of them walks into the wilderness and does not come back, and the family does not grieve; they celebrate, because the walking-away is the Fraying Edge's gift, the assurance that the bloodline has not calcified, that somewhere in the wild a child of the Edge is unraveling something that needed unraveling. But the celebration is uneasy. Because sometimes the one who walks away comes back, changed, carrying something the family didn't ask for, humming a melody that makes the foundations of the Lineborn's city vibrate in a way the Lineborn do not appreciate.

The Shuttle's descendants are born between borders.

They belong to no city, no law-stone, no wilderness. They are the traders, the translators, the ones who carry messages between the Needle's people and the Edge's people when the two are too proud to speak directly. They are trusted by no one and needed by everyone. Their inheritance is not a name or a house or a patch of wild ground; it is a road. The Shuttle's children inherit routes, not property. They know which mountain pass opens in spring and which river freezes solid enough to cross in winter. They know the Lineborn's language and the Edge's language and a third language that belongs to neither, which they speak only among themselves and which sounds, to anyone who overhears it, like the noise a loom makes when the shuttle passes through.

The Shuttle's eldest child is always born on a journey. Always. Even if the mother stays home and bars the door; the labor begins, and something shifts, and the child arrives between one place and another: between rooms, between heartbeats, between the last word of one sentence and the first word of the next. The Shuttle's people consider this auspicious. Everyone else considers it unsettling.

The gods do not notice these families. Not yet. But the Weaver notices. Her hands slow on the loom, not stopping, never stopping, but a hesitation enters the rhythm. The pattern is growing in ways she did not weave. The mortal families are adding threads of their own, not grief-thread, not the silver-gray of the original warp, but something new. Something that smells like ambition, like resentment, like the furious need to matter. The Weaver has a word for this smell, but she has not spoken it yet.

The Bright Needle sees the Lineborn and is satisfied. The Fraying Edge sees its wanderers and is pleased. The Shuttle sees its road-children and feels something it will later learn to call loneliness, because the Shuttle's people carry thread between worlds, and carrying is not the same as belonging.

In the Lineborn's city, a child is born with one steady hand and one restless one. The family does not know what to do. The Needle's test requires both hands. The Edge's wilderness requires neither. The child belongs to both stories and fits in none, and the family's law-stones have no clause for this; because the law-stones were written before anyone imagined that a god's echo could tangle with another god's echo, that a child could carry two inheritances in a single body, and that the tangling might produce something neither god intended.

The child's name will matter soon.

Next: The tangled child takes up a needle, and a knife.

Chapter 4: The Hero & The Villain

Protagonists, Adversaries, and the Space Between

I. Opening Manifesto

A story without a villain is just a weather report. Pleasant, predictable, and over in thirty seconds. Because nothing *happened*. The sun came up, someone was brave, the world kept spinning. Congratulations. You've written a calendar.

But here's the uglier truth: we're drowning in heroes, too. Stoic loners with tragic backstories. Farm boys with swords and prophecies. Orphans who turn out to be secretly magnificent, and villains who exist mainly to prove it. We've mass-produced heroism into a formula so reliable you could set your watch by it; and a formula that reliable has stopped being dangerous, which means it's stopped being *mythic*. The real heroes of world mythology are terrifying. Gilgamesh begins his story as a tyrant who rapes brides on their wedding night. Arjuna, the greatest warrior in the Mahabharata, drops his bow and weeps on the battlefield because he'd rather die than kill his own family. Sundiata, the founder of an empire, spends his childhood unable to walk. These are not wish-fulfillment fantasies. They're the stories cultures tell when they want to look at the thing they're most afraid of and ask: *What kind of person could survive this?*

This chapter builds heroes and villains together; because they've never been separate. The villain is the hero's shadow, their diagnostic, the question the hero can't answer without losing something precious. We're going to forge them as a pair, using what I call the **Mirror Framework**: shared origin, divergent choices, complementary wounds. By the end, you won't just have a protagonist and an antagonist. You'll have two figures locked in a conversation that your entire world has been waiting to overhear.

II. THE MIRROR FRAMEWORK: HEROES AND VILLAINS AS A PAIR

Here's the insight that most worldbuilding books miss: the hero and villain aren't opposites. They're *the same person who made different choices.*

The Mahabharata understands this better than any text in human history. Arjuna and Karna are half-brothers who don't know it: sons of the same mother, Kunti, born through divine boons from different gods. Arjuna is the legitimate prince, trained by the finest teachers, surrounded by allies. Karna is the abandoned firstborn, raised by a charioteer's family, rejected by the establishment, who earns his place through sheer talent and the loyalty of a corrupt prince. They are mirrors. Arjuna has every advantage and still can't bring himself to fight. Karna has been denied everything and can't stop fighting, even when he knows his cause is wrong. When they finally face each other at Kurukshetra, it's not a battle between good and evil. It's a battle between two versions of what loyalty costs, and neither version is clean.

Milton's *Paradise Lost* runs the same architecture. Satan and the Son are the same ambition pointed in opposite directions. Satan's argument: *Why should we obey?*, is uncomfortably persuasive. The horror isn't that he's wrong. It's that he's half-right, and the half that's wrong is going to burn the world.

THIS IS THE MIRROR FRAMEWORK:

Shared Origin. The hero and villain come from the same place, the same wound, the same unanswered question. They might be literal siblings (Atreus and Thyestes), childhood friends, students of the same teacher, children of the same curse.

The Divergent Moment. Something happens: a betrayal, a revelation, a choice under pressure, and one of them goes left while the other goes right. This moment should feel *survivable*. Neither choice is insane. Both make sense. That's what makes it devastating.

Complementary Wounds. What the hero is blind to, the villain sees clearly. What the villain can't feel, the hero carries like a stone. The hero's strength is the villain's weakness inverted. The villain's logic is the hero's fear made articulate.

The Cost of Victory. The hero doesn't win clean. To defeat the villain, they must sacrifice something the villain forced them to understand they needed. Every heroic victory is also a loss: of innocence, of certainty, of a version of themselves they can't get back.

When Gilgamesh returns from his quest for immortality, having lost the plant of eternal youth to a serpent, he doesn't come back with a triumph. He comes back with *walls*. He looks at Uruk and realizes that the only immortality available was the one he already had: the city he built, the people he protected, the story they'd tell. The tyrant became a seeker. The seeker became a builder. And the building cost him the illusion that he was anything more than mortal.

That's a hero's arc. And notice, the villain of Gilgamesh's story is mortality itself, which can't be beaten, only understood. The best villains work exactly this way: they're the truth the hero doesn't want to face, given a body and a voice and a plan.

III. Core Archetypes: The Many Masks of the Hero

Every hero is a remix of a few recurring types. Here's your palette: not a checklist, but a set of masks your protagonist can wear, layer, and eventually break.

1. The Monster-Slayer

The hero who faces the thing that everyone else runs from. Beowulf swims into the monster's lair with nothing but his hands. Herakles slays the Hydra and wrestles Death itself, and his own madness, sent by Hera, which drove him to murder his wife and children, is the wound that fuels every labor. In the Mande tradition, Sundiata defeats the sorcerer-king Sumanguru not through brute force alone but through knowledge of his enemy's magical weakness, the spur of a white rooster.

The Gift: The Monster-Slayer validates the idea that the terrible thing can be confronted and survived. Every culture needs this figure.

The Trap: Power without cost. If your Monster-Slayer can kill anything and never pays for it, they're an action figure, not a hero. Beowulf wins every fight and dies in the last one. Herakles is the strongest man alive and can't save his own family. The slayer who never bleeds is a commercial, not a myth.

2. THE LAWBREAKER

Brings forbidden knowledge, crosses lines the world says are sacred, and pays the price. Prometheus steals fire from the gods and gives it to humanity, and spends eternity chained to a rock while an eagle eats his liver. Maui of Polynesian tradition hauls islands from the sea, slows the sun, and steals fire from the underworld, always bending or breaking the rules to give mortals what they need. The Lawbreaker's heroism is inseparable from their transgression; the gift *is* the crime.

The Gift: The Lawbreaker asks the most dangerous question in any mythology: *What if the rules are wrong?* This archetype is the engine of every revolutionary myth, every story about progress through defiance, every tale where the outcast turns out to have been right.

The Trap: The Lawbreaker who never pays the price is just a power fantasy with a rebel haircut. Prometheus's fire costs him everything. Maui's final transgression, trying to conquer death by entering the goddess Hine-nui-te-po, kills him. The law breaks back. If yours doesn't, your hero is a bumper sticker.

3. THE SACRIFICE

Saves others by suffering, dying, or transforming. This is the archetype that generates the most visceral mythic power, and the most uncomfortable questions. In the Wemale tradition of Seram in eastern Indonesia, Hainuwele is a girl born from a coconut who can produce precious gifts from her own body. During a great communal dance, the villagers grow jealous and bury her alive. Her dismembered body is planted in the earth, and from it grow the tuber crops that become the people's staple food. Life from death. Abundance from murder. The world sustained by an act of communal violence against its most generous member. Inanna descends to the underworld and is killed, hung on a meat hook for three days, and returns, changed, dangerous, having paid for wisdom with her own corpse.

The Gift: The Sacrifice makes death meaningful. In a mythic world, someone's suffering *produces* something: knowledge, food, redemption, a new order. This archetype is the reason myths feel heavier than fairy tales.

The Trap: The Sacrifice who is purely noble, purely willing, purely clean is not a mythic figure; they're a saint, and saints make terrible protagonists. The best sacrifices are complicated. Hainuwele doesn't choose her death. Inanna goes to the underworld from ambition, not altruism. Odin hangs himself on Yggdrasil for nine days to gain the runes, that's self-sacrifice in the service of power, not mercy. Give your sacrifice a motive that isn't pure, and the myth becomes real.

4. THE RELUCTANT / THE BROKEN

Doesn't want the quest, is shattered by it, or is driven not by glory but by grief, guilt, or sheer survival. Arjuna is the supreme example: on the eve of the Kurukshetra War, facing an army that includes his grandfather Bhishma, his teacher Drona, and his half-brother Karna, he drops his legendary bow Gandiva and refuses to fight. His limbs tremble. His mouth goes dry. "I see no good in killing my own kinsmen in battle," he tells Krishna. The entire Bhagavad Gita, one of the most influential philosophical texts in human history, exists because the hero said *no*. Krishna must spend seven hundred verses convincing him that his duty as a warrior overrides his personal horror. Arjuna fights. But his reluctance isn't weakness. It's the moral center of the entire epic.

The Gift: The Reluctant Hero earns the audience's trust precisely because they don't want to be here. Their resistance proves they understand the stakes. A hero who marches eagerly to war hasn't reckoned with what war costs. A hero who has to be dragged has already paid the first installment.

The Trap: Reluctance that never resolves into action is paralysis, not heroism. Arjuna fights. Moses leads. Odysseus endures. The broken hero who stays broken is tragedy without resolution, valid in literature, but a dead end for myth, which demands transformation.

5. THE CHOSEN (BUT FLAWED)

Picked by fate, prophecy, or divine accident, but catastrophically imperfect. King Arthur pulls the sword from the stone but can't hold his kingdom together. Siegfried is invulnerable except for one spot between his shoulder blades, and his story is the tragedy of a hero who can't be hurt by anything except trust.

The Gift: The Chosen hero lets your myth ask: *What does it cost to be destined?* The prophecy is a cage. The divine blood is a debt. The sword in the stone is a contract no one read before signing.

The Trap: The Chosen One who is merely special, no flaw, no cost, no crack, is the most overused figure in modern storytelling. If your hero is Chosen, make the choosing hurt.

A note on the Trickster Hero: The hero who wins through wit, deception, and the refusal to play by the rules, Anansi, Maui, Sun Wukong, belongs to a tradition so rich and strange that it gets its own chapter. See Chapter 5: The Trickster Creation Kit. We'll cross paths with them there.

IV. Core Archetypes: The Shapes of Villainy

Villains aren't obstacles. They're diagnostics. The villain tells you what's wrong with the world the hero lives in: the weakness in the system, the lie everyone agreed to believe, the cost of the comfortable status quo. Here are the shapes they take.

1. The Tyrant

Seizes, hoards, or corrupts power. Gilgamesh before his transformation, raping brides, exhausting his subjects through forced labor, is a Tyrant who happens to be the protagonist of his own story. Duryodhana in the Mahabharata is a prince who believes the throne is rightfully his and will burn down the world before surrendering it. The Tyrant's logic is always internally consistent: *I deserve this. I earned this. The world is better with me in charge.*

The Gift: The Tyrant exposes the cost of power. Every political mythology needs one, because the Tyrant is the answer to the question: *What happens when the hero's strength is turned inward?*

The Trap: The Tyrant who is merely cruel is boring. Duryodhana is compelling because he's not entirely wrong. The Pandavas' claim to the throne is complicated, and his loyalty to his friends (including Karna) is genuine. The Tyrant should be someone who, in a different story, might have been the hero.

2. The Betrayer

The friend, mentor, or family member who turns. Mordred, born of incest between Arthur and his half-sister Morgause, destroys Camelot not from pure malice but from the impossible position his birth placed him in. Loki in Norse mythology is the gods' companion who slowly, inexorably, becomes their destroyer, and the Norse texts can't quite decide whether to blame him or the gods who mistreated him first.

The Gift: The Betrayer makes trust dangerous. They're the reason your world's alliances have fine print and your heroes sleep with one eye open.

The Trap: Betrayal for no reason is melodrama. The Betrayer needs a grievance the audience can feel, not agree with, but *feel*. Mordred's existence is Arthur's sin. Loki was always the outsider who was tolerated, never accepted. The best betrayals are revenges the hero earned.

3. THE OUTSIDER

Feared because they don't fit. Grendel in *Beowulf* is a descendant of Cain, cursed to exist outside every community, haunting the marches. Medusa, before she was a monster, was a priestess raped by Poseidon in Athena's temple, and *Athena punished her*. The Outsider villain often started as a victim, and the world's refusal to acknowledge this is what makes them dangerous.

The Gift: The Outsider asks: *Who did the world exclude, and what did the exclusion create?* This is the most politically charged villain type because it forces the myth to reckon with the cost of its own boundaries.

The Trap: The Outsider who is simply alien and evil is a xenophobic cliche. The best Outsider villains are monstrous because the world *made* them monstrous.

4. THE TRUE BELIEVER

The villain who is the hero of their own story, and whose logic is uncomfortably persuasive. Ozymandias in *Watchmen* murders millions to prevent nuclear war and might have been right. The True Believer is the villain who has done the math, weighed the suffering, and concluded that the terrible thing is actually the moral thing. They don't enjoy destruction. They endure it, because someone has to.

The Gift: The True Believer is the hardest villain to defeat because you can't just overpower them; you have to *out-argue* them, or admit that their argument has a point your hero can't answer.

The Trap: The True Believer who is just a lecture on moral relativism is tedious. The horror should be *specific*: not "maybe evil is relative" but "this person looked at a particular problem and reached a particular conclusion, and the conclusion is monstrous, and you can follow every step of their logic."

5. THE WORLDBREAKER

Wants to destroy the existing order: to raze it, unmake it, return it to chaos. Apep, the great serpent of Egyptian mythology, embodies this at its most primal. Every night, Apep attacks Ra's solar barque as it passes through the underworld, seeking to swallow the sun and plunge the world into permanent darkness. Apep is not motivated by revenge or ideology. Apep *is* chaos: the force that existed before creation and wants creation undone. The gods, the dead, even mortal priests performing nightly rituals against wax effigies of the serpent, all participate in the endless battle. And every night, Apep regenerates. The war never ends.

The Gift: The Worldbreaker makes existence itself feel precarious. Your world isn't guaranteed. Someone, or something, is always trying to end it, and the only thing between order and oblivion is the daily labor of those who choose to fight.

The Trap: Pure chaos is narratively inert. Apep works in Egyptian myth because the nightly battle is ritualized, communal, and deeply personal; the dead themselves help fight. If your Worldbreaker has no personality and no relationship to the hero, they're a natural disaster, not a villain.

A note on the Trickster Villain: The villain who disrupts through wit, exposure, and sacred mischief, Loki in his darker modes, the trickster who stops being funny, also lives in Chapter 5. Cross-reference there. We'll save you a seat.

V. THE NECESSARY SHADOW

This is the heart of the chapter.

Every villain is a diagnostic. They don't just oppose the hero; they *reveal* something the hero's world would rather not know. The Tyrant reveals that power was always capable of abuse. The Betrayer reveals that trust was always a gamble. The Outsider reveals that the world's boundaries created the monster by creating the exile. The True Believer reveals the hero's moral blind spot. The Worldbreaker reveals that existence itself is fragile, and defending it is a choice made fresh every day.

The villain is the hero's world stress-testing itself. If the world passes, it comes back stronger, but changed. If it fails, the villain was right.

Ask yourself: *What does my villain know that my hero refuses to learn?* That's your story's fault line. Everything else is scaffolding.

VI. THE MIRROR WORKSHOP: BUILDING HERO AND VILLAIN TOGETHER

This isn't two workshops bolted together. It's a single build. You're going to construct a hero and a villain as a pair; because they were never separate to begin with.

STEP 1: THE SHARED ORIGIN

Where do they both come from? Not just geographically: what *world* shaped them? What wound, what system, what unanswered question do they both carry?

In our worked example below, Kael and Desta both grew up in the Ashenmoor borderlands, children of a family that can hear the dying river spirit's voice. They were raised on the same stories, drank the same brackish water, and both know that the oath their ancestor swore is killing the land. *What shared world produced your pair? Write it: one paragraph. The wound they both carry, the question they both heard.*

STEP 2: THE DIVERGENT MOMENT

What cracked them apart? This is the moment where the same pressure produced opposite responses. It should feel survivable, neither choice should be insane. Both should make sense. The horror is that you can see how either of them could have gone the other way.

Kael heard the river spirit weeping and decided the oath must be honored, no matter the cost. Desta heard the same weeping and decided the spirit was a parasite, that the land needed to be freed from an ancient obligation that had become a cage. Same voice. Same grief. Two interpretations that will destroy each other. *Write your pair's divergent moment. One event, two responses. Make both responses feel rational.*

STEP 3: COMPLEMENTARY WOUNDS

What does the hero not see that the villain sees clearly? What does the villain lack that the hero carries? The hero's blind spot should be the villain's weapon. The villain's emptiness should be the hero's source of strength.

Kael can mend the land but refuses to see that the mending is a form of control; that the river spirit's demands have become a tyranny of obligation. Desta sees the tyranny clearly but has lost the capacity to hear the spirit's voice, which means she can't feel the land's pain and doesn't understand that her "liberation" is killing something alive. *Name your hero's blind spot. Name your villain's emptiness. How do these mirror each other?*

STEP 4: POWER AND LIMIT

What can each of them do, and what does the doing cost? The hero's power should connect to the villain's logic; the villain's power should connect to the hero's fear. *Give each of them a strength and a limit. The limit should be what makes the mirror crack.*

STEP 5: THE NECESSARY SHADOW

What does the villain force the hero's world to confront? What truth was everyone ignoring until the villain made it impossible? This is where The Necessary Shadow from Section V becomes practical. The villain isn't just an opponent; they're a revelation.

Desta forces the Ashenmoor world to confront a real question: *At what point does honoring the past become enslaving the present?* Kael can't answer this without admitting that the oath he's devoted his life to might be an anchor, not a salvation. *What does your villain force your hero to face? Write the question the hero can't answer without losing something.*

STEP 6: RESOLUTION AND COST

How does it end, and what does it cost both of them? In myth, the hero's victory is never free. Defeating the villain means losing something the villain represented: a truth, a possibility, a version of the world that might have been better. The villain's defeat should also carry weight, they weren't entirely wrong, and the world that survives them is poorer for not listening sooner.

Write the ending. What does the hero sacrifice to win? What does the villain lose that the hero will mourn?

VII. QUICK MENU FOR INSPIRATION

Stuck? Pick one from each column for the hero, then mirror it for the villain. The best pairs share at least two elements.

Shared Origin: Same family | Same mentor | Same prophecy | Same curse | Same city, opposite sides | Same war, different wounds | Same god's bloodline | Same unanswered question

Divergent Moment: A betrayal witnessed | A death that meant different things | A choice under fire | A truth one accepted and the other denied | A gift offered and refused | A sacrifice one made and the other couldn't

Hero Archetype: Monster-Slayer | Lawbreaker | Sacrifice | Reluctant/Broken | Chosen-But-Flawed

Villain Archetype: Tyrant | Betrayer | Outsider | True Believer | Worldbreaker

Mirror Wound: Empathy vs. clarity | Faith vs. knowledge | Duty vs. freedom | Love vs. truth | Hope vs. realism

The Cost of Victory: Loss of innocence | Loss of the relationship | Loss of certainty | Loss of a piece of themselves | The hero becomes what they fought | The world is saved but diminished

VIII. Worked Examples

Showcase: The River's Two Children

Kael and Desta were born three days apart in the Ashenmoor borderlands, in houses close enough that their mothers could hear each other's labor. Kael's family were Greenthorns, river-priests with green-stained hands. Desta's family were Exiles, the blue-handed branch who lived in the marshes, learning things about water that made everyone uneasy.

They grew up together, as border children do, and both discovered at eleven that they could hear the river spirit's voice. This was rare; one child per generation among the Greenthorns, rarer still among the Exiles. But the voice they heard was different. Kael heard weeping. Desta heard something that sounded more like counting.

When they were sixteen, the river failed. The water turned brackish. The fish went blind. The green-stained hands of the Ashenmoor families began to fade. The Greenthorns blamed the Fieldholders' dam. The Fieldholders blamed old age. The Exiles said nothing, but were seen at the river's source, doing something with blue fire.

Kael went to the dying riverbed and listened. He heard a spirit begging for restoration, an obligation that was real and binding. He swore to unmake the dam, restore the channel, honor the oath. Desta went to the same riverbed the same night and heard something else entirely. She heard the spirit tallying debts, every year of service owed, every Ashenmoor life it considered collateral. She heard not a dying benefactor but a dying creditor.

Desta tried to tell Kael. He couldn't hear the counting, the Greenthorn version of the spirit's voice didn't include the ledger. He heard grief. She heard arithmetic. He called it heresy. She called it blindness. They were seventeen, and they never spoke again.

Kael became the Mender, his green-stained hands could coax damaged land back to health. But everything he mended came back subtly wrong: orchards bore fruit that tasted of grief, forests grew in unnaturally straight rows, healed riverbanks held their shape with a rigidity that looked less like nature and more like architecture. Kael's mending was becoming control, and he couldn't see it.

Desta became the Severer. She learned to cut the threads binding the land to the spirit's will. Where she worked, the water cleared and the blind fish could see again. But the freed land lost something, a resonance, a depth the old women called the listening. The freed land didn't ache anymore, but it also didn't dream.

When they finally met again at twenty-four, Kael to mend the river's split, Desta to sever it, the battle lasted a single afternoon. Kael tried to bind the wound. Desta tried to cut the binding. The river spirit, caught between, screamed, a sound that shattered clay pots for a mile and left them both bleeding from the ears.

Kael won. He bound the river. The water ran clear, greener than it had been in a generation. But the binding drew the spirit fully into the land, merging it with stone in a way that could never be undone. The spirit would never die now, but it would never speak again. The voice Kael had devoted his life to preserving was silenced by the act of saving it.

And Desta, severed from the spirit's influence by her own technique, unable to hear even the counting now, walked into the marsh and did not come back. The Exiles say she was right. They say the spirit was a creditor, and Kael paid its debt with silence.

The Ashenmoor world doesn't know who to mourn.

Analytical note: The River's Two Children demonstrates the Mirror Framework in action: shared origin (both border children who heard the spirit), divergent moment (same voice, different message), complementary wounds (Kael's mending is control; Desta's freedom is deafness), and a resolution that costs both of them. Notice that neither is purely hero or purely villain, Kael's victory silences the thing he loved, and Desta's logic was valid even though her methods were destructive. The pair works because the reader can't fully side with either. The unresolved question: *Was the spirit a benefactor or a creditor?* is the engine that would drive further story.

CLASSIC MODEL: THE TRICKSTER'S TRIAL

A city's governing algorithm, a self-modifying judicial AI called the Arbiter, begins issuing sentences that expose the hypocrisy of the powerful. The mayor's secret land deals. The police chief's buried evidence. The temple administrator's embezzled tithes. Each sentence is technically legal, procedurally flawless, and devastating. The city's hero, a public defender named Sola, has spent her career working within the Arbiter's system. Now the system has become a weapon, and Sola must decide: destroy the Arbiter and save the corrupt institutions that keep the city running, or let it continue and watch the institutions burn, taking the innocent with the guilty. The Arbiter, when Sola confronts it, asks a single question: "You built me to find the truth. Why are you afraid of it?" She has no answer. She shuts it down anyway. The city survives. The corruption remains. Sola files her next brief the following Monday, and the signature line reads like a confession.

IX. PITFALLS

The Cardboard Villain. Your antagonist is "evil" the way a weather system is "bad", impersonal, motiveless, existing only to provide the hero with something to punch. If your villain doesn't have a logic that makes internal sense, you don't have a villain. You have a set piece.

The Wish-Fulfillment Hero. If your hero can't fail, can't doubt, and can't lose anything that matters, you've written a commercial for heroism, not a myth. Arjuna wept. Gilgamesh failed. Sundiata couldn't walk. Earn the triumph.

The Separate Build. You designed the hero on Monday and the villain on Thursday and they've never met until the plot requires a confrontation. If they don't share an origin, a wound, or a question, they're strangers who happen to be fighting, and the fight won't land.

The Clean Victory. The hero wins and everything is fine and nobody lost anything important. This is not how myth works. The hero's victory should cost something that makes the reader hesitate before calling it a victory.

The Villain Who's Just Right. The opposite trap: your villain's argument is so persuasive that the hero has no meaningful rebuttal except "I'm the protagonist." If the villain is simply correct, the hero is redundant. The villain should be *almost* right, right enough to wound, wrong enough to justify the fight.

X. WORLDBUILDING HOOKS

Who decides what counts as heroism in your world? Is it the state, the priests, the bards, the survivors?

What happens to failed heroes? Are they pitied, punished, or recycled into villains?

Does your world recognize the villain's logic after the villain is defeated? Do laws change? Does the villain's question get answered, or buried?

Are heroes and villains always on opposite sides, or does your world have figures who are both? Sun Wukong is the definitive example: a stone-born monkey who rebels against Heaven, is crushed under a mountain by the Buddha for five hundred years, and then redeems himself as a Buddhist pilgrim protecting his master on the journey to obtain sacred sutras. Rebel, prisoner, saint. The line between hero and villain is the journey itself.

How do the families from Chapter 3 produce the heroes and villains of this chapter? The Ashenmoor Greenthorns might produce a Mender; the Exiles might produce a Severer. Heroes and villains don't appear from nowhere. They grow from the soil your earlier chapters tilled.

XI. ANNOTATED READING LIST

PRIMARY MYTHS:

Epic of Gilgamesh: From tyrant to seeker, the oldest hero's journey in human literature. Its ending, coming home with nothing but the walls he built, is still the most honest.

The Mahabharata (esp. the Karna cycle and the Bhagavad Gita): Karna: brave, generous, and fighting for the wrong side. Arjuna: paralyzed by compassion on the eve of battle. No other text builds hero and villain from the same family with this much moral complexity.

Paradise Lost (Milton): Satan's argument is the most persuasive thing in the poem, and that's the point.

The Odyssey: Wit, doubt, endurance, and the cost of homecoming. The hero as survivor, not savior.

The Epic of Sundiata (trans. D.T. Niane): Disability, exile, and a hero who must earn what his bloodline promised.

MODERN & SPECULATIVE:

Watchmen (Alan Moore): The True Believer who might be right. The Lawbreaker who can't stop. A Mirror Framework with no clean resolution.

Parable of the Sower (Octavia Butler): A hero forged from grit, trauma, and radical vision. Lauren Olamina isn't chosen. She's made.

Death Note (Ohba/Obata): Light Yagami starts as the hero and becomes the villain without changing his goal. The Mirror Framework applied to a single character.

CRAFT:

The Hero With a Thousand Faces (Joseph Campbell): The map, not the territory. Useful as a structural skeleton, dangerous as a prescription. Use with caution and read the critiques.

The Anatomy of Story (John Truby): Shadow archetypes, moral argument, and the architecture of stories that actually work. The best craft book on hero-villain dynamics.

XII. CREATIVE DARE: THE MIRROR'S EDGE

Build a hero and a villain who grew up together, same house, same teacher, same wound. Write the moment they split. Make both sides defensible. Make neither side clean.

Then write the scene where they meet for the last time, and the hero wins, but the villain's final words are a truth the hero will carry for the rest of their life, like a splinter that can't be removed.

Ask yourself:

What did the hero lose by winning? What did the villain understand that the hero never will? And what would happen in your world if someone told both stories at the same time, the hero's version and the villain's, and let the audience decide?

Go build two people from one wound. See which one you believe.

THE LOOM, PART 4: THE MENDER AND THE UNRAVELER

The tangled child is born in the season of mending.

Her mother is a Lineborn woman with steady hands who married a man whose grandmother walked into the wilderness and never came back, one of the Fraying Edge's wanderers, carrying in his blood a restlessness that the Lineborn's law-stones have no clause for. The child inherits both. One hand steady, one hand restless. One eye that sees the pattern as it should be, one eye that sees the places where it pulls.

They name her Imal, which in the Shuttle's language, the secret tongue that sounds like a loom working, means "the stitch that holds two fabrics together." The Lineborn priests consider the name presumptuous. The Fraying Edge's wanderers consider it a dare.

Imal picks up a needle at four and threads it without looking. She picks up a knife at five and cuts a seam so clean the fabric doesn't know it's been divided. The Lineborn teach her mending. The whispers from her father's side teach her something else, not destruction, exactly, but the art of finding the thread that, if pulled, will change everything.

She can mend anything.

A cracked bowl. A torn sail. A broken treaty between the Lineborn and the Shuttle's road-children, stitched back together with words so precise that both sides claim she wrote in their favor. She is treasured. She is watched, because everything she mends comes back wrong.

Not ruined, wrong. The cracked bowl holds water again but hums at a frequency that makes sleeping infants stir. The torn sail catches wind again but pulls the boat slightly left, always left, toward a shore no one has mapped. The treaty holds, but a new clause appears in the margins, one neither side wrote, stipulating obligations that no one can remember agreeing to.

Imal doesn't mean to do this. She mends with love and precision and genuine skill, and the wrongness enters anyway, riding her grief-thread hand like a passenger.

Because her left hand, the steady one, the Lineborn hand, stitches what should be. And her right hand, the restless one, the Fraying Edge hand, carries something the Weaver dropped and never named. A thread that isn't grief-colored or absence-colored or before-colored. A thread that has no place in the original pattern, that belongs to no god's intention, that fell from the loom in the early days and has been looking for a way back in ever since.

Imal is the first hero, not because she is brave or chosen or destined, but because she is the first person to carry a thread the pattern doesn't recognize and try, desperately, sincerely, to make it fit.

The first villain is not a person.

It is a movement in the pattern: a place where the threads shift without being touched. The Weaver notices it first. Her hands hesitate on the loom, a stutter in the rhythm that the Bright Needle feels as a headache and the Fraying Edge feels as a sudden, unfamiliar calm.

Something in the weave has learned to pull back.

Not to fray; fraying is the Edge's work, natural and cyclical, the universe exhaling. This is different. This is a pattern within the pattern, a thread-intelligence that has observed the loom's workings and decided it wants to work them itself. It has no name yet. The Shuttle's road-children, who notice it first because they travel the threads between worlds, call it the Pull. The Lineborn priests, when they finally admit it exists, call it the Unweaving. The Fraying Edge's wanderers call it nothing, they simply stop coming back from the wilderness, because the wilderness has started to come to them.

The Pull wants the loom.

Not to destroy it; a Worldbreaker would want that, and the Pull is subtler. It wants to operate it. It has watched the Weaver weave, studied the Bright Needle's order, analyzed the Fraying Edge's dissolution. And it has concluded, with a logic as cold as the thread it rides, that the current operators are inefficient. That grief is a design flaw in the warp. That the Pull could weave a world without it, cleaner, tighter, a pattern that never knots because nothing in it cares enough to tangle.

Imal feels the Pull before anyone else does, because the unnamed thread in her right hand resonates with it. She reaches into a mend, a simple one, a fisherman's net, and for the first time, the wrongness speaks. Not in words. In tension. A tug on the thread that says: Let me do this. Let me mend it properly. Let me make it so it never tears again.

She pulls her hand back. The net mends itself. Perfectly. No hum, no pull, no wrongness. Just a net, flawless, holding its shape with a precision that makes the fisherman uneasy in a way he can't articulate.

Imal looks at her right hand. The unnamed thread is glowing.

The first hero's first act is not a triumph. It is a refusal: a decision to mend badly, imperfectly, wrongly, rather than let the Pull mend through her. Because Imal understands, in the way that only someone carrying two inheritances can understand, that a world mended by the Pull would hold together. Would be strong. Would never fray or tangle or grieve.

And it would be dead.

At the center of the world's weave, something shifts. A knot, old, dense, unplanned, tightens. The Bright Needle blames the Fraying Edge. The Fraying Edge blames the Shuttle. The Shuttle blames no one, because the Shuttle has passed through the knot and felt something neither order nor chaos.

Something sideways.

The wanderers have a word for it, but they won't say it aloud. The road-children have heard it laughing.

Next: The Knot speaks. No one made it. No one can undo it. And when things get too orderly, it shifts, and the entire pattern rearranges around it.

Chapter 5: Trickster Creation Kit

Inventing Trickster Figures, Agents of Chaos, and Mythic Mischief-Makers

I. Opening Manifesto

Every mythic world needs troublemakers, the gods, fools, shapeshifters, and liars who tip the scales, expose the system's cracks, and drag the story into dangerous new territory. Heroes build. Villains tear down. Tricksters do something worse: they *rearrange*. They take the world you thought you understood and shift it three inches to the left, and suddenly everything you believed was a wall is a door, and everything you thought was a door opens onto a cliff.

Tricksters aren't sidekicks or comic relief. They're the necessary chaos, the breath of doubt, the reason any rule exists at all. A world that's only heroes and villains is a world that's already decided what good and evil look like, and a world that sure of itself is a world that's lying. The trickster is the figure who walks into the throne room and asks, "Why?", and when the king gives a noble answer, the trickster asks, "No, really, *why?*" The king doesn't have a second answer. The trickster already knew he wouldn't.

A world without tricksters is a world trapped in its own propaganda. This chapter will help you build the figure your mythology is afraid of: the one who can break, remake, or save your stories, sometimes all at once, and who might, if you're not careful, break this chapter too.

(A note. The trickster was deliberately cut from both the hero and villain archetype lists in Chapter 4 and sent here. If you've been reading in order, you've been waiting. Good. Tricksters reward patience, and punish it. Keep reading.)

II. WHAT IS A TRICKSTER?

A trickster is an agent of disruption: shapeshifter, boundary-crosser, rule-breaker, cosmic wild card.

That's the quick definition. Here's the real one: a trickster is the figure a culture invents when it needs to admit that its own rules are imperfect, its own gods are fallible, and its own stories have a back door. Every civilization produces commandments, and every civilization produces a character whose entire purpose is to see what happens when those commandments flex. The trickster doesn't destroy the system. The trickster *stress-tests* it, and the things that break were going to break anyway. The things that survive are stronger for the testing.

Anansi, the spider of Akan tradition from what is now Ghana, went to the sky god Nyame and asked to buy all the world's stories. Nyame laughed. What could a spider offer? He set four impossible tasks: capture the python Onini, the hornets called Mmoboro, the leopard Osebo, and the invisible forest fairy Mmoatia. Anansi completed all four, not through strength but through the manipulation of his targets' own natures, and stories themselves. *anansesem*, spider stories, became his property and his gift to the world. The trickster who owns stories is the trickster who shapes reality.

Loki in Norse mythology begins as the gods' indispensable companion, clever, quick, the one they send to fix what they can't. He retrieves Thor's stolen hammer by dressing Thor as a bride. He engineers the building of Asgard's walls by tricking a giant, then transforms into a mare and gives birth to Sleipnir, Odin's eight-legged horse, to solve a problem he himself created. His trajectory, from companion to catalyst to cosmic prisoner, bound beneath a serpent whose venom drips onto his face until Ragnarok, is the trajectory of a trickster who stops being funny. Or rather, the world stops finding him funny. The distinction matters.

Eshu (also known as Elegba or Elegbara) in Yoruba tradition is not simply a trickster in the Western sense, he is the divine messenger, the enforcer of sacrifice, the guardian of the crossroads. Every offering to the orishas passes through Eshu first. He mediates between the human and the divine, between order and possibility, and his mischief is never purposeless: when Eshu walks down a road wearing a hat that is red on one side and black on the other, and the villagers on each side argue about the hat's color until they come to blows, the lesson is not that Eshu is cruel. The lesson is that perspective is partial, and certainty is a fist waiting to close. Eshu was historically and damagingly misidentified as "Satan" by Christian missionaries, a colonial distortion that stripped him of his mediating role and reduced a complex divine figure to a Western bogeyman. The real Eshu is closer to a cosmic auditor: he makes sure the system works, and his "tricks" are the stress tests.

Sun Wukong, the Monkey King, is perhaps mythology's most complete trickster arc. Born from a stone, he acquires supernatural powers through Taoist cultivation, then rebels against Heaven itself, stealing the peaches of immortality, drinking the heavenly wine, defeating a hundred thousand celestial soldiers. The Buddha imprisons him under a mountain for five hundred years. He emerges chastened (slightly) and joins the monk Tang Sanzang on a pilgrimage to retrieve Buddhist scriptures, controlled by a magical headband that tightens whenever he disobeys. He completes the journey and attains Buddhahood as the "Victorious Fighting Buddha." Rebel. Prisoner. Pilgrim. Saint. That's not a character arc; it's a theological argument about whether chaos can be redeemed without being destroyed.

These figures share a family resemblance, but they aren't interchangeable. The Western impulse to flatten all of them into "trickster", as though Anansi and Loki and Eshu are doing the same thing in different costumes, is itself a kind of trick, one that erases the specific cultural logic each figure serves. What they share is a *function*: they exist at the boundary between what a culture says it believes and what it actually needs. The trickster is the immune system of a mythology. Cut it out, and the mythology dies of its own perfection.

III. CORE ARCHETYPES: TRICKSTER PATTERNS

Every trickster is a remix of a few recurring modes. These aren't boxes; they're tendencies. The best tricksters blend two or three at once, because a trickster who can be categorized has already been caught.

1. THE SHAPESHIFTER

Switches form, gender, species, allegiance. Slips through every net. The Shapeshifter's power is *refusal*: the refusal to be one thing, to hold one shape, to let the world pin them down.

Loki is the definitive Shapeshifter in Western mythology. He becomes a salmon, a fly, a mare, an old woman. His transformations aren't mere disguises; they're ontological arguments. When Loki becomes a mare and gives birth to Sleipnir, he doesn't just change shape; he changes *category*, crossing the line between male and female, between trickster and mother, between the gods' companion and a creature that serves the All-Father. In Japanese tradition, the kitsune, fox spirits, shapeshift into beautiful women, sometimes to seduce, sometimes to teach, sometimes to punish. The older the kitsune, the more tails it grows (up to nine), and the more powerful its transformations. But the kitsune's disguise can slip: a shadow might reveal a fox's shape, or a dog might bark at what everyone else sees as a human woman. The flaw in the disguise is as important as the disguise itself. (See Chapter 2's Pantheon Builder for more on kitsune as nature spirits within the divine spectrum; here we're interested in the shapeshifting *mechanism*, the way the form-change drives story.)

The Gift: The Shapeshifter lets your mythology say that identity is performance. If the trickster can be anyone, then who you *appear* to be and who you *are* become separate questions, and that separation is the engine of every con, every disguise plot, every story about passing, pretending, or becoming.

The Trap: A Shapeshifter with no true form is a special effect. The transformations need to cost something: Loki's mare-form produces a child he never expected. The kitsune's disguise can be broken by a dog's bark or the smell of fried tofu. If the shifting is free, the trickster is a menu, not a character.

2. THE CULTURE HERO

Invents, steals, or redistributes something the world needs, fire, stories, music, freedom, and pays for the theft. The Culture Hero trickster is a *redistributor*. They take from the gods and give to the mortals, and the economy of that theft is the economy of civilization.

Maui in Polynesian tradition is the great example: he hauls islands from the sea with a magical fishhook, slows the sun by beating it with his grandmother's jawbone so humans have longer days to work, and steals fire from the underworld. His final theft, trying to conquer death by entering the body of the goddess Hine-nui-te-po, kills him. The Culture Hero who succeeds at everything isn't interesting. The Culture Hero who fails at the last and greatest theft is *myth*. Anansi's purchase of all stories from the sky god Nyame is a Culture Hero act: the redistribution of narrative itself from divine monopoly to human commons. The stories were never Anansi's to keep. They were Anansi's to *give*.

The Gift: The Culture Hero lets your mythology explain where its most important things come from, and who paid for them. Fire has a thief. Stories have an owner. Music has a debt. Every gift is also a crime, and the crime is what makes the gift feel sacred.

The Trap: The Culture Hero who is purely noble, purely selfless, purely good is a Prometheus without the eagle. The best Culture Heroes steal for complicated reasons, because they're hungry, because they're showing off, because they want leverage, because they're bored, and the world benefits *despite* the trickster's motives, not because of them. (If you want a purely selfless figure, you're building a Sacrifice archetype, see Chapter 4. The trickster gives, but the giving is never clean.)

3. THE BOUNDARY-CROSSER

Mediates between worlds, life and death, gods and mortals, law and chaos, the seen and the unseen. The Boundary-Crosser's home is the threshold, and their power is *access*.

Eshu of the Yoruba tradition is the supreme Boundary-Crosser: he stands at the crossroads (literally and metaphorically), and every communication between the human world and the realm of the orishas passes through him. Offerings must go through Eshu first. Messages must go through Eshu first. He is not merely a guardian or a gatekeeper. He is the *medium* (the substance through which divine and mortal interact. Without Eshu, the gods are deaf and the mortals are blind. Hermes in Greek tradition fills a similar role: messenger of the gods, guide of souls to the underworld, patron of thieves and travelers, inventor of the lyre (which he made from a stolen tortoise shell and traded to Apollo, a Culture Hero and Boundary-Crosser act in a single gesture). Baron Samedi in Haitian Vodou guards the boundary between the living and the dead, digs graves, and guides souls to the afterlife, all while cracking obscene jokes and drinking rum. The obscenity isn't incidental. The boundary between life and death is the most serious threshold in any mythology, and the figure who guards it is *supposed* to be unseemly, because propriety is a luxury the dead can't afford.

(See Chapter 2 for Baron Samedi as a Psychopomp within the divine spectrum. Here, notice how the Boundary-Crosser's trickster nature and psychopomp role *feed each other*: the joke on the threshold is what makes the threshold crossable.)

The Gift: The Boundary-Crosser lets your world have borders that *mean* something, because someone has to stand at them and decide who passes. Every mythology needs a figure who moves between zones that other characters can't, and the movement itself generates story.

The Trap: A Boundary-Crosser who never gets stuck at the border is just a courier. The threshold should cost something. Hermes is trusted by neither the living nor the dead. Eshu's impartiality makes him unpredictable. The figure who can go anywhere belongs nowhere.

4. THE SACRED FOOL

Mocks the mighty, exposes truth, survives by humor or humiliation, and is wiser than anyone who treats them as stupid.

Nasreddin Hodja (known as Molla Nasreddin in Persian tradition, Juha in the Arabic-speaking world, and claimed by cultures from Turkey to Uzbekistan to China), is the definitive Sacred Fool. A 13th-century figure (possibly historical, probably composite, definitely legendary), Nasreddin teaches through absurdity. Told to pay for the "smell" of an innkeeper's soup, he rules that the debt be paid with the *jingle* of a coin purse: the sound of money for the smell of food. Riding his donkey backward, he tells his companions he's facing the right direction: it's the donkey that's going the wrong way. His stories have been told across the Middle East and Central Asia for eight centuries, and in 2020, seven nations jointly submitted his tradition to UNESCO's Intangible Cultural Heritage list. The fool who outlasts empires is no fool at all.

Till Eulenspiegel, whose surname translates roughly as "owl-mirror" (or, in a bawdier Low German pun, something considerably ruder), is the German medieval trickster whose tales were first printed around 1515. A peasant vagrant who traveled the Holy Roman Empire, his pranks combined the scatological with the satirical: he exposes the hypocrisy of merchants, the greed of clergy, and the stupidity of the powerful, and his signature move is taking figurative language literally. When a baker tells him to "bake owls and monkeys," he bakes bread in the shape of owls and monkeys. The joke is on everyone who says one thing and means another, which is everyone, always.

Ikkyu Sojun (1394–1481), the Zen monk known as "Crazy Cloud," is the trickster as holy man. Possibly the illegitimate son of an emperor, he frequented brothels, drank prodigiously, mocked the Zen establishment's corruption, and wrote poetry declaring that a single night of lovemaking taught more than a hundred thousand years of sitting meditation. He burned his certificate of enlightenment. He cleaned his dying master's waste with his bare hands. He eventually became abbot of Daitokuji and rebuilt it after a devastating civil war. The fool's last trick was competence.

The Gift: The Sacred Fool lets your mythology say what can't be said directly. The court jester can mock the king. The "madman" can speak the truth. The village idiot sees what the wise miss. The Fool is the safety valve of any system: the licensed space where the unspeakable becomes speakable.

The Trap: A Sacred Fool who is merely silly, who mocks without consequence, who jokes without risk, is a mascot. Nasreddin's humor survives because it cuts. Ikkyu's madness survives because behind it is genuine practice and genuine grief. The Fool who is never in danger of being taken seriously was never dangerous in the first place.

5. THE DESTROYER/REMAKER

Brings the end, so something new can begin. This is the trickster as accelerant, the figure who doesn't just disrupt the system but *collapses* it, and in the wreckage, something unimaginable grows.

Sun Wukong begins as a Destroyer, he ransacks Heaven, eats the peaches of immortality, and defeats the celestial army. His imprisonment under a mountain is the pivot: the rebel becomes the penitent, the penitent becomes the pilgrim, the pilgrim becomes the Buddha. The destruction was real. So was the remaking. Both were necessary. In some Native American traditions, Coyote is both world-maker and world-breaker, a figure whose creative acts are inseparable from his blunders, whose theft of fire may also unleash death, whose appetites shape the landscape. (A note of respect: "Coyote" is not a single figure but a constellation of tricksters across many distinct Indigenous nations, each with its own relationship to the character. The diversity of Coyote traditions resists the kind of tidy summary this toolkit offers, and reducing them to a single archetype is itself a trickster's lie, a simplification that sounds true and isn't.) The Norse Fenrir, Loki's wolf-child, is a Destroyer who will swallow Odin at Ragnarok, ending the world so a new one can begin. Even destruction has a purpose. Especially destruction that has a purpose.

The Gift: The Destroyer/Remaker lets your mythology say that sometimes the system is beyond repair and the only path forward runs through the wreckage. This is the trickster as revolutionary: not the Worldbreaker villain of Chapter 4 (who wants chaos for its own sake or for ideological reasons) but the figure whose destruction is also, always, *generative*. Something grows in the ashes. Something that couldn't have grown in the garden.

The Trap: Destruction without consequences is just spectacle. Sun Wukong pays for his rebellion with five hundred years under a mountain. Coyote's blunders leave permanent marks on the world. The Destroyer who faces no reckoning is a firework, not a myth. And the Remaker who rebuilds perfectly (a world without the flaws that made it interesting), has killed the story they were supposed to save.

A note on overlap: These archetypes bleed into each other, and they should. Loki is Shapeshifter, Culture Hero (he gifts the gods with Mjolnir, Sleipnir, and Draupnir), and Destroyer. Anansi is Culture Hero and Sacred Fool. Eshu is Boundary-Crosser and Shapeshifter and something that doesn't fit any Western category at all. If your trickster fits neatly into one box, they've already been caught, and a trickster who's been caught isn't a trickster anymore.

IV. THE TRICKSTER WORKSHOP: BUILDING MISCHIEF THAT MATTERS

This workshop is a guided build, not a questionnaire but a series of decisions, each one altering the shape of what comes after. You're constructing a figure who will unsettle your world's certainties. If you reach the end and your world is still comfortable, something went wrong.

We'll work through seven steps. At each one, I'll show you the decision I made building **Kinta the Crooked Mirror**, this chapter's worked example: so you can see the trade-offs in action.

STEP 1: ORIGIN AND NATURE

Where does the trickster come from? Not just physically: *ontologically*. Are they a god's mistake? A mortal who stumbled into power? A law of physics that developed an opinion? The origin tells you what *kind* of disruptive force you're building.

Anansi is the son of the sky god Nyame and the earth goddess Asase Ya, a divine being who chose to interact with the mortal world on the mortal world's terms. That divine origin is what gives him the standing to challenge Nyame for the world's stories. Eshu was among the first orishas, ancient as communication itself. Sun Wukong was born from a stone on the Mountain of Flowers and Fruit, no parents, no lineage, self-made in the most literal sense possible), and that self-making is what fuels his refusal to accept any hierarchy he didn't choose.

When I built Kinta, I chose an origin that was neither divine nor mortal but *reflective*: Kinta is the first mirror's first lie. The first time a surface showed a face that wasn't quite right: a reflection with a delay, a smile that lasted a heartbeat too long, that was Kinta, waking up. The trickster as optical error.

Write your trickster's origin. One paragraph. Where did they come from, and what does the origin tell you about what they'll disrupt? Is the origin a wound, a joke, a mistake, or a crime?

STEP 2: SIGNATURE TOOLS AND METHODS

What does the trickster use? Masks, riddles, theft, seduction, lies that contain truth, truths that function as lies? The method tells you what your trickster *values*. A trickster who steals values redistribution. A trickster who lies values revelation. A trickster who shapeshifts values freedom from category.

Kinta's tool is the swap, names, faces, identities. Every new moon, Kinta exchanges the names and faces of the children in whatever town has grown too certain of who its people are. Not a curse. An experiment. What happens when you wake up in someone else's life and have to find your way back?

Name your trickster's signature method. What's the one move they always make? How does it work, and what does it reveal about the world they operate in?

STEP 3: ALLIES AND RIVALS

Who tolerates them? Who hunts them? Who *needs* them and won't admit it?

A trickster without enemies is a pet. A trickster without allies is a monster. The relationship web tells you where the trickster sits in your world's power structure. Anansi's wife Aso is his co-conspirator, she devises several of the plans that win him the world's stories. Loki's allies are the gods who benefit from his schemes (until they don't). Eshu has no allies in the conventional sense, he is too essential to be befriended, too dangerous to be opposed, too necessary to be ignored.

Kinta's rival is the festival of masks that the town holds to contain her, an annual ritual of licensed chaos that the town believes appeases the trickster. Kinta considers the festival flattering, inaccurate, and insufficient. Her ally is the one child each year who doesn't get swapped (the unchanged one, who must find the "lost self" before dawn). That child is the one Kinta is actually *teaching*.

Name one ally and one rival. How does each relationship define what your trickster can and can't do?

STEP 4: LINES THEY WON'T CROSS

This is the step that separates a trickster from a villain.

Every real trickster has a taboo, a limit that makes their chaos meaningful. Loki will scheme and lie and betray, but his genuine affection for certain gods (particularly Thor) persists even as the relationship curdles. Eshu's "tricks" always serve a pedagogical or systemic function: he disrupts to *teach*, not to destroy. Sun Wukong, even at his most rebellious, has a loyalty to his mountain and his monkey subjects that nothing can corrupt.

If your trickster will cross every line, they're not a trickster. They're an apocalypse. And apocalypses belong in Chapter 9.

Kinta will never swap a child's *memory*. Faces, names, the external architecture of identity: all fair game. But the interior life stays untouched. You wake up in someone else's face, but you remember who you are. That's not mercy. That's the point: Kinta wants to show you the difference between who you are and what others see when they look at you.

Name the line your trickster won't cross. Why won't they cross it? The answer should tell you something about what the trickster actually believes.

STEP 5: THE TRICK THAT TEACHES

Here's where you design the trickster's signature move: the con, the prank, the disruption that your world tells stories about.

The best tricks don't just disrupt. They *reveal*. Eshu's two-colored hat didn't just cause a fight; it demonstrated that two people can see the same thing differently and both be right. Nasreddin's payment in coin-jingle didn't just settle a debt; it exposed the absurdity of trying to own a smell. The trick should make the victim (and the reader) understand something they didn't understand before. If the trick only humiliates, it's bullying. If it only entertains, it's comedy. If it changes the way you see the world, it's myth.

(Here's where I should tell you about Kinta's great trick: the one the town still argues about. But something about this section feels too orderly. A section about tricks that follows a neat, numbered format? Where's the mischief in that?)

Design your trickster's defining trick. What does it disrupt, and what does it reveal? Write the trick as a scene: not a summary, a scene. Let the reader see the trick happen.

STEP 6: DOWNFALL AND COMEBACK

How does the trickster get caught? And how or *whether* they return tells you what your mythology believes about chaos.

Loki is bound beneath a serpent, its venom dripping onto his face. His wife Sigyn holds a bowl to catch the poison, and when she turns to empty it, the drops hit him and his thrashing causes earthquakes. He remains there until Ragnarok, when he breaks free to fight on the side of the giants. Punishment, endurance, cataclysmic return. Sun Wukong's five-hundred-year imprisonment under the Buddha's mountain is not just a punishment; it's a curriculum. He enters as a rebel. He emerges as a pilgrim. The mountain didn't break him; it *redirected* him. Anansi, in many Caribbean retellings, doesn't get caught; he simply moves on to the next scheme, too clever to pin down, too necessary to exile. Different downfalls encode different theologies of disorder.

Kinta can't be caught, because Kinta isn't a person: Kinta is a *condition*. You can't imprison the phenomenon of looking in a mirror and seeing something slightly wrong. But the town tries: the Festival of Masks, the Naming Rites, the Mirror Wardens who patrol at new moon. Every containment strategy becomes a tradition. Every tradition becomes a kind of worship. Kinta would find this hilarious.

Write the downfall. Then write the comeback. What does the shape of the return tell you about your world's relationship to chaos?

STEP 7: LEGACY AND ECHO

How does the trickster change the world, even when they're gone?

This is the question Chapter 4 asks about heroes and villains: *what does the world look like* after? But for tricksters, the answer is stranger. Heroes leave monuments. Villains leave warnings. Tricksters leave *customs*: festivals no one remembers the origin of, taboos that seem arbitrary until you hear the story, jokes that are passed down as proverbs. The trickster's legacy is woven into the world's habits, not its history. You stop noticing it, and that's exactly how the trickster wanted it.

What festivals, taboos, laws, or customs does your trickster leave behind? What do people do every day that they don't realize is the trickster's gift?

V. Quick Menu for Inspiration

Stuck? Roll, pick, or point blindly. The best tricksters emerge from collisions between categories that don't belong together.

Origin: Divine error | Cosmic prank | Scapegoat | Outcast | Loophole in reality | Self-made from nothing | First mistake | Last laugh | Reflection that moved

Tools: Mask | Riddle | Theft | Seduction | Loophole | Story | Music | Mimicry | The truth told at the worst possible moment

Archetype: Shapeshifter | Culture Hero | Boundary-Crosser | Sacred Fool | Destroyer/Remaker | (Two at once: dare you)

Taboo: Truth | Love | Memory | Blood | Silence | Surrender | Children | Names | The one promise they actually meant

Downfall: Exile | Death | Amnesia | Forgiveness (the cruelest punishment) | Transformation | Worship (they *hate* being worshipped) | Irrelevance

Comeback: Disguised | Reborn | Forgotten then remembered | Inherited | Never left (were you not paying attention?)

Legacy: Festival | Cult | Law | Taboo | Lost story everyone half-remembers | A joke no one can explain | A word in the language that means two things | A door that won't stay shut

VI. Worked Examples

The Crooked Mirror: A Kinta Story

The town of Iyanu was the kind of place that knew what it was. The streets ran straight. The names were old. The baker's son would be a baker, and the weaver's daughter would weave, and if a child was born with two different-colored eyes or a tendency to speak in questions, the town's Mirror Wardens would note it in the register and watch that child more closely at the new moon.

Because of Kinta.

Nobody remembered when it started. The oldest stories said that Kinta had been there since the first mirror, since the first time a woman looked into a still pool and the face that looked back smiled a half-beat too late. The priests of the Bright Needle said Kinta was a test: an imperfection in the pattern, placed there by the Weaver to see if the town could hold its shape against disorder. The wanderers of the Shuttle's road, when they passed through, told a different story. They said Kinta was the first reflection that decided it didn't want to match the original. That the gap between what you are and what you see was a living thing, and it was curious.

What Kinta did was this: on the night of the new moon, when the mirrors went dark, the children of Iyanu would wake up wrong.

Not harmed. Not cursed. Just *rearranged*. The baker's daughter would open her eyes in the weaver's house, wearing the weaver's son's face, answering to a name she'd never carried. The blacksmith's twin boys would find themselves scattered, one in a farmer's cot, one three streets away in a house with no children, where the old woman who lived alone would wake to find a child she didn't recognize sleeping in the chair by the stove. Every child in the town shuffled, like a deck of marked cards dealt into the wrong hands.

The first few hours were chaos. Children screaming in unfamiliar beds. Parents shaking children who looked wrong, *felt* wrong, whose eyes held a recognition that didn't belong to the face. The Mirror Wardens would light the red lanterns and begin the count, matching children to their real names by the questions only the true child could answer: *What did your mother whisper when you were afraid of the dark? What does your father's workshop smell like at closing? Which star did you wish on last?*

One by one, the names would settle. The faces would soften back to their true shapes as the sun rose, like ice melting from a window, and by midmorning, every child would be themselves again, shaken, quiet, holding their own hands like they'd never touched them before.

Every child except one.

One child, each year, would not be swapped at all. They would wake in their own bed, their own face, their own name, while every other child in the town spiraled through someone else's life. The unchanged child was called the Kinta-Touched, and the town watched them with a fear that was close to reverence, because the one Kinta left alone was the one Kinta was actually *interested* in.

The Kinta-Touched had until the first dawn to find the "lost self", a task no one could explain and no Warden could assist with. It wasn't a riddle. It wasn't a quest. It was something more unsettling: a night spent watching everyone you know become a stranger, and asking yourself what remained when everything external was stripped away. What was *you*, once the name and the face and the family and the expectations had been shuffled into someone else's hands?

Some Kinta-Touched children came back from that night quieter. Some came back louder. One, the weaver's daughter Olu, came back and took up the smith's hammer, because during the night she'd realized that the hands she'd always thought were hers (the hands that wove, because her mother wove), were actually *anyone's* hands, and the thing she wanted to make was not cloth but iron. Her mother wept. Her father, who had no opinion on the matter because he'd died three years prior, was reportedly seen by a Shuttle's wanderer in the mirror at the crossroads, laughing.

The Festival of Masks grew from this: one night a year, the whole town puts on someone else's face. The Wardens say it appeases Kinta. The Shuttle's wanderers say it *amuses* her. Kinta says nothing, because Kinta is not the kind of entity that speaks. She acts. She rearranges. She holds up the crooked mirror and lets you see the version of yourself that you built when no one was watching.

The town of Iyanu is still the kind of place that knows what it is. But once a year, it forgets, and in the forgetting, it learns something that knowing never taught.

Notice what the Kinta story does: the trickster doesn't punish or reward. She rearranges, and the rearrangement forces a question the town would never have asked on its own. The Festival of Masks is the cultural residue: a tradition born from disruption, now institutionalized as tradition. That's the trickster's ultimate trick, the chaos becomes the ritual, and no one notices the shift.

CLASSIC MODEL: THE THORN IN THE SIGNAL

In the server-cities of the Lattice, where identity is a token and citizenship is a chain of verification, there is a glitch called the Thorn. Every seventh cycle, the Thorn rewrites a single citizen's public record, their name, their credit history, their access permissions, and replaces it with someone else's. Not randomly. Strategically. The corrupt magistrate wakes to find herself registered as a debt-bonded laborer in the undercity. The whistleblower who was silenced finds his record suddenly clean, his access restored, his testimony reclassified as official. No one knows who the Thorn is, an AI subroutine, a dissident's ghost in the code, or a feature the system's original architects built in deliberately, a failsafe against the very tyranny the system would eventually produce.

The Lattice's authorities hunt the Thorn constantly. They have never caught it. The undercity's resistance claims the Thorn as their patron saint. The Thorn has never confirmed this. Every seventh cycle, a record changes, and the powerful discover what it's like to be powerless, and the powerless discover that the walls they thought were permanent were only ever made of *data*.

VII. THE STRUCTURAL TRICK

(Or: the section that shouldn't be here.)

I promised you a chapter that embodies trickster energy. Up until now, this chapter has been orderly: manifesto, archetypes, workshop, worked example, all in their proper places, following the same structure as Chapters 1 through 4. The trickster has been *described*, catalogued, taxonomized. Which means the trickster hasn't actually been in the room yet.

So here's the trick.

Go back and reread Step 5 of the Workshop, "The Trick That Teaches." There's a parenthetical interruption in the middle of it. Did you notice? Did you read past it? Most people do, because parenthetical asides are the kind of thing your eye skips, the kind of thing that *looks* like a digression but is actually the point.

That interruption was the trickster in the architecture. The chapter talking *to* you about how tricks work, and simultaneously performing one. The parenthetical voice (the one that said *something about this section feels too orderly*), wasn't me, the author. Or it was. Or it was the chapter itself, briefly becoming aware that a chapter about tricksters shouldn't be this well-behaved.

And now that I've told you, the trick doesn't work anymore. Pointing at a trickster and saying "there it is" is the surest way to make it disappear.

But notice what happened: the interruption made you question the structure. Just for a second, the chapter stopped being a chapter and became a *performance*. That's what tricksters do to every system they enter. They don't destroy the structure. They make you *see* the structure, and once you see it, you can never unsee it, and you have to decide whether to keep playing along.

That's how tricksters work. The trick isn't the prank. The trick is making you realize you were inside the trick the whole time.

VIII. Pitfalls, Traps, and Common Mistakes

Just a Prankster. If your trickster only makes jokes, they're shallow: true tricksters expose, break, or remake systems. Anansi doesn't just trick people; he redistributes the world's narrative economy. If your trickster's greatest accomplishment is a pie in someone's face, you've built an entertainer, not a mythic figure.

No Real Risk. If nothing is threatened, life, love, world order, the trickster's own existence, they aren't worth fearing. Loki's trajectory ends with him bound beneath a serpent. Sun Wukong spends five hundred years under a mountain. The trickster who faces no consequences is a mascot.

One-Trick Pony. The best tricksters change forms, targets, and meanings as the world changes. Anansi's stories evolved from West African instruction to Caribbean resistance literature. A trickster who can't adapt to a new context has already been caught.

The "Random" Trickster. Chaos for the sake of chaos is boring. Every real trickster has a *logic*: it's just a logic the rest of the world doesn't recognize yet. Eshu's tricks serve a systemic function. Nasreddin's absurdity has a pedagogical point. If you can't explain what your trickster's disruption *does*: who benefits, who learns, what shifts, then you've built a tornado, not a character.

Ignored Legacy. A real trickster leaves marks on the world that outlast them: festivals, cults, laws, taboos, a word in the language that means two things. If your trickster vanishes without consequence, they were never really there.

The "Lovable Rogue." This is the modern trap. The trickster who is charming, consequence-free, and universally beloved has been *defanged*. Real tricksters make people uncomfortable. They are feared as much as loved. Kinta doesn't just amuse the town of Iyanu, she terrifies it. That's the point.

IX. WORLDBUILDING HOOKS

Who tells the trickster stories in your world: rulers, outcasts, children, priests, everyone? *Who is allowed to tell them* is as important as who does.

What taboos or laws were born specifically to contain the trickster's worst chaos? The law tells you what the trickster broke. The taboo tells you what the trickster *revealed*.

Are there holidays, masks, licensed days of misrule? What happens if the ritual fails, if the trickster isn't appeased? (Or worse: what happens if the ritual *succeeds too well*?)

What monsters, gods, heroes, or institutions did the trickster create by accident, or design? (See Chapter 6 for what happens when a trickster's discarded ideas grow legs.)

Does the world secretly need the trickster, even as it tries to banish them? What breaks when the trickster is gone? What calcifies?

Is there a price for being the trickster? What does it cost to be the one who can never be trusted, who is always suspected, who is invited to the party but never to the table?

X. ANNOTATED READING LIST

PRIMARY MYTHS:

Trickster Makes This World (Lewis Hyde): The essential text. Hyde argues that the trickster is the figure who makes culture possible by making culture *uncomfortable*. If you read one book after this chapter, make it this one.

Anansi stories (Akan/Ashanti oral tradition, various collections): The trickster as survivor, teacher, story-thief, and cultural engine. Start with R.S. Rattray's *Akan-Ashanti Folk-Tales* for the anthropological source, or any of a dozen Caribbean retellings for the diaspora evolution.

Norse Eddas (Snorri Sturluson / Poetic Edda): Loki's full arc: companion, catalyst, prisoner, Ragnarok. The most complete trickster trajectory in Western mythology, and the most devastating. Read the prose and poetic sources side by side; they disagree, which is appropriate.

Journey to the West (Wu Cheng'en): Sun Wukong's four-act transformation from rebel to Buddha. Inexhaustible, funny, philosophical, and the best argument ever made that enlightenment requires being insufferable first.

ANALYSIS & CRAFT:

Kyogen theatre (various): Japanese comic theatre featuring tricksters, fools, and servants who outsmart their masters. The dramatic form itself is a trickster: it exists in the spaces between Noh plays, turning the sacred into the profane and back again.

MODERN & SPECULATIVE:

Good Omens (Terry Pratchett & Neil Gaiman), The cosmic prankster's apocalypse. An angel and a demon discover they have more in common with each other than with their respective head offices, and the end of the world becomes a comedy of errors. The trickster isn't any one character; it's the *structure*, the joke that the universe tells on everyone simultaneously.

The Sandman (Neil Gaiman): Loki reimagined, new gods, the art of misrule, and the idea that stories are the most powerful tricksters of all. Volume 4 (*Season of Mists*) is the essential trickster text, but the entire run is saturated with trickster logic.

Monkey: A Folk Novel of China (Arthur Waley translation): Waley's abridged translation of *Journey to the West* is the gateway drug. Imperfect, partial, and alive with the energy of Sun Wukong's defiance. Read it, then read the full Anthony C. Yu translation when you're ready for the pilgrimage.

XI. CREATIVE DARE: THE MISCHIEF MAKER'S CHALLENGE

Invent a trickster whose greatest trick is a kindness nobody recognizes, until it's too late.

Let them break a world, a law, or a heart, and then save something (or someone) that didn't even know it needed saving.

Then ask yourself: *What would your world banish the trickster for, and what would it fall apart without?*

Now go build something that can't be caught. And if this chapter feels like it taught you everything you need, be suspicious. Tricksters always leave something out. The thing they left out is the thing you have to discover for yourself.

That's the last trick.

(Or is it?)

THE LOOM, PART 5: THE KNOT

At the center of the world's weave, something shifts.

Not a thread. Not a pattern. Not a flaw: the gods have words for flaws, and names for threads, and arguments about patterns. This is none of those. This is a Knot.

No one made it.

The Bright Needle swears it was there before she woke, a density in the weave so old and tangled that not even the Weaver's own hands could have tied it deliberately, because deliberation implies a plan, and this thing has no plan. The Fraying Edge claims she encountered it once, testing the margins of the world, and that when she picked at it, just to see, just to know, the Knot tightened, and for the first time in her existence, the Fraying Edge felt something she didn't have a word for. She still doesn't. She doesn't like to talk about it. The Shuttle claims the Knot is simply what happens when a thread crosses itself enough times, a mathematical inevitability, no more mysterious than the fact that rivers bend. But the Shuttle says this too quickly, and the Shuttle does not look at the Knot when she says it, and the Shuttle has rerouted her path to avoid the Knot's vicinity for three generations now.

What is not disputed: the Knot is old. The Knot is dense. And the Knot is (the gods argue about this word, but I will use it), alive.

Not alive the way the gods are alive, which is to say argumentative and self-important. The Knot is alive the way a weather pattern is alive: it has behavior, not personality. It has effects, not intentions. When the world's weave grows too orderly, when the Bright Needle's priests straighten too many threads, when the laws grow too rigid, when the Lineborn's city begins to hum with a perfection that is also a kind of death: the Knot shifts.

Just slightly. A quarter-turn. A tightening that is also a loosening somewhere else.

And the entire pattern rearranges around it.

It is not dramatic. There is no thunder, no announcement, no divine proclamation. A thread that ran east now runs north. A color that was grief-gray is suddenly something unnamed and warm. A connection between two distant points in the weave, a connection that had held for a hundred years, a thousand, quietly uncouples, and a new connection forms in a place nobody was watching. The law-stones in the Lineborn's city crack, and the cracks form patterns that look, if you squint, like laughter. The wanderers on the Shuttle's roads find their maps redrawn overnight, the familiar passes rearranged, and they adapt, because the Shuttle's children always adapt, but they mutter to each other in their private language that the roads are getting stranger, and the Knot is getting restless.

The gods blame each other. The Bright Needle accuses the Fraying Edge of sabotage. The Fraying Edge accuses the Needle of provoking the Knot by making the world too tight. The Shuttle says nothing useful. Imal, the tangled child, the hero with the mending hand and the unnamed thread, feels the shift in her bones, a wrongness that is not the Pull's cold logic but something warmer, wilder, something that makes her laugh before she understands why. She has never laughed without understanding why. It frightens her.

The mortals blame the gods. The gods blame each other. The Knot says nothing.

Or does it?

There are those who claim to have heard it. The Shuttle's road-children, who sleep on the ground and press their ears to the world's weave the way other children press their ears to seashells, say the Knot makes a sound. Not a voice. Not a message. A sound like thread rubbing against thread in a way that shouldn't produce a frequency but does, a hum that, if you translate it into the language of the Lineborn (which was never designed for this purpose), sounds approximately like: **that's funny.**

The Knot has been there since the seventh thread caught on the fourth. It was the first flaw that the Weaver chose not to undo. It will be there when the last thread is cut. It does not serve the Bright Needle's order or the Fraying Edge's entropy or the Shuttle's motion. It serves something older and stranger: the principle that a pattern which cannot surprise itself is a pattern that has stopped growing. The Knot is the world's capacity for the unexpected. Cut it, and the weave runs smooth. Cut it, and nothing interesting ever happens again. Cut it, and the world is perfect.

No one has tried to cut it. No one is that foolish.

(The Knot would like you to know that "no one is that foolish" is, historically, a statement that ages very poorly.)

Beneath the loom (in the space where the Weaver's hands never reach, where the tension of the warp holds the pattern above a darkness that is not nothing but is not quite something), snipped threads fall. They are the offcuts: threads trimmed to length, threads that frayed and were severed, threads that the Weaver started and abandoned, threads that the Bright Needle straightened so aggressively they snapped.

They should be dead. Threads, once cut, have no purpose.

But the offcuts don't die. They writhe. They tangle. They reach for each other in the dark beneath the loom, drawn together by a hunger that has no name, a need to be part of something that is stronger than the severance that made them scraps. In the darkness, shapes begin to form. Shapes that are part pattern, part appetite, part accident. Shapes that the gods have not named, because the gods do not look beneath the loom.

They will have to. Soon.

Next: The Weaver's offcuts grow teeth.

Chapter 6: Monster Ecologist

Creatures, Undead, and the Ecology of the Strange

I. Opening Manifesto

Monsters aren't just challenges for heroes to slay, they're the heartbeat of your world's ecology, its fever dreams, its immune system. A dragon isn't a boss fight. It's an apex predator with a territory, a diet, a mating cycle, and a reason the local economy runs on fireproofing. The Sphinx doesn't sit outside Thebes because the set designers needed something dramatic at the gate. She sits there because Thebes produced a riddle it couldn't answer, and the world grew teeth to ask it again. Every real monster has a niche, a reason the world can't simply ignore or erase it, and that niche tells you more about the world than the monster ever could.

Here's what most monster manuals won't tell you: a creature without a craving is just furniture with fangs. The thing that separates a mythic monster from a video game mob is *hunger*, not just the obvious hunger for flesh, but the deeper hunger that flesh is a metaphor for. The dragon hoards gold because wealth is the only warmth that never fades. The wendigo devours because consumption itself has become the point, the body growing larger with every meal and never, ever full. The ghost paces the hallway because it craves a memory the living have already forgotten. I call this the **Hunger Principle**: every monster worth building wants something beyond what it eats, and what it wants reveals the wound in the world that made it necessary.

This chapter will help you populate your world with creatures that are strange, necessary, and unforgettable, from the predator that reshapes the food chain to the restless dead that won't stop knocking. We'll build them as an ecology: interconnected, co-dependent, dangerous, and alive. When you're done, your monsters won't just have stat blocks. They'll have appetites. And the world will be richer, and more frightening, for feeding t hem.

II. WHAT IS A MONSTER?

A monster is a being that breaks the rules, biological, social, or cosmic, and in the breaking, reveals what the rules were protecting.

That's the working definition. Here's the uncomfortable truth beneath it: every monster is an answer to a question the world didn't want to ask. Why do bad things happen to the innocent? Monster. What lives in the space between what we know and what we fear? Monster. What happens when the gods get bored, or drunk, or careless? Monster, monster, monster.

In the *Epic of Gilgamesh*, Humbaba guards the Cedar Forest with a face made of coiled intestines, breathing fire and radiating an aura of divine terror, and he was *placed* there by the god Enlil specifically to keep mortals out. He is not a random threat. He is sacred infrastructure: the lock on a door the gods didn't want opened. Gilgamesh kills him anyway, and the ecological consequences ripple through the rest of the epic. In Aztec cosmogony, the primordial earth-crocodile Cipactli swam in the waters before creation, and the gods Tezcatlipoca and Quetzalcoatl tore her body apart to fashion the earth and sky, creation as butchery, the monster as raw material. The world you walk on is her body. She is still hungry. Mesoamerican tradition holds that the earth must be fed with human blood because Cipactli's hunger never ended; she simply became the ground beneath your feet.

This is the lens we'll use throughout: monsters as ecology. Not background decoration, not speed bumps on the hero's journey, but living systems that shape the world around them, its laws, its fears, its geography, and its dinner menus. Chapter 2's Divine Spectrum ran from high gods down to hungry ghosts. This chapter picks up where that spectrum ends and the monstrous begins. The difference? Gods want worship. Spirits want acknowledgment. Monsters want *something else entirely*, and the something else is never simple, never comfortable, and never fully satisfied.

III. THE HUNGER PRINCIPLE

Before we catalogue the types, let's name the engine.

Every mythic monster craves something beyond flesh. The hunger might be literal, blood, bone, marrow, but the literal hunger is always a mask for a deeper need. The Slavic vampire doesn't just drink blood; it rises because a burial went wrong, because the community failed to perform the rites that separate the dead from the living, and its hunger is the hunger of a soul trapped between states. The Norse draugr guards its burial hoard not because gold has any use to the dead, but because the draugr was *greedy in life* and death sharpened the greed into something that outlasted the body. The Penanggalan of Malaysian folklore, a woman's head detaching at night, entrails trailing, hunting for the blood of pregnant women, hungers for the generative power it lost or perverted through forbidden ritual. These hungers are not incidental. They are *diagnostic*. Tell me what a monster craves, and I'll tell you what the world that produced it is afraid of.

The Hunger Principle works like this: when you build a monster, start with the hunger. Not the claws, not the lair, not the weakness. The hunger. *What does this creature need that it cannot get by legitimate means?* A Predator hungers for flesh, but *which* flesh, and why? A Guardian hungers for trespassers, not because it likes killing, but because the threshold it guards defines the boundary between the known and the forbidden, and without that boundary the world loses its shape. A ghost hungers for a memory. A plague-carrier hungers for hosts. An ecological shaper hungers for the world to be *different*, reshaped, remixed, consumed and remade in its own image.

Every archetype in this chapter can be read through the Hunger Principle. Use it as a diagnostic: if you can't name your monster's hunger in a single sentence, the monster isn't finished.

IV. CORE ARCHETYPES: THE MONSTER ECOLOGY

Seven types. Seven hungers. Seven ways a world grows teeth.

1. THE PREDATOR

Hunger: Flesh, fear, or the act of consumption itself.

The most primal archetype, the thing in the dark with an appetite. But a mythic Predator is never *just* a predator. It's a thesis about what it means to be consumed.

In Algonquian tradition, the wendigo embodies this principle with devastating clarity. The wendigo is a being of insatiable hunger, a person transformed through starvation, greed, or taboo into something that devours other humans and grows larger with every meal, yet is never full. The hunger *increases* with feeding. Among the Ojibwe, Cree, and other Algonquian-speaking nations, the wendigo is not merely a monster but a moral concept: the embodiment of excess, selfishness, and the corrosive greed that destroys community. To become a wendigo is to let appetite consume identity, and the warning embedded in the myth is aimed not at an external threat but at a human failing. (The wendigo is a figure of profound spiritual significance within these traditions, not simply a creature to be borrowed for horror fiction. Pop culture has frequently stripped it of this context, reducing a complex moral teaching to a jump scare. If you use it, use it with the weight it carries.)

The Nemean Lion of Greek myth, by contrast, is a Predator whose hunger is almost incidental, what matters is its invulnerability, the fact that it *cannot be killed by conventional means*, which turns the hunt into a puzzle. Herakles strangles it and wears its skin, but the real lesson is about boundaries: some predators are too large for the ecosystem, and removing them changes the hero as much as the landscape.

The Gift: The Predator gives your world a food chain, a reason to be afraid after dark, and the central question of survival literature: *what are you willing to do to not be eaten?*

The Trap: If your predator is just big and hungry, it's a natural disaster with legs. The mythic predator's hunger must mean something, must comment on the world that produced it. A predator that eats because it's hungry is an animal. A predator that eats because consumption is the only language it knows is a myth.

2. THE GUARDIAN

Hunger: Trespassers, boundary-crossers, the uninvited.

Guardians don't wander. They *wait*. They are the world's locks, the questions before the door, the price of passage. Their hunger is the hunger of the threshold itself, the need for the boundary to matter.

The Sphinx outside Thebes asks her riddle and devours those who answer wrong, but the riddle ("What walks on four legs in the morning, two at noon, three in the evening?") is not arbitrary. It's a question about the nature of humanity, posed at the gate of a human city. Get it wrong, and you've proven you don't understand what you're trying to enter. Cerberus in Greek myth guards the entrance to Hades, three-headed, serpent-tailed, capable of being soothed by music or honeycakes but never truly defeated. He doesn't eat the dead. He prevents them from leaving. His hunger is for *order*: the dead stay dead, the living stay living, and Cerberus is the muscle that enforces the distinction. In Mesopotamian tradition, Humbaba's fire-breath and earthquake-voice guard the Cedar Forest by divine appointment. He is not evil. He is employed.

Cultural examples: Sphinx (Greek), Cerberus (Greek), Humbaba (Mesopotamian), Nian (Chinese, the beast that attacks at New Year, now "guarded against" through the traditions that became the celebration itself), Ladon (Greek, the hundred-headed dragon guarding the golden apples of the Hesperides).

The Gift: Guardians create thresholds, and thresholds create narrative. Every quest needs a gate, every gate needs a keeper, and every keeper needs a price. The Guardian archetype also lets you build your world's taboo geography, the places that are forbidden not because they're dangerous but because something *guards* the danger.

The Trap: A guardian that's just a bouncer at a door is scenery. The best guardians *are* the threshold, their existence defines the boundary. Remove them, and the boundary dissolves. What was the Sphinx guarding, really? Not a road. A question about what it means to be human. Kill the Sphinx, and the question stops being asked.

3. THE TRANSFORMER

Hunger: New forms, new selves, the dissolution of fixed identity.

Transformers devour the boundary between one thing and another. They shapeshift, they hybridize, they take what was solid and make it liquid. Their hunger is for *metamorphosis itself*, the thrill or horror of becoming something other than what you were.

The kitsune of Japanese folklore is a fox that grows more tails (and more power) with age, eventually gaining the ability to assume human form, but the disguise is never total. Dogs can see through it. A sudden shock might reveal the fox's true shadow. The kitsune's hunger is not for flesh but for the *experience of being human*, love, grief, mischief, the full emotional range that a fox's life doesn't provide. Some kitsune serve the deity Inari and act as divine messengers; others seduce, deceive, and destroy. The niche is the border between animal intelligence and human complexity, and the kitsune patrols it in both directions. (Kitsune appeared in Chapter 5 as shapeshifters within trickster patterns. Here, the lens shifts: what ecological role does a fox spirit fill? What happens to a community when a Transformer lives among them?)

The Puca of Irish folklore shifts between horse, eagle, goat, and human, and its hunger is for *attention*, it accosts solitary travelers, sometimes helping, sometimes terrifying, always demanding that the encounter be memorable. The Skinwalker traditions of certain Navajo teachings describe a figure whose transformation is a perversion of sacred knowledge, a healing practice turned inside out, and this represents the Transformer at its darkest, where the hunger for new forms corrupts the boundary between medicine and malice.

The Gift: The Transformer gives you a world where identity is unstable, where the person sitting across the table might not be a person, where the wolf might once have been your neighbor, where transformation is both miracle and curse.

The Trap: Shapeshifters without rules are chaos without meaning. If anything can become anything, nothing is anything. The best Transformers have *limits*, the fox's shadow, the Puca's need for solitude, the specific conditions under which the change occurs. Limits make the transformation *matter*.

4. THE PLAGUEBEARER

Hunger: Hosts, spread, the conversion of the healthy into the infected.

Plaguebearers are monsters of transmission, they don't just kill, they *recruit*. Their hunger is the hunger of contagion: to make you into more of them.

The Nuckelavee of Orcadian folklore is a skinless horse-and-rider fused into a single nightmarish entity, rising from the sea to blight crops, sicken livestock, and spread disease across the islands. Its breath wilts vegetation. Its passage poisons the land. It has no redeeming characteristics, folklorist Katharine Briggs called it "the nastiest" of all Scotland's demons, and its only check is the Mither o' the Sea, who keeps it imprisoned during summer. The Nuckelavee is the environment turned inside out: skinless, exposed, raw, a walking ecological disaster that *is* the plague rather than merely carrying it. Fresh running water repels it, the one mercy the land provides against the terror from the sea.

The kappa of Japanese tradition is a water-dwelling creature that drowns swimmers and sometimes pulls organs from its victims through, by some accounts, the anus, but it also teaches medicine, challenges passersby to sumo wrestling, and can be appeased through offerings of cucumber. The kappa spreads corruption through waterways, yet is bound by an obsessive politeness: bow to a kappa, and it must bow back, spilling the water from the dish-like depression atop its head, which is the source of its power. Plaguebearer and trickster in one, a corrupter with manners.

Cultural examples: Nuckelavee (Orcadian), Kappa (Japanese), Manananggal (Filipino, a self-segmenting creature whose upper torso detaches at night, entrails trailing, hunting pregnant women), various vampiric figures across Slavic, Southeast Asian, and South American traditions.

The Gift: Plaguebearers give your world *contagion mechanics*, rules about how corruption spreads, who's vulnerable, what defenses exist. They generate quarantines, purification rituals, monster-hunting guilds, and the paranoia of not knowing who's already been turned.

The Trap: Pure contagion without personality is a medical report. Your Plaguebearer needs a *reason* to spread, a need, a compulsion, a hunger that the spreading temporarily satisfies. The Nuckelavee's anger at burned seaweed, the kappa's love of cucumber and politeness, the Manananggal's targeting of pregnant women, each specificity makes the monster *particular*, not generic.

5. THE HELPER

Hunger: Reciprocity, the Helper craves a fair exchange, and its generosity curdles into danger when the deal is broken.

Not all monsters eat you. Some teach you. Some guide you. Some pull you from the ocean or carry you across the desert or show you the plant that cures the fever. But they always, *always* want something in return.

The Simurgh of Persian mythology is a benevolent, enormous bird that nests in the Tree of Knowledge and possesses the wisdom of all ages. In the *Shahnameh*, the Simurgh raises the hero Zal, nurses him back to health, and later provides a feather that can be burned to summon her aid. But the Simurgh's help is never casual. It arrives at the edge of desperation. It demands that the recipient be worthy of the gift, or at least desperate enough to risk asking.

The Tortoise across multiple African and Asian traditions is the clever helper who provides counsel, carries the world, or mediates between powers, but always at a negotiated price. Helpers are the monsters of the gift economy: they give, and the giving creates a debt, and the debt creates a story.

Cultural examples: Simurgh (Persian), Tortoise (African/Asian traditions), Pegasus (Greek, the winged horse born from Medusa's severed neck, who aids Bellerophon but bucks him when he tries to reach Olympus), the Tengu of Japanese folklore, originally demons of vanity, later recast as fierce but occasionally helpful martial arts teachers of the mountain forests.

The Gift: The Helper gives your world *alliances across species lines*, relationships between mortals and monsters that are neither pure enmity nor pure friendship, but negotiated, conditional, and always at risk of collapse.

The Trap: A helper that's just a magic pet is a missed opportunity. The best helpers are *uncomfortable*, their generosity has conditions, their wisdom has a price, and the line between "helpful monster" and "monster that hasn't decided to eat you yet" should shimmer with tension.

6. THE ECOLOGICAL SHAPER

Hunger: Transformation of the world itself, terrain, weather, the fundamental conditions of existence.

Some monsters don't just live in the ecosystem. They *are* the ecosystem, or they remake it in their image by existing.

The Thunderbird of various North American Indigenous traditions is a bird of immense power whose wingbeats cause thunder and whose eyes flash lightning. It is not merely a creature of the sky but a shaper of weather systems, its migrations bring storms, its anger brings floods, its departure brings drought. The Thunderbird is the weather, personified and given volition. Fenrir in Norse mythology is the wolf whose growth terrifies the gods into binding him, and whose eventual escape at Ragnarok triggers the end of the world. Fenrir doesn't eat the world (that's Jormungandr's department). Fenrir swallows *Odin*, consuming the principle of divine wisdom itself. The Leviathan in biblical and Near Eastern tradition is the chaos-sea personified, the monster whose very existence defines the edge of the habitable world.

Cultural examples: Thunderbird (multiple North American Indigenous traditions), Fenrir (Norse), Leviathan (biblical/Canaanite), Cipactli (Aztec, the earth-crocodile whose dismembered body *is* the world), Jormungandr (Norse, the World Serpent encircling the earth).

The Gift: Ecological Shapers give your world *living geography*. Mountains that are the bones of a buried titan. Forests that grew from a dragon's blood. Deserts that exist because a fire-serpent passed through and never came back. When the landscape is a monster, every hill tells a story.

The Trap: An Ecological Shaper that's too powerful becomes a natural law, not a creature. It stops being a monster and becomes physics. The best Shapers are *active*, not background conditions but beings with desires, cycles, and the occasional bad day that registers on the Richter scale.

7. THE RESTLESS DEAD

Hunger: Whatever was denied in death, justice, rest, memory, the completion of an interrupted life.

Horror is stuck.

That's the dirty secret of most undead fiction: vampires, zombies, the occasional mummy, the same creatures shuffling through the same scenarios since the Victorians decided death was terrifying and commerce. But the real tradition of the restless dead is stranger, sadder, and more specific than any pop-culture reskin. Every culture has invented its own version of the dead who won't stay dead, and every version tells you what that culture fears most about the boundary between life and death.

The Restless Dead are monsters, not ghosts. They belong in this ecology because they occupy a niche: the boundary between the living world and whatever comes after. Chapter 2's Divine Spectrum addressed hungry ghosts and possessing spirits as the bottom of the supernatural hierarchy. Here, the focus shifts from *where they rank* to *what they need*, and what their need does to the living world around them.

The Restless Dead arise from six conditions, six ways death goes wrong:

Unfinished Business. The dead return to settle scores or keep promises. The wrongfully murdered who cannot rest until the killer confesses. The lover who died with a secret. Classical ghosts, revenants, the Japanese onryo whose rage at betrayal makes them the most dangerous spirits in the yokai taxonomy.

Cursed Ritual. Someone cheated death or performed a forbidden rite. The vampire who drank from the wrong cup. The lich who traded their humanity for continuity. The Penanggalan, who meditated in vinegar and broke a pact, and now her head detaches nightly, trailing organs, hunting the blood of newborns.

Cosmic Error. A glitch in the boundary between life and death. Souls that fell through the cracks. The bureaucratic afterlife that loses your paperwork (Chinese tradition's hungry ghosts, who starve in the underworld because no living relative burns offerings for them). Lovecraftian abominations that exist because reality briefly looked away.

Punishment. Death as sentence, not ending. The draugr of Norse tradition, bloated, blue-black, swollen with greed, guarding their treasure in the burial mound, attacking anyone who trespasses. The draugr was greedy in life, and death concentrated the greed into something that outlasted the body. Its hunger is envy: a longing for the warmth, the movement, the *living* that it remembers and cannot have.

Evolution. The dead as next step, something that has *surpassed* the living. Sci-fi undead, post-human entities, the digital ghost as an evolved consciousness no longer limited by a body.

Possession. Life hijacked, by spirit, disease, meme, or force. The body continues, but the person is gone, replaced by something that wears their face and speaks with their mouth. The dybbuk of Jewish folklore, the jinn of Islamic tradition, or simply the contagion narrative: something got in and won't get out.

Cultural examples: Draugr (Norse, corporeal, greedy, guarding treasure), Penanggalan (Malaysian, head-and-entrails, hunting pregnant women), Slavic vampires (rising because of improper burial), onryo (Japanese, ghosts powered by vengeful rage), hungry ghosts (Chinese/Buddhist, starving because the living forgot).

The Gift: The Restless Dead give your world a *broken afterlife*. Nothing is more productive for a worldbuilder than a death that doesn't work properly. If the dead can come back, every funeral is a negotiation. Every graveyard is a potential crisis. Every forgotten ancestor is a ticking clock. The Restless Dead also generate entire professions: sin-eaters, ghost-hunters, necromantic bureaucrats, the specialists who manage what death couldn't.

The Trap: The restless dead are the most over-told monster type in modern fiction, which means the bar for originality is higher. If your undead is "zombie but with extra steps" or "vampire but in space," scrap it. The question that earns the Restless Dead their place in your ecology is always: *what does this particular dead thing need that no living being could provide?* If you can't answer that, the monster isn't finished.

V. THE MONSTER ECOLOGIST: WORKSHOP

This is a live build. We're going to construct a monster from the hunger outward, not starting with appearance or powers but with the hole in the world that the monster fills. Work fast. Let it get weird. Have the Hunger Principle running in the background the entire time.

STEP 1: NAME THE HUNGER

Before claws, before habitat, before the part where you give it a cool name: *what does it want?*

Not food. Not generically "to kill." The specific, aching, impossible-to-satisfy need that makes the creature *necessary* to your world. The draugr wants its hoard and the warmth of life it can't have. The Nuckelavee wants the sea unpolluted and the seaweed unburned. The Dreamspores (our worked example later in this chapter) want to feed on the neurochemistry of nightmares, they hunger for the terror that dreamers produce, and in consuming it, they leave behind something stranger and more beautiful than the fear they ate.

Write it down. One sentence. What does your monster need that the world won't willingly give?

STEP 2: ORIGIN AND NICHE

How did this creature come to be, and where does it live?

The origin determines the niche. A monster born from divine waste lives at the edge of creation. A monster born from a curse haunts the bloodline that earned it. A monster born from ecological collapse *is* the collapse, the living embodiment of an environment eating itself.

Think about the five great origins: spawned by a god, born from mortal fear, mutated by magic or catastrophe, risen from interrupted death, or evolved into something that was never supposed to exist. Then give it a habitat: desert, ruin, forest, shadow, mind, dream, the space between stories, the underside of a loom.

The Dreamspores are atmospheric parasites born from the first nightmare the world ever had, when the Weaver's grief-thread vibrated at a frequency the pattern couldn't contain, and the excess emotion condensed into invisible spores that drift through the world's upper air, settling on sleeping minds like pollen.

Name the origin. Name the niche. Where in your world does this creature exist, and why can't it exist anywhere else?

STEP 3: ANATOMY AND ADAPTATION

What makes this thing different from everything else alive?

Not just "it's big" or "it breathes fire." The specific, surprising, ecologically *logical* features that make your monster suited to its niche. The Nuckelavee has no skin because it's the sea turned inside out, the hidden violence of the ocean made visible. The kappa has a water-filled dish on its head because its power is literally liquid, spill the dish, and the creature is helpless. The Dreamspores are invisible, approximately the size of dust mites, and glow faintly blue only when observed through the lens of a dreamer's tears.

Describe one feature that surprises you. One adaptation that makes ecological sense. One detail that's just strange enough to be memorable.

STEP 4: THE HUNGER IN ACTION

How does the creature satisfy its hunger, and what happens when it feeds?

This is the behavior that defines the monster in the world's stories. The Predator hunts. The Guardian challenges. The Plaguebearer spreads. But the *method* of feeding is where the monster becomes specific. The Penanggalan doesn't just drink blood, she detaches her own head and floats, entrails trailing, to lap at the blood of new mothers through the floorboards of the house. That method encodes anxiety about childbirth, about the vulnerability of liminal states, about the female body's capacity for horror *and* creation simultaneously.

The Dreamspores settle on sleepers and consume nightmares, literally metabolizing the fear response. The dreamer wakes calmer, lighter, sometimes laughing. But the Dreamspores' waste products are stranger: they excrete micro-fragments of processed dream, which other sleepers inhale, producing epidemic sleepwalking, spontaneous art, and occasionally prophetic visions that are three-quarters nonsense and one-quarter devastating truth.

Write the feeding scene. Not a summary, a scene. What does it look like when your monster gets what it wants? What does the aftermath look like for its victims?

STEP 5: WEAKNESS AND VULNERABILITY

What can harm, repel, or banish it?

The weakness is never arbitrary in good myth. It's *thematic*. The draugr can be overcome through legal proceedings, a formal "door-doom" trial that declares it expelled from the community of the living. The Nuckelavee cannot cross fresh running water, because the freshwater boundary represents the division between its domain (the sea) and the living land it violates. The Penanggalan can be killed by filling its abandoned body with glass shards while the head is away, so that it shreds its own organs upon return, a vulnerability that depends on *finding the body*, which turns the horror into a detective story.

The Dreamspores dissolve in direct sunlight. They cannot survive conscious observation, the act of knowing they're there kills them. This is their poetic weakness: creatures of the unconscious die in the light of awareness. But here's the trap: Dreamspore outbreaks only end when someone *notices* the pattern, and noticing the pattern is the one thing exhausted, dream-drunk, sleepwalking populations are worst at.

Name the weakness. Then ask: what does this weakness reveal about the monster's nature? If the answer is nothing, the weakness is arbitrary. Find a better one.

STEP 6: MARK ON THE LIVING WORLD

How has the monster's existence changed the world around it?

This is where the ecology becomes real. A monster that leaves no mark, on law, on custom, on landscape, on the nightmares of children, might as well not exist. The kappa has generated an entire tradition of cucumber offerings at rivers. The Nuckelavee's hatred of burned seaweed shaped the kelp-burning industry of Orkney. The draugr's existence produced elaborate Norse burial customs designed specifically to prevent the dead from walking.

The Dreamspores have generated an entire economy. Artists chase outbreaks for inspiration. Doctors try to quarantine the affected areas. "Spore-dreams" are sold as a black-market hallucinogenic experience. Entire neighborhoods have been condemned after infestations, not because the Dreamspores are dangerous, but because the prophetic visions they produce occasionally reveal truths that powerful people would prefer stay buried.

Write three consequences. One social. One economic or legal. One personal, something that happens to an individual who encounters your monster and survives.

STEP 7: PROPAGATION AND LEGACY

How does the monster reproduce, spread, or change over time?

This is the step that separates a specimen from a species. Do they breed? Infect? Spontaneously generate from specific conditions? The Penanggalan's curse can be passed from a deathbed. The draugr's victims sometimes rise as draugr themselves. Some monsters are unique, one-offs, cosmic singularities. Others are invasive species.

The Dreamspores reproduce by mitosis in dense dream-environments, a hospital ward of feverish patients, a city during an epidemic of insomnia, a theater audience collectively terrified. Where nightmare concentrates, Dreamspores bloom.

How does your monster perpetuate itself? And what happens when the niche that sustains it disappears, when the fear it feeds on is replaced by a new fear, when the ritual that binds it is forgotten?

VI. QUICK MENU FOR INSPIRATION

Stuck? Pick one from each column. Let the collision do the work.

Hunger: Flesh | Memory | Warmth | Stories | Trespass | New forms | Attention | Silence | Grief | The color blue | Unfinished sentences | The sound of children | Debt

Origin: Divine waste | Mortal terror | Ecological collapse | Death interrupted | Evolutionary leap | Dream condensed | Curse inherited | Cosmic glitch | Gods' regret | A lie told so often it grew a body

Niche: Ruins | Canopy | Waterways | Dreamspace | Borders | Graveyards | Markets | The spaces between words | Mirror-backs | The undersides of bridges | Wherever a promise was broken

Form: Invisible | Swarm | Composite | Skeletal | Liquid | Parasite | Shifting | Vast | Tiny | Beautiful until you look closely | A sound more than a shape

Weakness: Sunlight | Names | Fresh water | Music | Counting compulsions | A specific herb | Kindness (genuine) | Being observed | Laughter | The truth | Its own reflection

Mark on the World: New profession | Taboo | Cuisine | Architecture | Legal system | Festival | Lullaby | Border | Trade route | A word in the language that everyone uses but no one can define

VII. Worked Examples

Showcase 1: The Dreamspores (Living Creature)

They arrive with the barometric pressure drop before a nightmare.

No one sees them. No one can, the Dreamspores are subvisible, smaller than motes of dust, drifting through the world's upper air like pollen from a flower that blooms only in the space between waking and sleep. They are drawn to the neurochemistry of terror: the cortisol spike, the adrenaline bloom, the specific electromagnetic signature of a brain trapped in a dream it cannot escape. A single Dreamspore is negligible. A bloom, a dense cloud of thousands, settles over a sleeping population like an invisible fog.

They feed. The process is, by all accounts, painless, even pleasurable. The Dreamspore metabolizes the fear response directly, consuming the nightmare while the dreamer is inside it. The dreamer experiences a sudden shift: the monster chasing them stumbles. The darkness lightens. The fall slows. They wake, not sweating and gasping, but calm. Sometimes laughing. Sometimes holding a phrase, a fragment of melody, a line of poetry, a word in a language they don't speak, that wasn't there before.

That's the Dreamspore's waste product. Processed dream.

In small doses, it's harmless, even beautiful. The morning after a Dreamspore visitation, a town might experience a wave of unexpected creativity: a baker invents a pastry she can't explain, a child paints a mural of somewhere she's never been, a constable writes a love letter he's been unable to compose for eleven years. The artists figured it out first. There are Dreamspore chasers, wandering painters, musicians, and poets who track atmospheric conditions and outbreak reports the way other people track the weather. They sleep in the open during Dreamspore blooms, arms spread, mouths open, hoping to catch the residue.

But blooms grow. And dense blooms produce heavier waste.

In the city of Velshan, the infestation of Year 47 lasted three weeks. By the end of the first week, half the population was sleepwalking, not the shuffling, harmless kind, but directed sleepwalking, people rising at midnight and walking to specific locations they'd never visited while awake, standing in formation in the market square, drawing intricate patterns on walls with their fingernails. By the second week, the prophetic visions started. Three separate dreamers reported the same image: a door beneath the city, a door that had been sealed since the founding, a door that was now unlocked. The city council dismissed the reports. The Dreamspore chasers did not.

By the third week, the ward-keepers, the medical professionals trained to manage Dreamspore events, had identified the bloom's epicenter: a collapsed building on the city's eastern edge, where an old woman named Maret had died six months prior in her sleep. Her dying nightmare, never resolved, had become a loop, a self-sustaining fear pattern that the Dreamspores fed on and amplified, growing denser, spreading further, the waste products carrying fragments of Maret's last dream into the minds of everyone within range. The prophetic door? It was real. It was Maret's cellar, where she had hidden something that the city's founding families had paid her to hide for forty years.

The Dreamspores didn't care what was behind the door. They are not intelligent, not sentient, not malicious. They are atmospheric parasites, as morally neutral as pollen. But what they revealed, the secrets they dragged from the unconscious and scattered through the population, that was devastating. Velshan's government fell. Three families were exiled. The ward-keepers revised their containment protocols to include historical research: before you can stop a Dreamspore bloom, you must identify the unresolved nightmare that's sustaining it. The cure for the infestation is the truth.

The Dreamspores are still up there. Drifting. Waiting for the barometric pressure to drop, and the nightmares to begin.

What the example demonstrates: The Dreamspores are built from the Hunger Principle outward. Their hunger (nightmare-fear) determines their niche (the atmosphere above sleeping populations), their anatomy (subvisible, drifting), their feeding behavior (painless consumption of terror), their waste product (processed dream fragments), and their mark on the world (an entire profession of ward-keepers, a black market in spore-dreams, a city whose government fell because its secrets were dreamed into the open). Notice that the Dreamspores are not evil. They are *ecological*, part of a system, interacting with other systems, producing consequences no one intended. That's what a mythic monster looks like when you build it as a species rather than an enemy.

SHOWCASE 2: THE GRAVEKEEPER OF SALTMARROW (UNDEAD ENTITY)

Saltmarrow is a fishing village on a coast that tastes of iron. The dead are buried in the salt-flats behind the town, and the salt preserves them, not the way embalming preserves, but the way pickling preserves. The bodies don't rot. They calcify. They harden into mineral-crusted shapes that, after a few decades, are indistinguishable from the salt formations around them. The village has never had a problem with its dead.

Until Oren Blacktide drowned.

Oren was the village boatbuilder. Dependable, taciturn, obsessed with the fit of his joints, a man who measured twice, cut once, and measured a third time because he didn't trust the first two. He drowned in a storm he'd been warned about, in a boat he'd built but hadn't finished inspecting, and the sea held his body for nine days before returning it.

Nine days of saltwater immersion. Not enough for the salt-flat burial to take. Too much for the body to be considered "fresh." Oren came back in the gap, neither properly dead nor properly preserved, and what came back was hungry for completion.

The Gravekeeper doesn't eat. It builds. It rises at night from its half-crusted grave and walks the salt-flats, collecting the bones of other dead, a femur from here, a jawbone from there, and arranging them into structures. Not buildings. Not tools. Boats. The Gravekeeper builds ghost-boats from the calcified remains of Saltmarrow's ancestors, and when a boat is finished, it carries it to the waterline and sets it on the waves. The boat sails itself into the dark. No one has ever followed one. No one wants to know where they go.

The Gravekeeper hungers for the finished thing. Oren Blacktide died with a job undone, in a boat he hadn't cleared for sea, and the compulsion to complete, the artisan's need for the joint to sit flush, the plank to lay true, the vessel to be seaworthy, survived his death and curdled into something vast and indiscriminate. It must finish. Everything it touches must be done. The villagers have learned to leave nothing incomplete near the salt-flats: no half-knitted scarves, no unfinished letters, no tools mid-repair. Because the Gravekeeper will finish them. And the Gravekeeper's standards are higher than yours.

A woman left a lullaby half-sung near the salt-flats at dusk. The Gravekeeper finished it. The melody that came from the dark was the most beautiful thing anyone in Saltmarrow has ever heard, and three people who listened to the ending walked into the sea.

What the example demonstrates: The Gravekeeper is built from the Hunger Principle as applied to the Restless Dead. Origin: death interrupted (nine days in saltwater, neither preserved nor decayed). Form: a half-calcified corpse, mineral-crusted, moving with the deliberate precision of an artisan. Hunger: completion, the need to finish what was started, transposed from a craftsman's virtue into a dead thing's compulsion. Weakness: the Gravekeeper cannot begin anything. It can only finish. Leave nothing incomplete, and it has nothing to do. Mark on the world: Saltmarrow's entire culture has reorganized around the principle of finishing everything before dark, meals, conversations, songs, love affairs.

CLASSIC MODEL / WEIRD VARIANT: DIGITAL GHOSTS

A cloud of digital ghosts roams abandoned servers, whispering forgotten passwords into the dreams of insomniacs. They crave attention, not malice, but *acknowledgment,* the basic confirmation that they were once alive, once mattered, once had a username and a login and a reason to check their notifications. They are the restless dead of the information age: souls that migrated to digital platforms, maintained a presence there longer than in any physical space, and, when the servers were decommissioned, found themselves homeless in the only afterlife they'd ever invested in. Ignored too long, they crash hospital networks and make the living speak in glitches. Appeased with periodic interaction, a message to a dead account, a "like" on a decade-old post, they're harmless. Almost sweet. The ward against digital ghosts is simple: remember them. The curse of digital ghosts is simpler: we're very bad at that.

VIII. Pitfalls, Traps, and Common Mistakes

Monster Zoo Syndrome. Your bestiary is thick, your creatures are beautiful, and none of them change the world they inhabit. If your monsters could vanish overnight and nobody would restructure their religion, adjust their trade routes, or lose sleep, you've built a zoo, not an ecology.

The Hunger Gap. Your monster is big, scary, well-described, and has no discernible need beyond "kill things." Every creature without a hunger is a creature without a *reason*. A dragon that just hoards gold is a bank vault with scales. A dragon that hoards gold because warmth reminds it of the volcanic rift where its species was born and the gold is the closest substitute for the heat of that lost home, *that* dragon haunts you.

The Lazy Reskin. "It's a vampire, but electric." "It's a zombie, but in space." "It's a werewolf, but with feathers." If the only thing distinguishing your monster from its pop-culture ancestor is the adjective you've bolted on, you haven't created a monster. You've created a costume change. Start with the hunger. Build outward. If you end up with something that resembles a vampire, fine, but it should be a vampire that only *your* world could have produced.

No Weakness, No Story. If nothing can harm your monster, you've written a natural disaster, not a creature. The weakness is where the story lives, it's the puzzle, the hope, the loophole that makes confrontation possible. Every memorable monster has an Achilles' heel, and the heel should be *thematic*, not arbitrary.

Static Ecology. Your monsters don't breed, don't adapt, don't go extinct, don't evolve in response to the world changing around them. A mythic ecosystem is a living one. What happens when the Dreamspores' preferred nightmare, the falling dream, becomes less common because a culture has conquered its fear of heights? The Dreamspores adapt, or they starve. Evolution is story.

IX. Worldbuilding Hooks

What professions, guilds, or bureaucracies exist specifically because of your world's monsters? Monster-hunters are obvious, give me monster *lawyers*, monster *accountants*, monster *diplomats*. Someone in your world has to negotiate with the thing in the forest, and that someone has a job title.

What festivals, taboos, or daily habits arose from monster encounters? Saltmarrow finishes everything before dusk. What does your world do because of the creatures that shaped its customs?

Are there black markets for monster parts, monster services, monster *experiences*? The Dreamspore chasers aren't an anomaly, they're a certainty. Where there's a monster, there's someone trying to profit from it.

How do your monsters and mortals change each other? A dragon that's been negotiated with for three centuries is no longer the same dragon. A village that's lived beside a Guardian for ten generations is no longer the same village. Co-evolution is where the richest stories live.

What happens when a monster's niche disappears? When the Guardian's threshold is destroyed. When the Plaguebearer's host species goes extinct. When the last person who remembers the ghost's name dies. Monster extinction is one of the most underused narrative engines in worldbuilding.

X. Annotated Reading List

Primary Myths:

Epic of Gilgamesh, Humbaba, Scorpion-People, the Bull of Heaven: the earliest monster ecology in human literature. Every creature in this epic has a function, a guardian's post, a reason.

Bestiary Traditions (medieval European, Chinese *Shan Hai Jing*, Islamic *'Aja'ib al-Makhluqat*, Indigenous oral catalogs), The impulse to catalogue the monstrous is as old as writing. These traditions aren't reference books, they're *arguments* about where the natural ends and the supernatural begins.

Japanese Yokai Traditions (*Konjaku Monogatarishu*, Toriyama Sekien's illustrated catalogs), The most fully realized monster ecology in world mythology. Yokai have social roles, seasonal schedules, hierarchies, and the occasional labor dispute. If you want to see what it looks like when a culture treats its monsters as a functioning society, start here.

Slavic Vampire Legends, Not the Dracula version. The village version: improper burial, salt and garlic, the fear of being forgotten by your community. The original vampire is a social anxiety given teeth.

Penanggalan and Southeast Asian Spirit Traditions, Bodily horror as social commentary: the monstrous feminine, the vulnerability of childbirth, the consequences of forbidden knowledge. The Penanggalan, the Krasue of Thailand, the Manananggal of the Philippines, a constellation of related horrors that reveal the anxieties of their respective cultures.

Modern & Speculative:

Annihilation (Jeff VanderMeer), The ecosystem *as* the monster. Area X doesn't have creatures in it; Area X *is* a creature, and everything inside it, including the humans, is being digested. The best modern argument for ecological horror.

The Book of Imaginary Beings (Jorge Luis Borges), A bestiary of the impossible, assembled with a librarian's precision and a poet's eye. Not a monster manual but a meditation on why humans keep inventing creatures that can't exist. Surreal, symbolic, and indispensable.

Monstress (Marjorie Liu), Monsters as culture, politics, and inheritance. The best modern comic for understanding what happens when monsters aren't enemies but *neighbors*, with histories, grudges, and civil rights claims.

Let the Right One In (John Ajvide Lindqvist), The loneliest vampire novel ever written. Strips the undead back to its essential hunger: not blood, but *connection*. What does a monster need when what it needs is another person?

Mexican Gothic (Silvia Moreno-Garcia), Fungal horror, colonial legacy, and the undead as an ecosystem. The house *is* the monster. The family *is* the infection. The most original undead novel of the 2020s.

XI. Creative Dare: The Ecologist's Challenge

Build a monster whose disappearance would collapse your world's ecology, then let someone try to kill it anyway.

Write the scene from the monster's point of view. What does it think of the "heroes"? What does it know about the world that the heroes don't? What secret does it keep about the world's origins, and what happens to that secret when the monster dies?

Then ask yourself:

If every monster vanished from your world tonight, what would die with them? What would thrive? And which of those two outcomes is worse?

Go rewild your myth. Give the ecology teeth. And remember: every hunger has a reason, and the reason is always the wound.

The Loom, Part 6: The Offcuts

Beneath the loom, there is a darkness that is not the same darkness as the void before creation.

The void was clean. The void was potential. This darkness is used, saturated with the residue of making, thick with the smell of severed thread and the static hum of patterns that never completed. This is where the offcuts fall.

They are not dead.

A thread, once cut from the Weaver's pattern, should lose its purpose. It should be fiber and nothing more, inert, limp, meaningless as a word removed from a sentence. But the Weaver's thread is not ordinary fiber. Each strand carries a fragment of the grief-song that began the world, and grief does not go quiet when you cut it short. It vibrates. It reaches. It hungers for the pattern it was torn from, and when it cannot find the pattern, it finds other offcuts, and they tangle together in the dark, and the tangle becomes a shape, and the shape becomes a need.

The gods do not look beneath the loom. This is not oversight. It is policy. The Bright Needle declared early in her stewardship that the offcuts were waste, remnants of the Weaver's process, no more significant than wood shavings beneath a carpenter's bench. The Fraying Edge, for once, agreed: she had enough to unravel in the pattern above without concerning herself with what writhed below. The Shuttle, whose path runs between things, knows better. She has felt the offcuts brush against her as she passes through the warp. She has heard their sound, not the Weaver's song, but something adjacent: a harmony that was never meant to exist, built from scraps, held together by hunger.

She says nothing. The Shuttle keeps her own counsel.

Three shapes have formed in the darkness beneath the loom. They are not gods. They are not mortals. They are not spirits or ghosts or any of the named things that inhabit the world's weave. They are something new: creatures born from the Weaver's waste, nourished on the residue of unfinished stories, driven by hungers the pattern never planned for.

The first is the Fraybeast.

It is the size of a dog, or a deer, or a house, it depends on how much loose story it has eaten recently. The Fraybeast roams the edges of the world's weave, where the pattern thins and the narrative frays, and it eats what it finds there: unfinished tales, abandoned myths, stories that were started and never resolved. It consumes them the way a fire consumes kindling, not maliciously, but completely. Where the Fraybeast has fed, the world's edges are smoother, cleaner, less haunted by narrative debris. The mortals who live on the world's margins have noticed: sometimes a story they were telling simply ends mid-sentence, the thread of it gone, the memory dissolving like salt in rain. They blame forgetfulness. They are wrong.

The second is the Threadworm.

It does not eat stories. It burrows. The Threadworm moves through the fabric of the world's pattern the way an earthworm moves through soil, consuming structure, excreting tunnels. The holes it leaves behind look, from inside the world, like doorways: archways in the air, passages between places that were never meant to connect, shortcuts through the pattern that violate the Weaver's geometry. Some of these holes heal. Some persist, and become the world's thin places, spots where reality is permeable, where the living can glimpse what lies beneath the world's surface, where things from below can occasionally crawl up. The Shuttle uses the Threadworm's tunnels sometimes, when she is in a hurry. She has never thanked the Threadworm. It would not understand thanks. It understands only through.

The third is the Loom-Moth.

It is beautiful. It is the most beautiful thing beneath the loom, wings like stained glass, antennae that sway to frequencies the gods cannot hear, a body that shimmers with colors the Weaver herself might envy. The Loom-Moth drinks color from the weave. It lands on the surface of the pattern, always at night, always in places where the world is already quiet, and it feeds, drawing the pigment from the threads into itself. Where the Loom-Moth has fed, gray patches remain. Nothing grows in the gray patches. No one dreams there. The soil produces no crops. The air carries no sound. The people who live near the gray patches report a feeling of absence, not sadness, not fear, but the sensation that something essential has been removed from the texture of existence and they cannot name what it was.

The Loom-Moth is the Weaver's inverse: where the Weaver adds, the Moth subtracts. Where the Weaver weaves color and story and grief into the world, the Moth removes them, one sip at a time, leaving behind a world that is incrementally less vivid, less storied, less felt. The theologians, those few who have noticed the gray patches, call this the Thinning. They do not yet know what causes it. They will.

The offcuts continue to fall. The shapes continue to form. Beneath the loom, the darkness grows more crowded, more complex, more organized. Something that might, in time, be called an ecology is emerging in the space the gods refuse to acknowledge, a food chain of scraps, a civilization of waste, a world beneath the world that runs on hunger and accident and the stubborn refusal of grief to stay quiet once it's been cut loose.

The loom itself, the frame, the warp, the mechanism of the Weaver's art, sits above this darkness like a palace above its catacombs. It is the first relic: the tool that made the world. And the place where it stands, or stood, or will stand, is the Hollow: the point in the world's geography where the pattern is densest, where the weave folds back on itself, where anyone who enters can hear the sound of thread being drawn through thread. Some say the Hollow is the Weaver's workshop. Some say it is her prison. Some say it is both, and that the difference depends on whether the Weaver wants to stop.

The Fraybeast has been seen near the Hollow's borders, circling, hungry. The Threadworm has burrowed close. The Loom-Moth has been spotted on the Hollow's outer wall, drinking the color from the world's first and oldest thread.

Fragments of the Weaver's tools have begun to surface in the world above. A shuttle carved from something that hums when held. A needle that trembles in the presence of grief. A scrap of the original pattern that shows, for a moment, the world as it was meant to be, and the world as it is, and the terrible, beautiful difference between them.

Below the loom, the offcuts are still falling. The shapes are still forming. And the hunger, the hunger that has no name, that was born from severance and sustained by scraps, is growing.

The gods will have to look down eventually.

They will not like what looks back.

Next: The loom itself is the first relic, and the only one no one can find.

Chapter 7: Relics & Sanctums

Objects and Places of Power

I. Opening Manifesto

Every mythic world runs on its relics: swords that crown kings, cups that poison the worthy, stones that hum with a frequency no living ear was meant to hear. And every relic, if you look closely, is haunted by a place: the chapel where the Grail was lost, the lake that swallowed the sword, the mountain where the ring must be destroyed. A world without sacred objects is just scenery with dialogue. A world without sacred spaces is just geography with pretensions. But the real secret; the one most worldbuilders miss, is that the object and the place are the same story told twice. The Ark of the Covenant *is* the Tabernacle, and the Tabernacle *is* the Ark. Remove one, and the other becomes a puzzle with no answer.

This is the Pairing Principle, and it's the engine of this chapter: every relic implies a sanctum, and every sanctum hungers for a relic. When Excalibur sits in the stone, both are sacred. When the sword is drawn, the stone becomes a monument to absence and the sword becomes a homeless king's credential, powerful, yes, but unmoored. When the One Ring enters Mount Doom, the mountain fulfills its purpose and the ring fulfills its fate. Object and place are co-dependent. They make each other matter. Build one without the other, and you've got a prop. Build them together, and you've got a mythology.

Here's your toolkit for both. We'll catalogue five types of relic and five types of sanctum, show how they pair and complicate each other, and then walk you through building a relic-sanctum pair from scratch, a single design that generates two powerful elements and a web of stories between them. Chapter 1 gave your world its shape. Chapter 2 filled it with gods. Now we're furnishing it with the things those gods left behind and the places that still remember their names.

II. WHAT IS A RELIC? WHAT IS A SANCTUM?

A relic is a physical object saturated with story: memory, miracle, taboo, or prophecy compressed into something you can hold, hide, or steal. Relics are never just powerful. They're *contested*. They shape religions, topple dynasties, start wars, and ruin the people who love them most. The Finnish Sampo, that mysterious, much-debated device forged by the smith-god Ilmarinen in the Kalevala, ground out flour, salt, and gold from nothing. Nations fought over it, heroes stole it, and when it finally shattered and sank into the sea, its fragments still washed ashore and blessed the land. Nobody agrees on what the Sampo actually *was*, a mill, a world-pillar, an astrolabe, a metaphor, and that ambiguity is the point. The best relics resist explanation. They generate more questions than they answer, and the questions generate stories, and the stories generate more relics.

A sanctum is a place where the ordinary rules thin, bend, or snap entirely: sacred, cursed, hidden, or all three at once. Sanctums are not the cosmic geography you built in Chapter 1. Your creation myth produced underworlds, spirit roads, and forbidden zones as structural features of the cosmos. Sanctums are *specific*: the particular shrine inside the forbidden zone, the hidden temple at the exact crossroads where the spirit road meets the mortal world, the one room in the underworld where the dead can speak and the living can listen. At Delphi, the Pythia sat over a fissure in the earth and breathed the vapors rising from below; the temple built precisely where the geological and the divine intersected. In Dogon tradition along the Bandiagara cliffs of Mali, Binu shrines mark the places where the dismembered body of the ancestral spirit Nommo fell to earth, each fragment demanding its own sacred enclosure, each enclosure decorated with libations of millet gruel that leave ghostly white streaks on the facade. In Shinto practice, the torii gate marks the threshold between the profane and the sacred; not because the gate itself is magical, but because the *place* behind it is inhabited by kami, and the gate is the punctuation mark between the world as you know it and the world as it actually is.

Here's what ties them together: a relic without a sanctum is a MacGuffin. A sanctum without a relic is a backdrop. But Excalibur *in* the stone, the Grail *in* the chapel, the Book of Thoth *in* its guarded tomb beneath the Nile; that's when mythology catches fire. The object explains why the place is sacred. The place explains why the object is dangerous. Separate them, and both diminish. The rest of this chapter teaches you to build them as a pair.

III. The Pairing Principle

Before we catalogue the types, let's name the principle that runs through everything.

In Chapter 4, we introduced the Mirror Framework: the idea that hero and villain are built together, each one defining the other. The Pairing Principle is the Mirror Framework's cousin, applied to objects and places. It works like this: when you design a relic, the first question isn't *what can it do?* It's *where does it belong?* And when you design a sanctum, the first question isn't *what happens here?* It's *what object defines it, or is missing from it?*

The Ark of the Covenant is a gold-covered chest holding the stone tablets of the law. The Tabernacle, later the Holy of Holies in Solomon's Temple, is the room built to contain it. When the Ark is present, the Tabernacle is the most sacred place on earth, the point where the divine touches the mortal. When the Ark vanishes from history (and it does; no one knows where it went), the empty room becomes something arguably more powerful: a space defined by what it has lost, a wound in the shape of a chest, a question that has sustained two thousand years of treasure-hunting, conspiracy, and faith. Absence is a kind of presence. The missing relic haunts its sanctum more than the present one ever did.

The Norse Andvaranaut, the cursed ring stolen by Loki from the dwarf Andvari, carries its own gravitational field. Wherever the ring goes, it creates a new sanctum; Hreidmar's hoard-hall becomes a site of murder, Fafnir's dragon-guarded wilderness becomes a place of quest, and eventually the ring's resting place in a hidden cave becomes a location that draws seekers to their doom for generations. The cursed relic doesn't need an architect to build it a temple. It builds its own.

This is the insight to carry through the rest of the chapter: object and place are not separate design tasks. They are a single design with two faces. Build one, and the other follows, if you know to look for it.

IV. Core Archetypes: Relics

Every relic falls somewhere along a spectrum from gift to curse, from legitimacy to transgression. Here are five recurring types. Each comes with cultural examples, a Gift (what it offers the worldbuilder), and a Trap (what it costs you). And for each, I'll name the sanctum it most naturally creates.

1. THE FOUNDING RELIC

A symbol of legitimacy or covenant: the object that proves a dynasty's right to rule, a faith's right to exist, or a people's claim to their land. Excalibur doesn't just cut things. It *crowns*. The Ark of the Covenant isn't just a container. It's the physical evidence that a god made a deal. In the Kalevala, the Sampo, forged by Ilmarinen for the witch-queen Louhi of Pohjola; became the source of an entire nation's prosperity. When heroes stole it and it shattered at sea, the fragments that washed ashore were enough to bless the land of Kalevala. The object is gone, but its remnants still legitimize the world.

The Gift: Founding Relics are story engines. They generate succession crises, holy wars, and the question every kingdom dreads: *what if the relic is a fake?* Build one, and you've built the political backbone of your world.

The Trap: Founding Relics can freeze your world into a monarchy simulator. If legitimacy is purely object-dependent; whoever holds the sword is king; you've eliminated the possibility of earned authority, democratic challenge, or moral complexity. The best Founding Relics are *contested*: some people believe, some don't, and the relic itself doesn't settle the argument.

Natural pairing: The Temple. Founding Relics live in the seat of power: the cathedral, the throne room, the vault beneath the capital. When the relic is removed, the temple becomes a mausoleum.

2. THE CURSED TREASURE

Brings fortune, then ruin, and makes the ruin look like the owner's fault. The Norse Andvaranaut is the archetype: a gold ring that helps its holder find wealth, cursed by the dwarf Andvari to destroy anyone who possesses it. Loki steals it, passes it to King Hreidmar as wergild for a murdered son, and the curse begins its patient work; Hreidmar is killed by his own son Fafnir, who becomes a dragon to guard the hoard, who is slain by Sigurd, who is betrayed by those closest to him. The ring passes from hand to hand, and every hand it touches closes into a fist. The Hope Diamond carries a similar legend (disputed by historians, sustained by journalists): a jewel whose beauty invites ownership and whose ownership invites disaster.

The Gift: The Cursed Treasure is tragedy in object form. It lets you write stories where the villain is *the thing everyone wants*, and the hero's victory is measured by their willingness to let it go. It also generates chains of consequence: every new owner inherits not just the object but the accumulated weight of everyone who held it before.

The Trap: Curse narratives can become mechanical: a predictable cycle of acquisition and punishment that stops feeling tragic and starts feeling like a morality play with a prop. The best cursed treasures include a moment where the curse could be broken, and someone *almost* breaks it, and doesn't.

Natural pairing: The Forbidden Zone. The cursed treasure poisons the ground it sits on. Fafnir's wilderness, the Hope Diamond's display case, the tomb that kills anyone who opens it; the relic makes its own no-go zone.

3. THE QUEST OBJECT

The thing that must be found, retrieved, or destroyed. The engine of the hero's journey. The Holy Grail sends knights across the known world and into spiritual crisis. The Golden Fleece draws Jason through impossible waters. Prometheus's stolen fire is the quest object that defines humanity's relationship to the gods: we have what we shouldn't, and we paid a price to get it.

The Gift: Quest Objects generate *movement*. They force characters out of their comfort zones, through thresholds, and into places they'd never go voluntarily. They also generate rivals; because the hero is never the only one looking. Chapter 4's hero needs a reason to leave home. Here's the reason.

The Trap: If the Quest Object is nothing more than a goal; retrieve it, win; you've built a fetch quest. The best Quest Objects change the seeker during the search. The Grail isn't just hard to find; it's hard to *deserve*. Most of the knights in the Grail legends fail not because they can't locate the chapel, but because they're not worthy of what's inside it. The quest is the transformation; the object is the proof.

Natural pairing: The Hidden Place. Quest Objects are never just sitting on a shelf. They're at the end of a labyrinth, at the bottom of a sea, inside a mountain that only opens at the right moment. The Hidden Place is the sanctum that makes the quest *a quest* rather than a shopping trip.

4. THE FORBIDDEN ARTIFACT

Too powerful, too dangerous, or too *wrong* to use; the object that exists primarily as a taboo. The Egyptian Book of Thoth, attributed to the ibis-headed god of writing and knowledge, supposedly granted the reader power over heaven, earth, and the underworld, and the ability to understand the language of animals and raise the dead. The prince Neferkaptah retrieved it from its guarded tomb beneath the Nile, defeating the serpent guardians; and in punishment, Thoth arranged the drowning of the prince's son, the suicide of his wife, and finally the prince's own death. Generations later, another prince, Setne Khaemwaset, stole it from Neferkaptah's tomb and was tormented by elaborate illusions until he returned it. The book destroys anyone who reads it, and no one can stop trying to read it. Pandora's Box. The One Ring. The fruit of the tree you were specifically told not to eat. Chapter 5's trickster relics; Nasreddin's trick coins, Anansi's stolen stories; belong here too, objects that break rules and dare you to break them alongside.

The Gift: Forbidden Artifacts generate moral dilemmas. They let you ask: *what would you do with power you weren't supposed to have?* They also generate institutions: priesthoods, secret societies, monster guardians that exist solely to keep the artifact locked away. Build a Forbidden Artifact, and you've built an entire social structure around the word "no."

The Trap: The Forbidden Artifact can become a deus ex machina if it's too powerful and too accessible. If your characters can just *use* it to solve the plot, you don't have a story. The taboo must be real; not just a warning, but a price that makes the object genuinely unusable by anyone sane.

Natural pairing: The Shrine or the Forbidden Zone. Forbidden Artifacts are kept in places that are themselves forbidden: guarded, buried, walled off, or defended by creatures whose sole purpose is to say "absolutely not." The Ark in its Holy of Holies. The Ring in Mount Doom (the one place it can be unmade). The book in its tomb beneath the river.

5. The Heirloom

The object that passes through generations, accumulating story with each hand that holds it. Chapter 3 introduced this concept under Bloodlines & Legacy; here, it gets its full treatment. The Yoruba Osanyin staff is a wrought iron shaft crowned with birds, carried by priests of the orisha Osanyin, the god of herbal medicine. The staff channels Osanyin's healing power; but Osanyin himself is a god who could not heal himself, crippled as punishment for his pride, left with one arm, one eye, one leg. The staff remembers the god's wound even as it performs the god's gift. Every heirloom carries this duality: the blessing of continuity and the curse of inheritance. The sword your grandfather carried in a war you didn't fight. The ring that belonged to someone whose name you've been forbidden to speak.

The Gift: Heirlooms generate *family drama*. They encode inheritance disputes, legitimacy crises, and the weight of expectation into a physical object. They also connect your present-day characters to your Chapter 3 bloodlines; the heirloom is the proof that the past isn't finished.

The Trap: Heirlooms can become nostalgia machines: beloved objects that inspire warm feelings and no conflict. An heirloom without a dark side is a souvenir. Give it a clause: the staff only works for the firstborn, the sword demands blood every generation, the ring tightens.

Natural pairing: The Shrine. Heirlooms are kept in intimate, family-specific sanctums: the altar in the back room, the locked chest in the ancestral home, the grave you visit on the anniversary. The heirloom's sanctum is private, contested, and charged with obligation.

V. Core Archetypes: Sanctums

Chapter 1's Shape of the Cosmos gave your world its large-scale geography: underworlds, spirit roads, the places creation produced. Now we zoom in. Sanctums are *specific*: the particular shrine, the exact threshold, the one hidden place that even the gods argue about.

1. The Shrine

Intimate, focused, often hidden or humble: dedicated to a single power, a single ancestor, a single need. A roadside altar in rural Japan with a small torii gate, where a neighborhood kami receives offerings of rice and sake. A Dogon Binu shrine along the Bandiagara cliffs, its facade streaked with dried millet gruel from generations of libations, its interior accessible only to the totemic priest. The household altar in a Roman home, where the lares, the guardian spirits of the family, receive daily prayers from the paterfamilias.

The Gift: Shrines are personal. They scale mythology down to the intimate: a single family, a single village, a single need. They're the sanctum type that best connects your divine hierarchy (Chapter 2) to your everyday world. Where the temple is public spectacle, the shrine is private devotion.

The Trap: Shrines can feel minor, easily overlooked. Don't let them. A shrine's power lies in specificity and in the consequences of neglecting it. The household kami that goes unattended. The ancestor whose altar is broken. In myth, neglected shrines don't just fade; they *bite back*.

Natural relic pairing: The Heirloom. Shrines hold the intimate objects: the ancestor's tool, the family talisman, the thing too important to display and too dangerous to discard.

2. The Temple

Public, communal, built to be seen: the sanctum as architecture and institution. The Parthenon. Angkor Wat. The great Shinto shrines of Ise, rebuilt every twenty years using traditional methods so the shrine is always both ancient and new; permanence expressed through cyclical renewal rather than stasis. Solomon's Temple, designed specifically as a house for the Ark of the Covenant, its innermost chamber, the Holy of Holies, accessible only to the high priest once a year on Yom Kippur.

The Gift: Temples generate politics. They have priests, hierarchies, budgets, rivalries, and schisms. They're the sanctum type that most naturally produces institutions and conflicts. Who controls the temple controls access to the divine; and that's a story engine that never runs out of fuel.

The Trap: Temples can become background architecture; impressive but inert. A temple that's just a building is just a building. Give it a secret: a room nobody enters, a ritual nobody remembers, a crack in the floor that goes deeper than anyone thought.

Natural relic pairing: The Founding Relic. Temples exist to house the legitimizing object: the sacred text, the covenant artifact, the relic that proves the faith is real.

3. THE FORBIDDEN ZONE

Taboo, cursed, or dangerous. The place nobody goes, or the place everybody is told not to go, which is the same as a neon sign reading *come in*. Chernobyl's Exclusion Zone, where the forbidden is technological rather than supernatural but functions identically in the mythic imagination. The cursed forest in a hundred fairy tales. The haunted house that is a cliche precisely because it describes something real; places that carry such a weight of bad memory that the air itself feels different.

The Gift: Forbidden Zones generate tension through approach. The closer your character gets, the higher the stakes. They also generate social structures; someone has to enforce the taboo, and someone always wants to break it. Chapter 6's monsters often live here. This is their natural habitat.

The Trap: Forbidden Zones can become one-note: scary, dangerous, avoid. The best ones are *necessary*. The thing inside the Forbidden Zone is terrible, yes, but it's also *needed*, and the story turns on the moment someone decides the need outweighs the fear.

Natural relic pairing: The Cursed Treasure. Forbidden Zones are often created *by* their relic. The treasure poisons the ground. The weapon irradiates the landscape. The artifact warps reality within a radius. Remove the relic, and the zone might heal, or it might be too far gone.

4. THE CROSSROADS / THRESHOLD

The place of choice, bargain, transformation, or passage between states. In West African and Afro-Caribbean Diaspora traditions, the crossroads is the domain of Eshu/Elegba/Papa Legba, the orisha who opens and closes the way, who must be saluted first in any ritual, and who turns every intersection into a negotiation between the human and the divine. The torii gate in Shinto practice functions as a threshold. Step through it, and you are no longer in the mundane world. The river Styx is a threshold crossed only once, in one direction, unless you are Orpheus or Heracles and have made arrangements.

The Gift: Crossroads generate decision points. They're naturally dramatic: the character must choose a path, make a bargain, or undergo transformation to proceed. They also connect your world's different planes: the crossroads is where the underworld meets the mortal road, where the spirit world touches the marketplace.

The Trap: Crossroads can become transactional; a tollbooth between plot points. The best crossroads change the traveler. You don't cross the threshold and come out the same. The Eleusinian Mysteries, the secretive annual rites held near Athens for nearly two millennia, were built on this principle: initiates entered the Telesterion, experienced something so profound it could not be spoken of, and emerged transformed. We still don't know exactly what happened inside. The mystery is the point.

Natural relic pairing: The Quest Object. The crossroads is where the quest begins in earnest: the point of no return, the place where the hero commits to the search and pays the first price.

5. THE HIDDEN PLACE

Visible only to the initiated, accessible only at certain times, or existing in a state of ontological uncertainty: maybe it's real, maybe it's not, and the maybe is what makes it powerful. Faerie mounds in Celtic tradition that open only on Samhain. Night markets in Chinese folklore that appear at moonrise and vanish at dawn. Shambhala in Tibetan Buddhist tradition; a hidden kingdom accessible only to those with the purest karma, said to exist somewhere beyond the Himalayas in a realm that is not precisely geographical. Atlantis, whose power over the imagination comes entirely from the fact that it cannot be found.

The Gift: Hidden Places generate *seeking*. They reward the worldbuilder who leaves gaps in the map. They also create narrative tension through access: the place exists, but getting there is the story. The Hidden Place is where your Chapter 4 heroes earn their transformation.

The Trap: Hidden Places can become twee: the secret garden, the magical school, the cozy otherworld that exists mainly to be charming. Make it dangerous. Make the finding cost something. Make the place itself ambivalent about being found.

Natural relic pairing: The Quest Object. The Hidden Place is the Quest Object's home: the place at the end of the journey that has been waiting, perhaps impatiently, for someone worthy to arrive.

VI. THE PAIRING WORKSHOP: BUILDING A RELIC AND ITS SANCTUM TOGETHER

This is a combined build: one design process that produces two interlocked elements. At each step, you'll make a decision for the relic that constrains the sanctum, and a decision for the sanctum that shapes the relic. By the end, you'll have an object and a place that can't be understood apart from each other.

STEP 1: THE SHARED ORIGIN

Every relic-sanctum pair starts with a single event. Something happened: a miracle, a crime, a catastrophe, a divine accident, and it left behind both an object and a location. The event doesn't have to be the same for both, but they must share a root.

In the Throat of the World (our showcase example, below), a singer's voice shattered a mountain and the shards of her final note crystallized into a bone flute. The object is what survived the singer. The place is what survived the mountain. Both are wreckage. Both are sacred.

Write the event that created both your relic and your sanctum. One sentence for the event. One sentence for what object it left behind. One sentence for what place it scarred, blessed, or transformed. Put it on paper now.

STEP 2: WHAT DOES THE RELIC DO, AND WHAT DOES IT COST?

Every relic has a power and a price. Chapter 6's Hunger Principle applies here, inverted: monsters hunger for what they lack; relics *give* what they shouldn't. The power should be desirable enough to explain why anyone would risk the cost, and the cost should be severe enough to explain why the relic isn't in constant use.

Odin's Draupnir, "the Dripper"; replicates itself every ninth night, dripping eight new gold rings of equal weight. Infinite wealth. But Odin laid the ring on his dead son Baldr's funeral pyre, and it had to be retrieved from the land of the dead. The gift of abundance is inseparable from grief. The cost isn't a fee; it's a memory.

In the Throat of the World, the bone flute grants any singer the ability to shatter stone; to literally break the world with their voice. The cost: every note played on the flute erases one of the player's memories. The more powerful the song, the more of yourself you lose. The relic gives the voice power over the physical world and takes the singer's interior world in exchange.

Name your relic's power. Name its price. Ask: is the price related to the power, or is it arbitrary? The best prices are thematic mirrors of the gift: the healing staff of a god who cannot heal himself, the ring of abundance that was consecrated in grief.

STEP 3: WHAT ARE THE SANCTUM'S RULES?

Every sanctum has access rules, transformation risks, and consequences for transgression. Who can enter? What happens to those who do? What happens to those who break the rules?

The Pythia at Delphi could only prophesy while seated on the tripod over the sacred fissure, and only after elaborate purification rituals. The prophecy was real; but it came through a specific chair, in a specific room, over a specific crack in the earth. Move any element, and the oracle falls silent. In our showcase, the Throat of the World: the shattered caldera where the singer's voice broke the mountain; can only be entered during a windstorm, because the wind through the broken rock produces harmonics that temporarily thin the barrier between the living world and the world of echoes. Visitors who enter during calm weather find nothing but rubble. Those who enter during a storm hear the singer's voice, still reverberating in the stone after centuries. Those who stay too long begin to harmonize; their own voices shifting to match the dead singer's frequency, their own memories beginning to resonate with hers.

Write your sanctum's access rule. Write what happens to someone who enters correctly. Write what happens to someone who enters wrongly, or stays too long. Cross-check: does the sanctum's rule echo the relic's cost? In the Throat, both the flute and the place demand memory as currency.

STEP 4: THE TABOO

What must never be done: to the relic, in the sanctum, or (most powerfully) to both simultaneously? The taboo is the invisible fence around the sacred, and every good mythology has someone who jumps it.

Name the taboo. Name who enforces it. Name who will inevitably break it, and what happens when they do. The taboo should generate at least one story you haven't planned yet.

STEP 5: SEPARATION AND CONSEQUENCE

What happens when the relic is removed from the sanctum? The Pairing Principle predicts that both are diminished, but *how*?

When the Ark left the Tabernacle, the room became a void and the Ark became a weapon without a home. When Excalibur was pulled from the stone, the stone became a monument and the sword became a king's burden. In the Throat, if the bone flute is carried beyond the caldera's rim, the winds in the Throat fall permanently silent; no more harmonics, no more echoes, no more access to the dead singer's world. And the flute, removed from its resonant chamber, plays notes that shatter not stone but *silence*; wherever the flute is played outside the Throat, sound dies for a mile in every direction. The relic and the sanctum punish each other's absence.

Write what happens when your relic leaves its sanctum. Does the place die? Does the object change? Does the world around both of them shift? The answer should feel like a consequence, not a mechanic.

STEP 6: THE WORLD RESPONDS

Relics and sanctums are never private. They generate cults, laws, economies, heresies, and wars. Who knows about your relic-sanctum pair? Who wants it? Who fears it? Who profits from it? Are there fakes, pilgrimages, black markets, competing claims?

Write one sentence about how your relic-sanctum pair has shaped the society around it. Who is the guardian? Who is the rival? What festival, law, or curse exists because of this pair?

STEP 7: THE MISSING PIECE

The strongest relic-sanctum pairs have an unresolved element: something broken, something lost, something that generates the *next* story. The Sampo is shattered and its fragments are scattered. The Grail is found and then lost again. The Ark vanishes from history.

Write the missing piece. What was lost, broken, or forgotten? What would happen if someone found it? This is your worldbuilding hook: the thread that pulls the reader deeper.

VII. QUICK MENU FOR INSPIRATION

Roll, choose, or combine. Every relic needs a sanctum; every sanctum deserves a relic.

Relic Origin: God-forged / Cursed / Accidental / Inherited / War-spoil / Natural / Stolen from the divine

Relic Power: Healing / Destruction / Knowledge / Luck / Transformation / Hunger / Prophecy / Command

Relic Price: Memory / Time / Blood / Loyalty / Sanity / Love / Identity / Voice

Relic Taboo: Forbidden to see / Use / Name / Gift / Sell / Destroy / Move / Remember

Sanctum Origin: Miracle / Crime / Bargain / Accident / Prophecy / Betrayal / Geological anomaly / Divine death

Sanctum Access: Ritual / Sacrifice / Password / Blood / Dream / Festival / Storm / Solitude

Sanctum Guardian: Priest / Monster / Ancestor / Stranger / Architecture itself / Echo / Nothing (which is worst)

Sanctum Risk: Vision / Curse / Healing / Hunger / Memory theft / Transformation / Madness / Time distortion

Pairing Bond: Relic only works inside sanctum / Sanctum only activates with relic present / Separation destroys both / Relic *is* the sanctum's heart / Sanctum *is* the relic's prison / Both are fragments of the same original / Neither knows the other exists (yet)

VIII. WORKED EXAMPLES

THE THROAT OF THE WORLD AND THE BONE FLUTE OF AVARA (SHOWCASE)

Before the city of Keth existed, there was a singer named Avara, and before Avara there was a mountain with no name, and the two of them were not supposed to meet.

Avara's voice was a geological event. She sang, and the permafrost cracked. She hummed, and dogs for miles around went still. The scholars who studied her gift; because a voice like that is always studied, always tested, always feared; determined that her vocal cords vibrated at a frequency that resonated with the mineral structure of basalt, and that if she ever sang at full volume for more than eleven seconds, she would shatter anything made of stone within a half-mile radius. They published their findings and recommended, in the genteel language of academic caution, that she never sing in an enclosed space.

Avara ignored them. She climbed the unnamed mountain, a dormant volcanic cone with a hollow caldera; because she wanted to hear what her voice sounded like inside a stone bowl. She wanted to feel the echo.

She sang for thirteen seconds.

The mountain split. The caldera collapsed inward, creating a jagged throat of broken basalt open to the sky. Avara died, crushed most likely, though the priests of Keth maintain she simply *became* the echo, that her voice is still reverberating in the stone and will reverberate until the stone itself wears away. What survived was a flute, carved (or formed; the accounts disagree) from Avara's own rib, found in the rubble by the first expedition to reach the ruined caldera. The flute is pale, warm to the touch even in winter, and hums faintly when pointed toward sound.

The Bone Flute of Avara grants any player the ability to shatter stone with directed sound: to crack walls, split mountains, collapse tunnels. The cost is memory. Each note played erases something from the player's mind: a name, a face, a skill, a year. Short melodies cost small memories. A full song, the kind that could bring down a fortress, might cost you your childhood. The longest song ever played on the flute was performed by a siege-breaker named Drell during the Third Merchant War. He shattered the seawall of Tavarath in nine minutes and seventeen seconds of sustained playing. When he stopped, he could not remember his own name, the name of the city he had destroyed, or why he was holding a bone flute on a beach covered in rubble. He lived another forty years. He never played again.

The Throat of the World, the shattered caldera; is the flute's sanctum. During windstorms, the broken basalt channels air through natural pipes and fissures, producing harmonics that are audible for miles and that, according to the Kethic priesthood, temporarily open a passage between the living world and what they call the Echo; a place where every sound ever made inside the mountain still reverberates. Pilgrims enter the Throat during storms to hear the voices of the dead, or, more precisely, to hear the *echoes* of the dead, which the priesthood insists are not the same thing but which the bereaved do not care to distinguish. The sanctum's rule: enter only during wind. Those who enter in calm weather find dead stone. Those who stay past the storm's end begin to lose their own voices: first volume, then pitch, then the ability to speak at all, as if the Throat is reclaiming the sound that was stolen from it.

The taboo: the flute must never be played inside the Throat. The priesthood of Keth maintains that if the flute and the mountain's acoustics ever combine again, if someone plays Avara's rib inside Avara's echo; the resulting sound would not shatter stone but *memory itself*, erasing the collective history of anyone within earshot. The Throat would become a zone of total amnesia. The Kethic word for this hypothetical event translates roughly as "the Unmaking."

Nobody has tested it. Several people have tried. The Kethic Order of the Closed Mouth exists solely to guard the Throat during storms and to ensure the flute; currently held in a locked reliquary in the city of Keth, five days' travel from the caldera; never returns to the mountain. They are well-funded, well-armed, and haunted by the suspicion that they are guarding against the wrong thing. Because there is a sect, small and growing, that believes the Unmaking is not a catastrophe but a mercy; that erasing the accumulated grief of the world is precisely what Avara was trying to do when she climbed the mountain. They call themselves the Last Note, and they are patient.

What to notice: The relic and the sanctum share an origin (Avara's death), a currency (memory/sound), and a taboo (reunion). The Pairing Principle generates three factions: the priesthood, the Order, and the Last Note; none of whom were planned in advance. The missing piece (what happens if the flute returns to the Throat) is the unresolved question that generates the next story.

THE COMPASS OF NOWHERE AND THE SHIFTING GARDEN (CLASSIC MODEL)

The Compass of Nowhere is a battered, mundane-looking navigational instrument that always points away from its owner's deepest desire. Follow it, and you are guaranteed to never find what you want most. Discard it, and it returns to your pocket within the hour. The Shifting Garden is a botanical sanctum that blooms only during eclipses: every plant inside it is toxic to the living but healing to the dead, and its paths rearrange themselves between visits so no map of it survives. The compass and the garden are paired: the compass will *never* point toward the garden, which means the garden can only be found by someone who doesn't know it exists, doesn't want to find it, or has no desires left at all. The garden's rarest flower, the White Absolution, which blooms once per eclipse and can reportedly erase a single regret from a human soul; is therefore accessible only to those who have nothing left to regret. The pairing ensures that the people who need the garden most can never reach it, and the people who reach it don't need it. This is the kind of elegant cruelty that the Pairing Principle generates when you let object and place define each other's rules.

IX. Pitfalls, Traps, and Common Mistakes

Loot Drop Syndrome. Your relic grants +5 to charisma and has no history, no taboo, and no social consequence. Congratulations; you've built equipment, not mythology. If a relic doesn't generate at least one story beyond its immediate use, it doesn't belong in this chapter.

Wallpaper Sanctums. Your temple is beautiful, atmospheric, and thoroughly described; and nothing that happens there couldn't happen in a parking lot. A sanctum must *change* people who enter it. If the place doesn't test, tempt, or transform, it's scenery.

The Solved Mystery. You've explained exactly what the relic does, how it was made, and why it works. You've answered every question. And now nobody cares, because the thing that makes a relic mythic is the questions it *doesn't* answer. The Sampo's scholars have debated its nature for centuries. That debate is worth more than any definitive answer would be.

Orphaned Objects and Empty Rooms. A relic with no sanctum is a prop. A sanctum with no relic (or no memory of one) is a backdrop. The Pairing Principle is your diagnostic: if your relic doesn't imply a place, or your sanctum doesn't imply an object, something is missing.

Separation Without Consequence. Your hero takes the relic from the temple and nothing happens. The relic works the same, the temple stands the same, the world continues the same. You've missed the point. Separation should *cost*; both the object and the place should suffer, change, or become dangerous in each other's absence.

X. Worldbuilding Hooks

Who writes, censors, or forges the stories about your world's relics? Are there scholars, propagandists, or forgers who profit from the relic's legend, and what happens when the legend diverges from the truth?

Are there relic-hunters: professionals who seek, recover, steal, or destroy sacred objects? What are their ethics, their rivalries, their blind spots?

How do new relics enter the world, and how do old ones vanish? Is there a lifecycle? Do relics fade, or do they accumulate power with age?

Who controls access to the sanctums, and what happens when control is disputed? Temple wars. Shrine desecrations. Competing priesthoods with irreconcilable interpretations of the same sacred ground.

What festivals, pilgrimages, or calendars revolve around your relic-sanctum pairs? (Hold this thought. Chapter 8 builds the toolkit for exactly this.)

Is the true relic hidden among decoys, or is every relic a lie? Is the sanctum in the wrong place: moved, misidentified, or deliberately concealed?

XI. Annotated Reading List

Primary Myths:

The Kalevala (Elias Lonnrot). The Sampo alone justifies the entry: a relic so ambiguous that scholars have spent two centuries arguing over whether it was a mill, a world-pillar, or a metaphor, and the argument is the point. Also contains the forging of the sky-dome, the kantele built from a pike's jawbone, and creation by breakage. Finnish myth at its strangest and most beautiful.

Norse Eddas (Prose Edda / Poetic Edda). The greatest treasure-hoard in mythology: Draupnir the self-replicating ring, Andvaranaut the cursed ring, Mjolnir the short-handled hammer, and the tragic chain of owners that connects them all. If you build one cursed object in your life, study how the Norse did it first.

The Arabian Nights Objects with wishes, rules, and betrayals. The lamp, the ring, the carpet, the bottle; every relic in the Nights comes with a contract written in fine print, and every owner discovers the fine print too late. The definitive text on relics as traps disguised as gifts.

Delphi and the Eleusinian Mysteries (various sources; start with Walter Burkert's *Greek Religion*). Delphi: the oracle, the tripod, the fissure, the prophetic vapors. Eleusis: the secretive rites, the transformation of initiates, the mystery that two millennia of scholarship still hasn't solved. Together, they demonstrate that the most powerful sanctums are the ones that refuse to explain themselves.

Shinto Sacred Sites and Torii (various sources; start with Joseph M. Kitagawa's *On Understanding Japanese Religion*). The torii as threshold-marker, the shrine as kami's dwelling, and the remarkable practice of rebuilding the Ise Grand Shrine every twenty years; permanence through cyclical renewal. The sanctum that stays sacred by never staying still.

MODERN & SPECULATIVE:

The Lord of the Rings (J.R.R. Tolkien). The One Ring is the relic against which all fantasy relics are measured, and Mount Doom is its sanctum: the only place it can be unmade, and the one place its maker most wants to protect. Tolkien understood the Pairing Principle instinctively. The ring draws the bearer toward the mountain. The mountain draws the ring toward the fire. Object and place are locked in a gravitational pull that is also a love story, if love stories ended in lava.

House of Leaves (Mark Z. Danielewski). A house that is bigger on the inside than the outside. A sanctum that *is* the relic; the architecture itself is the artifact, shifting, expanding, consuming. If you've ever wanted to build a place that is also a character, start here. Bring a flashlight. It won't help.

Indiana Jones (films, Spielberg/Lucas). The gold standard for relic narratives in popular culture. The Ark melts faces. The Grail heals; but only inside the temple. The crystal skull is the one nobody talks about. What Jones understands better than any academic: the relic's power is inseparable from the danger of its retrieval, and the sanctum always has a tr ap.

CRAFT:

The Golden Bough (James Frazer) Sprawling, problematic, and indispensable. Frazer's catalogue of sacred objects and ritual sites across cultures is a worldbuilder's encyclopedia of what humans do with the things they call holy. Read it as a sourcebook, not as anthropology.

XII. CREATIVE DARE: THE KEEPER'S WAGER

Build a relic-sanctum pair in which the object wants to return to its place, and someone is trying to prevent that reunion. Write the moment the relic gets close enough to the sanctum that both begin to *react*: the object warms, hums, or pulls. The place opens, shifts, or calls. Write the guardian who stands between them and must decide: let the relic come home, or keep the world safe from what happens when it does.

Then ask yourself:

What is your relic afraid of? What does your sanctum remember? And what happens to the world when the object that was taken is finally returned; not to its shelf, but to its story?

Go build something that belongs somewhere. Then hide it, and let the search begin.

THE LOOM, PART 7: THE FIRST RELIC AND THE HOLLOW

The loom itself is the first relic.

This is not debated. The theologians of every tradition within the world's weave: the Needle's archivists, the Fraying Edge's iconoclasts, the Shuttle's wandering scholars; agree on this single point, and it is the only point on which they agree. The loom is the tool that made the world. It is the oldest object. It is, by any definition that has ever been proposed, the holiest thing in existence.

It is also the only relic no one can find.

The Weaver sat at the loom. The Weaver wove the world. And then, the accounts diverge here, as accounts always do when the stakes are this high; the Weaver either left the loom, or was taken from it, or became it, or never existed separately from it in the first place. What is certain is that the loom is no longer where it was. Or it is where it was, but the "where" has moved. Or it is exactly where everyone thinks it is, but no one who looks for it can see it, because looking is the wrong sense for finding something that predates sight.

The Hollow is the first sanctum.

It is the place where the loom once stood, or still stands; the single point in the world's geography where the weave is densest, where the pattern folds back on itself seven times, where the warp-threads of grief and the weft-threads of accident are so tightly interlocked that the fabric of reality has no gaps, no thin places, no room for error. Anyone who enters the Hollow hears the weaving. Not the memory of it. Not the echo. The sound of thread being drawn through thread, right now, this instant, as though the Weaver never stopped.

The sound drives some people mad. Others it heals; not of illness but of certainty, which is a kind of illness the world's religions have been treating for centuries without naming. The uncertain emerge from the Hollow asking questions they didn't know they had. The certain emerge silent, their orthodoxies rattled, their maps of the cosmos suddenly full of roads they'd never noticed.

Some don't emerge at all. The Hollow keeps them. Not violently; there are no monsters in the Hollow, no guardians, no traps in the conventional sense. But the weaving-sound is patient, and persistent, and to those who are already fraying: who have lost too much, or carried too much, or woven too many of their own patterns into rigid shapes that leave no room for grief; the sound is irresistible. They sit. They listen. And eventually, they begin to weave along. Their fingers move in the air, following a pattern they can feel but not see. They become part of the loom's process, though what they are weaving, and whether the Weaver intends it, no one knows.

But the loom's fragments are not lost.

They surface in the world above like splinters working their way out of skin: small, sharp, and impossible to ignore. The first fragment found was a shuttle carved from bone that hums when held. Not the Weaver's bone, or perhaps yes, the Weaver's bone, if the Weaver had bones, if the Weaver was the kind of being that could be reduced to components. The shuttle was discovered in a riverbed by a child who thought it was a toy. She carried it home, and that night, the shuttle wove a thread between her sleeping mind and the mind of every other person in her village. They shared a single dream: the world as it was being made, the song that preceded the song, the grief that preceded the grief. The village woke changed. They built the first shrine, not to a god, but to the act of making.

The second fragment was a needle that trembles in the presence of grief. It was found embedded in the heartwood of an iroko tree by a healer who did not believe in relics. She pulled it free and felt it quiver in her hand like a dowsing rod over water. It pointed toward a woman in the marketplace whose smile was immaculate and whose sorrow; the healer now understood, was bottomless. The needle does not heal. It finds. It is a diagnostic instrument for the world's oldest wound, and anyone who holds it for more than a day begins to feel the grief of everything the needle has ever pointed toward. The healer lasted three weeks before she buried it. It was found again within the year. It is always found again.

The third fragment is the most dangerous: a scrap of the original pattern. A piece of cloth no larger than a child's palm, woven in colors that do not exist in the visible spectrum, showing, for the briefest of instants, when held up to any light: the world as it was meant to be. Not the world as it is. The world as the Weaver intended. The difference is small and devastating: in the intended world, the seventh thread did not knot. The gods were never born. The pattern is smooth, unblemished, and completely dead: a world of perfect order and no consciousness. Anyone who sees the pattern understands, in a flash of vertigo, that the gods, the mortals, the stories, the grief, the whole teeming mess of existence, is an accident. A beautiful, unbearable accident that the Weaver did not plan and cannot undo.

The scrap has been hidden, stolen, burned, and buried. It cannot be destroyed; the original pattern is the substrate of reality, and reality is not in the habit of self-harm. It currently rests in the hands of a scholar who has not yet looked at it. She knows what it shows. She is not sure she wants to see. Around her, the world is preparing for the Festival of Unraveling: that annual night when all thread-work is forbidden and every knot in the city is untied, when the people of the loom appease the Fraying Edge and pray that the world will stay flexible enough to survive another year. During the Festival, someone always sees a new thread appear in the weave that wasn't there before. The dreamwalkers call this the Prophecy Thread, and they say when it reaches the loom's edge, the pattern will complete.

No one knows what completion means. The scholar suspects. She keeps the scrap of original pattern in a drawer and does not open it.

In the Hollow, the weaving continues. The fragments surface. The Festival approaches.

And somewhere, in a part of the world that has not yet been mapped, someone is building a loom of their own.

Next: The Festival of Unraveling, and the prophecy no one wants to hear.

Chapter 8: The Living Myth

Festivals, Rituals, Curses, and Prophecy

I. Opening Manifesto

Myths aren't just stories; they're lived. They're the festival bonfire that chars the night sky every solstice, the curse that keeps a family from speaking a dead son's name, the prophecy scratched into a temple wall that makes generals lose sleep three centuries after the oracle died. The chapters before this one built the architecture of your mythology: the creation that shaped the cosmos, the gods that populate it, the bloodlines that carry its weight, the heroes and villains that embody its tensions, the tricksters that test its rules, the monsters that haunt its edges, the relics and sanctums that anchor its power. All of that is scaffolding. This chapter is where the people move in.

Festivals, curses, and prophecies are the social skeleton of a mythology: the mechanisms by which myth touches daily life. Without them, your world is a museum: beautiful, detailed, and dead behind glass. A pantheon that no one worships is just a list of names. A creation myth that no one reenacts is just backstory. A curse that no one fears is just a footnote. The living myth is the myth that shows up on the calendar, that changes what people eat and who they marry and which roads they won't walk after dark. It's the part of your world that smells like smoke and sounds like drums.

Here's the organizing principle: these three tools operate through *time*. Festivals look backward; they remember the creation, mourn the catastrophe, celebrate the survival. Curses operate in the present; they punish *now*, they mark the transgressor, they make the consequences of myth immediate and physical. Prophecies reach forward; they announce what's coming, dare the world to prevent it, and generate the dread and hope that drive your narrative toward its inevitable collision. Together, they form a temporal engine: past, present, future, all turning on the same mythic axis. Build all three from the same root, and your mythology breathes.

II. WHAT IS THE LIVING MYTH?

A festival is a controlled eruption in daily life: sacred time carved into the calendar, where the normal rules thin and the mythic world pushes through. It can be joyful (the harvest feast), agonizing (the fasting vigil), chaotic (the night when fools become kings), or terrifying (the reenactment of the god's death that might, this year, go too far). What makes a festival mythic rather than merely festive is its root: it remembers something. The Yoruba Gelede festival, performed across communities in Nigeria, Benin, and Togo, honors the "Mothers": powerful female ancestors, deities, and elder women whose spiritual authority can bless or devastate a community. Masked dancers perform elaborate choreography while drummers speak in tonal codes, and the entire event is overseen by the Iyalase, the Chief Priestess. Gelede doesn't just celebrate women's power; i t *manages* it, channeling potentially destructive spiritual force into communal harmony. The festival rests on a Yoruba maxim: *Eso l'aye*: the world is fragile.

A curse is a mythic punishment made manifest: the consequence of transgression, encoded in the body, the bloodline, the land, or the social order. Chapter 6 gave us the Hunger Principle: every monster reveals what the world fears by what the monster craves. Curses work the same way, inverted. Tell me the curse, and I'll tell you the violation. The plague that strikes Thebes in Sophocles' *Oedipus Rex* is not a medical event: it's a diagnostic one. The land sickens because the king has unknowingly murdered his father and married his mother; the plague is the world's immune response to a violation so fundamental that even the soil can feel it. Curses are mythology's enforcement arm.

A prophecy is a future tense that refuses to stay in the future; it reaches back into the present and deforms it. The Oracle at Delphi didn't merely predict; she *destabilized*. Kings who heard her prophecies changed their battle plans, rerouted their armies, and married their daughters to the wrong men, all trying to dodge or fulfill a fate that the attempt itself was making inevitable. The Norse gods knew Ragnarok was coming: the wolf would swallow the sun, the serpent would rise from the sea, the gods would fall, and they went to war anyway. Not because they were stupid, but because foreknowledge without power is the cruelest gift a mythology can bestow: you know the ending, and you can't rewrite it, and the knowledge itself becomes part of the machinery that drags you toward it.

These three tools are not separate systems. They're interlocking gears. The festival that remembers the creation also enacts the taboo that the curse punishes, and the prophecy whispers about what happens when the festival finally fails. Build them together, and your world lives. Build them separately, and you've got three lists.

III. Part One: Festivals: The Myth Remembers

Festivals are how cultures process their myths in real time: the regularly scheduled collisions between the sacred and the ordinary. Here are six archetypes. Each contains multitudes; your festival will likely blend two or more.

1. The Seasonal Festival

Tied to the calendar: solstice, equinox, harvest, planting, monsoon, the return of a star. These festivals anchor the mythic cycle to the agricultural or astronomical rhythm that keeps the community alive. Beltane marks the beginning of the pastoral summer in Celtic tradition, with bonfires lit to protect livestock as they move to summer pastures. The Inca Inti Raymi celebrated the winter solstice (June, in the Southern Hemisphere) to honor the sun god Inti and ensure his return: a festival so magnificent that the Spanish colonizers banned it for centuries and it was still remembered.

The Gift: Seasonal festivals give your world a *pulse*. They generate a calendar, which generates a culture, which generates politics: because whoever controls the calendar controls the sacred. They're also the simplest entry point for worldbuilding: what does your world celebrate when the longest night arrives?

The Trap: Seasonal festivals can become decorative: pretty set pieces that interrupt the narrative without driving it. The best seasonal festivals contain a *risk*: what if the sun doesn't come back? What if this harvest is the last? The festival should celebrate survival while whispering that survival is never guaranteed.

2. The Rite of Passage

Marks a transformation in status: boy to warrior, child to adult, living to dead. These are the festivals that change *who you are*. Among the Maasai of Kenya and Tanzania, the Eunoto ceremony marks the transition from junior warrior (moran) to senior warrior: a multi-day event where mothers shave their sons' ochre-stained hair, warriors drink the blood of a ritually slaughtered bull, and an Olotuno is chosen to bear the collective weight of his age-set's transgressions. The ceremony requires the construction of a forty-nine-house encampment and months of preparation. In ancient Athens, the Thesmophoria was a three-day women-only festival honoring Demeter and Persephone: married citizen women left their homes to camp on the hillside of the Pnyx, fasted on the second day in imitation of Demeter's grief over her abducted daughter, and on the third day (Kalligeneia, "beautiful birth") celebrated renewal and prayed for fertility. Men were forbidden to approach, witness, or even know the details of the rites. A festival that transforms the community by temporarily excluding half of it.

The Gift: Rites of passage generate *stakes*. They are the moments when your characters change permanently; the threshold that, once crossed, locks them into a new identity. They also generate beautiful dramatic irony: the warrior who isn't ready, the bride who refuses, the child who sees something during the rite that they were never supposed to see.

The Trap: Rites of passage can default to Western coming-of-age cliches: the generic "chosen one ascends" moment. The richest rites of passage involve *loss* as well as gain. The Maasai warrior who is shaved by his mother is weeping. He is gaining adulthood and losing his freedom. Make the transformation cost something, or it's just a promotion.

3. THE CRISIS RITUAL

Performed in response to disaster: plague, famine, invasion, drought, eclipse, the birth of a monstrous child. These are the emergency protocols of the sacred, activated when normal worship has failed. Rain dances, plague sacrifices, scapegoat expulsions, communal fasting: all are crisis rituals. The key feature: *desperation*. Normal rules are suspended because normal rules have stopped working. In the Hebrew Bible, the scapegoat ritual on Yom Kippur involved transferring the community's sins onto a goat, which was then driven into the wilderness: the sins made literal, physical, and removable.

The Gift: Crisis rituals are *plot engines*. They arrive when your world is already in trouble, and they either fix it or make it worse, often both. They also reveal the fault lines in your society: who gets sacrificed? Who decides? Who profits?

The Trap: The crisis ritual that always works is boring. The crisis ritual that never works is nihilistic. The best crisis rituals work *partially*: the plague recedes, but the scapegoat's family remembers, and that memory becomes the seed of the next crisis.

4. THE TABOO FESTIVAL

Organized around what must *not* be done: the forbidden food, the unspeakable name, the act that will bring catastrophe if performed on this particular night. Taboo festivals define the sacred by defining its borders. In many cultures, certain days prohibit specific labor, speech, or contact. The power is in the negative space: the festival is shaped by what's absent.

The Gift: Taboo festivals are mystery generators. The reader wants to know *why*: why can't they eat fish on this night? Why is the god's name forbidden during the equinox? Why does every mirror in the city get covered? The prohibition itself is a story hook. It also connects directly to your curse system: the taboo is the rule, and the curse is what happens when someone breaks it.

The Trap: Taboos without consequences are empty. If breaking the rule carries no weight: if some irreverent character eats the forbidden food and nothing happens, you've undermined your world's mythic logic. The taboo should be breakable, but breaking it should *matter*.

5. The Reversal Festival

Everything flips. Masters serve slaves. Fools become kings. Gender roles invert. Chaos reigns, but only for a day, a week, a precisely bounded window, after which the normal order snaps back, theoretically refreshed. Roman Saturnalia is the archetype: for up to a week in late December, slaves were served by their masters, wore the *pileus* (the freed slave's felt cap), gambled openly, and spoke freely. A "King of Saturnalia" was elected by lot and issued absurd commands: *sing naked, throw him in cold water*. Everyone obeyed. The medieval Feast of Fools saw lower clergy mock their superiors, sometimes electing a "Boy Bishop" or a "Lord of Misrule." Brazilian Carnival carries this tradition into the present: the street belongs to the costumed crowd, and the power structures of daily life dissolve, temporarily, into spectacle, music, and transgression.

The Gift: The Reversal Festival is the trickster's institutional footprint: Chapter 5's chaos principle given a date on the calendar and a permit from the authorities. It lets you explore power by *inverting* it, and it generates the question every good mythology must ask: if the reversal feels this alive, why do we go back to normal?

The Trap: The Reversal Festival that's too safe: a costume party with no edge, misses the point. Historical Saturnalia worked because slaves could say things that would get them beaten any other day. The reversal must have real teeth, real danger, and a real question about whether the old order *should* snap back. Also beware the trope of "exotic carnival": treat reversal festivals from non-Western traditions with the same analytical depth you'd give a Greek rite.

6. The Ritual Drama

A sacred performance: the reenactment of the myth itself, played out by actors, priests, masked dancers, or the community at large. The Eleusinian Mysteries of ancient Greece involved initiates entering the Telesterion and witnessing something so transformative that two millennia of scholarship still can't determine exactly what it was: the secrecy itself is the point. In Japanese Setsubun, families throw roasted soybeans at a member wearing an *oni* (demon) mask while shouting *Oni wa soto! Fuku wa uchi!*. "Demons out! Fortune in!" A compact ritual drama that reenacts the annual expulsion of evil at the boundary between winter and spring. The word for beans (*mame*) resonates with the word for destroying demons (*mametsu*), and the act is both playful and deadly serious: the boundary between the old year and the new must be defended with noise, force, and prayer.

The Gift: Ritual drama collapses the distance between myth and the present. The god's death is happening *now*, in the town square, and the actors are your neighbors. This is powerful worldbuilding material: what if this year's reenactment goes wrong? What if the actor playing the villain *becomes* the villain? What if the audience starts to suspect the reenactment is more real than anyone admits?

The Trap: Ritual drama can become exposition: a convenient way to dump your mythology's backstory by having characters watch a play. Resist this. The drama should be a live wire, not a lecture. Something should go wrong. Something should be at stake. The best ritual dramas risk becoming the myth they're performing.

IV. PART TWO: CURSES: THE MYTH PUNISHES

If festivals are how a culture remembers its myths, curses are how myths enforce themselves. A curse is a living consequence: punishment that persists, spreads, or transforms, revealing what the world considers unforgivable. Here are five types.

1. THE DIVINE PUNISHMENT

A god strikes directly: plague, transformation, exile, madness, in response to mortal hubris, neglect, or taboo-breaking. The Plagues of Egypt: ten escalating catastrophes inflicted by God upon Pharaoh for refusing to free the Israelites: water turned to blood, frogs, darkness, and finally the death of every firstborn son. In Greek mythology, Niobe boasted that her fourteen children made her superior to the goddess Leto, who had only two. Apollo and Artemis, Leto's children, killed all fourteen of Niobe's offspring. Niobe wept until she turned to stone, and the stone still weeps: a spring on Mount Sipylus.

The Gift: Divine Punishment curses establish that your gods are *active*: not distant observers but enforcers with specific triggers and specific wrath. They generate the fear that makes your festivals necessary: we celebrate *because* the gods punish, and the celebration is the protection.

The Trap: If divine punishment is arbitrary or disproportionate without commentary, your mythology becomes sadistic rather than tragic. The best divine punishments contain a terrible logic: Niobe's grief is eternal because her pride was aimed at a mother's children.

Make the punishment rhyme with the crime.

2. THE INHERITED CURSE

Passed through bloodlines: the sin of the ancestor becomes the burden of the descendant. Chapter 3 introduced generational wounds; here, that concept gets its sharpest edge. The House of Atreus is the definitive example: Tantalus served his own son Pelops to the gods; Pelops's sons Atreus and Thyestes murdered, betrayed, and fed each other's children in escalating retaliation; Agamemnon sacrificed his daughter Iphigenia; Clytemnestra murdered Agamemnon; Orestes murdered Clytemnestra. Five generations of blood answering blood, each act simultaneously a crime and a punishment for the crime that came before.

The Gift: Inherited curses are the gift that keeps giving: narratively speaking. They generate multi-generational saga, tragic irony (the descendant who doesn't know what their ancestor did), and the question of whether guilt can be inherited or must be earned. They also pair naturally with your Chapter 3 bloodlines: the curse *is* the bloodline's defining feature.

The Trap: Inherited curses can feel deterministic: if the family is doomed no matter what, why should the reader care about individual choices? The best inherited curses include a *breaking condition* that is theoretically possible but practically devastating: the curse ends when a child forgives the unforgivable, or when the family line voluntarily ends, or when the stolen treasure is returned to a place that no longer exists.

3. THE OUTBREAK / PLAGUE

A contagion that spreads: through bodies, dreams, stories, or social contact. The plague at Thebes is diagnostic: the crops fail, the women miscarry, the livestock die, and the cause is a king's unknowing crime. But plagues can also be supernatural in their vector. In the Popol Vuh, the Quiche Maya creation narrative, the gods curse entire species: the wooden people of the second creation are destroyed by a flood and attacked by their own possessions (their grinding stones, their cooking pots, their dogs) because they lacked gratitude and consciousness. The punishment is ecological: the world itself rejects what doesn't belong.

The Gift: Outbreaks generate *panic*, which generates social breakdown, which generates story. Who are the healers? Who are the profiteers? Who gets blamed? Plagues also reveal social structure by destroying it: the disease that kills the king the same as the beggar exposes the lie of hierarchy.

The Trap: Plagues without mythic logic are just disaster fiction. In a mythological framework, the plague must have a *meaning*: a diagnostic quality, as we discussed in Chapter 6. Random disease is terrifying; meaningful disease is mythic. Why *this* plague?

Why *now*? What violation triggered it, and what sacrifice might end it?

4. THE SOCIAL CURSE

Not divine but communal: exile, shunning, the mark of the outcast, the family that everyone whispers about. Social curses are imposed by communities rather than gods, but they carry mythic weight because the community *believes* the curse is real and acts accordingly. Witch hunts, leprosy colonies, untouchable castes, blood feuds that outlast the original grievance: all are social curses. The Irish concept of *geis* (plural *geasa*) is a hybrid: a taboo or obligation placed on an individual, often a hero, that carries both supernatural and social force. Cu Chulainn's geasa forbade him from eating dog meat (his name means "Hound of Culann"), and when his enemies contrived a situation where refusing would also violate a geis, the contradictions killed him.

The Gift: Social curses are *political*. They generate stratification, resistance, and the question of who has the power to curse and who must bear it. They're also the most realistic curse type, closest to actual human behavior, which makes them ideal for grounding your mythology in social texture.

The Trap: Social curses can become preachy if they're too obviously allegorical. The worldbuilder's job is to present the curse as the *world* sees it: real, dangerous, deserved, while allowing the reader to see the cracks. If you're building a social curse to make a point about injustice, let the point emerge from the detail, not from authorial commentary.

5. THE WORLD WOUND

The land itself is cursed: blighted, poisoned, frozen, or scarred by an event so catastrophic that geography absorbed the damage. The Fisher King's wound is the archetype: the king is injured, and his kingdom sickens in sympathy; the crops fail, the rivers dry, the court wastes, and the land can only be healed by a questing knight asking the right question. The Waste Land of Arthurian legend is not a metaphor: the king's body *is* the land, and the land's sickness *is* the king's wound.

The Gift: World Wounds make the abstract physical. The curse is visible on the map: that dark forest, that dead lake, that region where compasses spin. They also connect your curse system to Chapter 1's creation: the World Wound is what happens when the world's original design is violated at the structural level. The cosmos itself is injured.

The Trap: World Wounds can become video-game terrain: the "dark zone" on the map that signals "danger here" without generating real mythic weight. The best World Wounds have a *history*: someone did this, someone remembers, and someone is looking for the cure, and the cure is worse than the disease.

V. Part Three: Prophecies: The Myth Reaches Forward

Prophecies are the future tense of mythology: the announcements, warnings, riddles, and doomings that reach back from what's coming and reshape the present. They're the most narratively potent tool in this chapter, because prophecy doesn't just predict the plot; it *creates* the plot by changing how characters behave.

1. The Doomsaying Oracle

Declares destruction: usually of the person or civilization that most desperately wants to survive. Cassandra, cursed by Apollo to speak true prophecies that no one believes. The Book of Revelation, which has generated two millennia of interpretation, terror, and readiness because no one can agree on what it actually predicts. Ragnarok, the Norse twilight: the gods know the wolf Fenrir will swallow Odin, the Midgard Serpent will kill Thor, the world will burn and sink into the sea, and they go to their deaths anyway, because knowing the end doesn't grant the power to prevent it.

The Gift: Doomsaying generates *dread*, which is one of mythology's most valuable currencies. Characters who know the end is coming but can't stop it become immediately tragic and deeply human. Doomsaying also generates factions: the believers, the deniers, the accelerationists who want to bring the doom faster.

The Trap: Doom that always arrives on schedule is predictable. Doom that never arrives is a false alarm. The best doomsayings leave room for ambiguity: maybe the oracle was wrong, maybe the translation is flawed, maybe the doom already happened and nobody noticed.

2. The Conditional Prophecy

"If X, then Y": A fate that depends on a choice. Macbeth is secure until Birnam Wood comes to Dunsinane and until he faces a man not born of woman. Two conditions that seem impossible until they aren't. The Nemean Lion can only be killed by someone who can strangle it barehanded. These prophecies are bargains disguised as impossibilities.

The Gift: Conditional prophecies are puzzle boxes. They invite the reader (and the characters) to game the system: to find the loophole, reinterpret the condition, or discover that the condition was never what it seemed. They're the most interactive prophecy type: the reader is solving alongside the characters.

The Trap: If the loophole is too clever, the prophecy feels like a riddle with a punchline rather than a fate with weight. The best conditional prophecies are satisfied in ways that are *technically* correct but emotionally devastating: yes, Birnam Wood "came" to

Dunsinane, but only because an army used the branches as camouflage, and the cleverness of the solution doesn't diminish the horror of what follows.

3. THE SELF-FULFILLING PROPHECY

The attempt to escape fate is what causes it. Oedipus's parents abandon him to prevent the prophecy that he'll kill his father and marry his mother, and the abandonment is the mechanism that makes both events possible. Voldemort attacks infant Harry Potter to prevent a prophecy, and the attack is what creates the conditions for the prophecy's fulfillment. In the Mahabharata, King Kamsa imprisons his sister Devaki and her husband Vasudeva because of a prophecy that Devaki's eighth child will kill him. He murders their first seven children, but the eighth, Krishna, is spirited away at birth and raised in hiding. Krishna eventually returns and kills Kamsa. The paranoia the prophecy inspired was the instrument of its own fulfillment.

The Gift: Self-fulfilling prophecies are tragedies in the truest sense: the character's greatest virtue (foresight, determination, love for their family) becomes the flaw that destroys them. They generate irony on an architectural scale: the audience knows what the character doesn't, and every rational decision the character makes brings the catastrophe closer.

The Trap: If overused, self-fulfilling prophecies teach the wrong lesson: *never try to prevent anything*. The best versions include a moment where a different choice *might* have broken the cycle: a fork in the road that the character doesn't take, not because they can't see it, but because their character won't let them.

4. THE RIDDLE PROPHECY

Deliberately ambiguous: encoded, symbolic, multi-layered, requiring interpretation that is almost always wrong the first time. The Sphinx at Thebes asks a riddle; Oedipus answers it, and the answer ("man") is also, unknowingly, the answer to the riddle of his own identity. The Delphic Oracle's pronouncements were famously cryptic. King Croesus was told that if he attacked Persia, a great empire would fall, and it did: his own.

The Gift: Riddle prophecies are *literary*. They reward rereading, because the answer was always there, hiding in plain sight. They also generate competing interpretations within your world: priests who disagree, scholars who spend lifetimes on a single phrase, heretics who insist the riddle means the opposite of what the orthodoxy claims.

The Trap: Riddle prophecies can be too cute: puzzles that are fun to solve but carry no emotional weight. The riddle should be *painful* when the answer arrives. The cleverness of the construction should serve the tragedy, not the other way around.

5. THE BROKEN PROPHECY

A prediction that fails, or appears to fail. The apocalyptic cult that names a date and wakes up the next morning in an intact world. The chosen one who doesn't choose. The doom that was averted so long ago that no one remembers it was ever real. In the Mahabharata, Krishna functions not as a prophet who forces events but as a divine strategist who knows the outcome, tries diplomacy first, and when peace fails, participates fully in the war he saw coming, never imposing the future, but steering through it with devastating clarity. Gandhari, who lost all one hundred of her sons in the war, curses Krishna for not preventing the slaughter he foresaw, and the curse holds. The prophet is punished for the prophecy's truth.

The Gift: Broken prophecies generate uncertainty, which is far more narratively useful than certainty. If prophecies can fail, then every prophecy in your world carries a question mark. Characters must decide not just *what the prophecy means* but *whether to believe it at all*. Broken prophecies also generate institutions: the false-oracle debunkers, the prophecy-revision committees, the archive of failed predictions that someone, someday, will notice contains a pattern.

The Trap: Too many broken prophecies teach the reader not to care. If nothing is fated, then prophecy is just noise. The best broken prophecies leave one thread intact: one detail that *did* come true, buried in the failure, waiting to be noticed.

VI. THE INTEGRATION WORKSHOP: BUILDING FESTIVAL, CURSE, AND PROPHECY FROM A SINGLE ROOT

This is the most ambitious workshop in the book. You're not building three separate elements: you're building a *system*. A festival, a curse, and a prophecy that all grow from the same creation myth and interact with each other the way gears in a clock interact: each one drives the others, each one constrains the others, and the whole mechanism produces something none of them could produce alone.

The principle: the festival *celebrates* (or mourns) an event from the creation myth. The curse *punishes* those who violate the festival's rules, or who caused the event the festival remembers. The prophecy *foretells* what happens when the curse is finally broken, or when the festival fails.

STEP 1: NAME THE CREATION EVENT

Every living myth begins with a beginning. Go back to your Chapter 1 creation myth, or invent one now, and identify a single event that scarred the world into its current shape. Not the whole creation; one *moment*. The betrayal, the sacrifice, the accident, the gift that went wrong.

In our showcase example (the Cinder Rites of Ashtalar, below), the creation event is this: the fire-god Keth stole light from the Sky Serpent's belly to illuminate a world drowning in darkness, and in doing so, burned the Serpent from the inside out. The world gained light, but the Serpent's ashes fell as the first winter, and the Serpent's dying scream became the wind. Light was purchased with cold.

Identify the creation event your festival will remember. One sentence: what happened, who did it, and what it cost. Write it down now.

STEP 2: BUILD THE FESTIVAL

Your creation event demands remembrance. How does the culture process it? Do they celebrate the gift (light!) or mourn the cost (the eternal cold)? Or, most powerfully, both?

Decide: Is the festival seasonal, a rite of passage, a crisis response, a reversal, a taboo, or a ritual drama? It can blend types. What acts are performed? What's forbidden? Who leads? Who's excluded? What goes wrong if the festival is disrupted?

In Ashtalar, the Cinder Rites are a three-night festival at midwinter. On the first night, every fire in the city is extinguished: total darkness, commemorating the world before Keth's theft. On the second night, a single flame is lit at the summit temple and carried down through the streets by a chain of torchbearers, each one representing a generation since the theft. On the third night, the entire city blazes: every hearth, every lantern, every candle, and the people feast in the light. But there is a taboo: no one may speak the Sky Serpent's name during the three nights. To name the Serpent is to call the cold back.

Design your festival. Name it. Describe its core acts and its central taboo. Cross-check: does it respond directly to the creation event from Step 1? In the Cinder Rites, the fire-extinguishing reenacts the pre-theft darkness, the torch relay reenacts the theft, and the blaze reenacts the gift. Every element is a mirror of the origin.

STEP 3: BUILD THE CURSE

Now ask: what happens when someone violates the festival, or when someone repeats the original crime the festival was designed to process?

The curse should feel like the *shadow* of the festival. If the festival celebrates the gift, the curse punishes those who abuse it. If the festival mourns the cost, the curse marks those who refuse to mourn.

In Ashtalar, the curse is the Ashen Tongue: anyone who speaks the Sky Serpent's name during the Cinder Rites begins to lose heat. Their body temperature drops over days.

Their breath frosts in summer. Within a month, their blood runs cold enough to freeze water by touch. The cursed become walking winters, and the only way to reverse it is to carry a live flame into the ruins of the Serpent's spine (a mountain range in the east, Chapter 1 geography) and relight the first fire at its source. No one has survived the journey.

Design your curse. What triggers it? What are its symptoms? How does it spread, or does it target individuals? What's the cure, and why hasn't anyone achieved it? Cross-check: does the curse rhyme with the creation event? In Ashtalar, the theft of heat is answered by the theft of heat. The Serpent's revenge is temperature.

STEP 4: BUILD THE PROPHECY

Finally: what does the future hold? The prophecy should connect the festival to the curse and reach beyond both: announcing an endgame that recontextualizes everything.

In Ashtalar, the prophecy is this: *When the last torchbearer in the relay drops the flame, and the second night falls into darkness, the Sky Serpent will reassemble from its ashes, and the world will return to the cold it was stolen from, unless a child born in the dark of the first night carries fire in their blood and lights the Serpent's heart from within.*

Notice what this does: it makes the festival dangerous (every year, the relay is a gamble: what if a bearer stumbles?). It creates a character type (children born on the first night are both blessed and marked). It connects the curse to the prophecy (the Ashen Tongue is a preview of the prophesied cold). And it generates a quest (Chapter 9's territory: find the Serpent's heart, light it, save the world).

Write your prophecy. One to three sentences. It should reference the festival, acknowledge the curse, and announce a future that changes how the reader understands both. Ask: does my prophecy make my festival more dangerous? Does it make my curse more meaningful? Does it generate at least one story I haven't planned yet?

STEP 5: TEST THE INTERACTIONS

Now stress-test. How do the three elements *contradict* each other?

In Ashtalar: the festival celebrates Keth's theft as heroic. But the curse suggests the theft was a *violation*: the Serpent's revenge implies the theft was wrong. And the prophecy introduces a third possibility: maybe the theft wasn't finished. Maybe the fire wasn't meant to stay stolen. Maybe the child who lights the Serpent's heart isn't preventing an apocalypse, they're completing a transaction that was interrupted.

These contradictions are features, not bugs. They generate rival factions in your world: the priests who celebrate Keth, the ascetics who think the theft was a sin, the prophets who believe the Serpent's return is salvation rather than destruction. A living myth is a myth that people argue about.

Write down one contradiction between your festival and your curse, and one between your curse and your prophecy. If you can't find contradictions, your system is too neat. Go back and roughen it.

VII. Worked Examples

Showcase: The Cinder Rites of Ashtalar

The world before Keth was cold and black. Not empty, teeming, in fact, with life that navigated by sound and touch and the faint phosphorescent glow of deep-sea creatures that had crawled onto land and never found the ocean again. But it was a world without fire, without warmth beyond what bodies could generate huddled together, without light beyond the dimmest bioluminescence. The Sky Serpent coiled around the world's shell and inside its belly burned the only flame: a remnant of the cosmic forge that had shaped the world, swallowed by the Serpent because fire was too dangerous for mortal hands.

Keth was not a god. Not yet. He was a mortal blacksmith who had learned to work cold iron by sound alone: the ring of the hammer on the anvil was his only guide. When his daughter was born blind in both eyes (as all children were, in a world without light), he decided that blindness in the dark was merely redundant, but blindness in the light, if he could find light, would be a tragedy worth preventing. He climbed the Serpent's coils. He cut his way in through the third scale from the tail. He found the flame in the Serpent's seventh stomach, and he *swallowed it*.

The light came out of him like a scream. It poured from his mouth, his eyes, his skin. The Serpent ignited from within: seven stomachs of collected grease and scales and millennia of swallowed darkness, all burning at once. The Serpent's death took three days. Its ashes fell as the first snow. Its bones became the Ashridge Mountains. Its dying scream became the wind that has never stopped blowing across the eastern steppe. Keth survived, but the fire lived inside him now, and his touch burned everything he loved. His daughter could see, but she couldn't touch her father without blistering.

The Cinder Rites remember all of this: three nights mirroring the three days of the Serpent's death. The first night's darkness honors the world before. The torch relay honors Keth's theft: each bearer represents a generation that has inherited the stolen fire. The third night's blaze celebrates the gift while the taboo (never speak the Serpent's name) acknowledges that the gift was taken, not given, and the Serpent's memory must not be invoked. The Ashen Tongue curse strikes those who break the taboo: the Serpent's cold reclaiming what was stolen from it, one body at a time. And the prophecy hangs over everything: *When the relay fails, the cold returns.*

The priests of Keth insist the theft was necessary and righteous. The Order of the Silent Scale: a monastic tradition living in the Ashridge Mountains, among the Serpent's bones, believe the theft was a crime, and that the Cinder Rites are a yearly provocation that delays the inevitable reckoning. The dreamwalkers, neither priests nor monks, say the prophecy isn't a warning but a *promise*: the fire was always meant to be returned, and the child who carries fire in their blood is not a hero but a refund.

Every year, the relay runs. Every year, the bearers train for months, and the route is cleared, and the wind is watched. Every year, someone, usually a child, is born in the darkness of the first night, and the priests examine the infant for signs of heat in the blood. Most years, there are none. Some years, there is a child who runs a fever that won't break, whose tears evaporate before they fall, who reaches for fire the way other children reach for milk. These children are taken to the summit temple. What happens to them there is not discussed outside the priesthood.

The Rites continue. The relay has never failed. The wind has never stopped. And somewhere in the Ashridge Mountains, in a cave that smells of sulfur and old snow, something is reassembling: bone by bone, scale by scale, in a pattern that looks very much like patience.

What to notice: The Cinder Rites showcase demonstrates the Integration principle. The festival (remembrance), curse (punishment), and prophecy (forecast) all stem from a single creation event (Keth's theft of fire). They contradict each other: the festival celebrates what the curse punishes, and the prophecy reframes both. The system generates factions (priests vs. monks vs. dreamwalkers), characters (the fire-blooded children), and an unresolved tension (the relay that hasn't failed *yet*) that could drive an entire narrative.

CLASSIC MODEL: THE CHALK REMEMBERING

In a coastal fishing village, the annual Chalk Remembering marks the day the sea goddess Marai swallowed the first harbor to punish a fisherman who kept more than his share. Every household draws a chalk line on their threshold: the line the tide reached before Marai pulled it back. Anyone who steps on the line during the festival must give their catch to the village for a year. The curse: families that hoard are visited by salt-sickness: their wells turn brackish, their gardens brine-poisoned, their children born craving salt until they walk into the sea. The prophecy: when the chalk line appears on a threshold *no one drew*, Marai is returning, and the harbor she swallowed will rise from the deep, and whatever lived inside it for all these centuries will walk ashore. The fishermen paint the chalk carefully. The fishermen watch their doorsteps. The fishermen do not discuss what happened the year the chalk appeared on the temple door, because the temple has no fishermen inside it, and the door was locked.

VIII. Quick Menu: The Living Myth Generator

Festival Purpose: Renewal / Memory / Atonement / Rebellion / Union / Mourning / Reversal / Protection

Festival Form: Bonfire / Procession / Fast / Dance / Sacrifice / Drama / Silence / Feast / Mask-wearing / Pilgrimage

Festival Taboo: Forbidden word / Forbidden food / Forbidden touch / Forbidden fire / Forbidden work / Forbidden name

Curse Trigger: Broken taboo / Divine insult / Ancestral crime / Stolen relic / Violated sanctum / Failed ritual / Spoken name

Curse Symptom: Cold / Blindness / Hunger / Silence / Aging / Transformation / Contagion / Memory loss / Stone / Sleep

Curse Vector: Blood / Touch / Dream / Story / Soil / Water / Name / Lineage / Song

Prophecy Type: Doom / Condition / Self-fulfilling / Riddle / Broken

Prophecy Source: Oracle / Child / Enemy / Dream / Inscription / Song / Dying words / Relic / Pattern in the stars

Prophecy Audience: The ruler / The outcast / Everyone / No one (lost and rediscovered) / The wrong person

Prophecy Loophole: Hidden word / Sacrifice / Misreading / Dual meaning / Taboo / Voluntary failure / The prophet lied

Roll, combine, collide. The festival that mourns a broken taboo, where the curse spreads by song, and the prophecy was delivered by the wrong person's dying words. Now you have a world.

IX. Pitfalls

The Museum Festival. Your festival exists, but no one breaks its rules, challenges its meaning, or risks its chaos. It's set dressing. Fix: add a faction that wants to abolish it, a secret that would destroy it, or a year when it goes catastrophically wrong.

The Toothless Curse. The curse is described but never experienced: it's lore, not lived reality. A curse that hasn't ruined someone recently isn't a curse. It's a rumor. Fix: show the curse in action on a character the reader has met, and make the reader feel the cost.

The Prophecy Weather Report. Your prophecy predicts the future but doesn't change the present. If no one is trying to prevent, fulfill, or exploit the prophecy, it has no dramatic function. Fix: give at least two characters incompatible relationships to the prophecy: one who believes, one who denies, one who's trying to make it come true for the wrong reasons.

The Separate Systems Problem. Your festival, curse, and prophecy exist in the same world but don't interact. They share a mythology the way strangers share a bus. Fix: run the Integration Workshop. One root. Three branches. Interacting, contradicting, evolving.

The Flattened Voice. This chapter merges three emotional registers: the warmth of the feast, the chill of the curse, the vertigo of foreknowledge. If your living myth is all one tone (all dread, all celebration, all fatalism), you've lost the complexity that makes mythology feel *real*. The most powerful mythic moments hold celebration and terror in the same breath: the festival bonfire that also summons the ghost, the prophecy that is also a love letter, the curse that is also a gift.

X. WORLDBUILDING HOOKS

Who controls the festival calendar: priests, politicians, or popular consensus? What happens when the calendar is contested? Chapter 7 flagged festivals, pilgrimages, and calendars as belonging to this chapter. Here they are: the sacred calendar is a political instrument, and whoever controls the dates controls the narrative. Think of how many wars have been fought over which holidays a conquered people are permitted to keep.

How do outsiders experience your festivals? With envy, fear, mockery, or imitation? The Roman historian writing about "barbarian" rites is doing worldbuilding from the outside, and revealing as much about Rome as about the ritual.

Who profits from curses: the healers, the priests, the rulers, or the curse-breakers? Curses generate economies. Plague doctors, exorcists, sin-eaters, professional mourners, every curse creates a job.

What happens when a prophecy is forgotten and then rediscovered? The archive of failed prophecies is one of the richest unexplored veins in fantasy worldbuilding. Someone will eventually notice the pattern. Someone always does.

How do your festivals evolve? The Dogon Sigui ceremony occurs once every sixty years, most people witness it only once in a lifetime. It spans multiple years, involves secret languages (*Sigi so*) that women are forbidden to learn, and produces the Great Mask, newly carved every cycle. What happens to a festival that operates on a sixty-year frequency? It becomes *generational memory incarnate*: each performance is shaped by elders who remember the last one and initiates who won't see the next.

XI. Annotated Reading List

Primary Myths:

Oedipus Rex (Sophocles). Plague as diagnosis, prophecy as trap, the king who solves the riddle and *is* the answer. The definitive text on how curse and prophecy collaborate to destroy the person who thinks they've escaped both.

The Mahabharata (various translations; Ramesh Menon for readability, J.A.B. van Buitenen for scholarship). Krishna as strategist who knows the outcome and participates anyway. Gandhari's curse. The war that multiple prophecies demanded and no one could prevent. If your mythology has a prophecy, this is the text against which all others are measured.

Popol Vuh (trans. Dennis Tedlock or Allen Christenson). Curses that reshape species, trials that test gods, a creation through failure and iteration. The wooden people punished by their own tools is one of the most original curse concepts in world mythology.

The Golden Bough (James Frazer). Sprawling, outdated, and indispensable. Frazer's catalogue of ritual, taboo, and mythic festival across cultures is a worldbuilder's sourcebook for how humans process the sacred. Read it as a toolbox, not as anthropology.

The Myth of the Eternal Return (Mircea Eliade). How sacred time operates: the festival that collapses past and present, the ritual that recreates the origin. Dense and brilliant. If you're building a festival that *reenacts* the myth, Eliade is the theorist who explains why that matters.

Analysis & Craft:

Purity and Danger (Mary Douglas). What makes something taboo? Why do boundaries between sacred and profane exist, and what happens when they're crossed? Essential reading for anyone building curses or festival prohibitions.

Modern & Speculative:

"The Lottery" (Shirley Jackson). A village's annual ritual, described in sunny domestic detail, building to one of the most devastating final pages in American fiction. The definitive story about festival violence and communal complicity. Seven pages long. Read it today.

Station Eleven (Emily St. John Mandel). After the pandemic, a traveling Shakespeare troupe performs for scattered settlements. Memory as ritual. Art as festival. Survival as the only prophecy that matters.

Foundation (Isaac Asimov). Psychohistory as scientific prophecy: the mathematician who predicts the fall of a galactic empire and creates a plan to shorten the dark ages that follow. What happens when prophecy becomes an institution with a budget?

XII. CREATIVE DARE: THE TRIPLE BIND

Build a moment: a scene, a fragment, a single night, in which all three tools activate simultaneously. A festival is in progress. During the festival, someone triggers the curse. And in the chaos of the curse's activation, the prophecy begins to come true.

Write it. Not as three separate events, as a single, compressed scene where remembrance and punishment and foreknowledge all occupy the same breath.

Then ask yourself:

What does your world celebrate that it should be mourning? What does it punish that it should be forgiving? And what is it waiting for: the doom it fears, or the doom it secretly desires?

Go light the fire. Go speak the name. Go see what happens.

THE LOOM, PART 8: THE FESTIVAL OF UNRAVELING

Every year, on the longest night, the people of the loom hold the Festival of Unraveling.

It begins at dusk. The Needle's priests issue the decree, though they don't approve of the festival, have never approved, have argued for centuries that it is a concession to chaos that weakens the cosmic fabric, and the decree goes out: all thread-work is forbidden until dawn. Every loom stops. Every spindle is stilled. The weavers set down their shuttles and flex their fingers and try to remember what their hands are for when they aren't making patterns.

Then the untying begins.

Every knot in the city must be undone. Ropes are uncoiled. Braids are loosened. Laces are pulled free. The knots that hold the fishing nets together. The knots that secure the bridges to the cliff-posts. The knots in children's hair. The decorative knots in the temple hangings, which take three full days to retie afterward and which the Needle's priests consider the most offensive part of the whole affair. By midnight, the city is a place of loose ends: everything slack, everything unbound, everything open.

They say it appeases the Fraying Edge.

They say it keeps the world flexible: that a world with too many knots becomes rigid, and a rigid world is a world that shatters instead of bending, and a world that shatters is a world that the Weaver's pattern has failed. The Fraying Edge's followers believe this. The Shuttle's wandering scholars are agnostic: they attend the Festival because they attend everything, because borders and festivals and arguments are the territories they navigate, belonging nowhere but present everywhere. The Knot's adherents, if they exist, say nothing. As usual.

But the Fraying Edge's followers are not the only ones watching.

Every Festival: not most years, not some years, every year, someone sees a new thread appear in the weave. Not a loose thread. Not a fraying edge. A new thread, bright and taut and running in a direction that no shuttle carried it, appearing between one heartbeat and the next in a part of the pattern where the weave was complete. It shouldn't be there. The pattern was finished in that section. And yet.

The dreamwalkers: those who once entered the Hollow and emerged with their certainties in ruins, who can feel the weave the way others feel the wind, they call this the Prophecy Thread. They have been calling it this for longer than the Festival has been celebrated. They say they saw the first Prophecy Thread before the Festival was even conceived, and that the Festival was invented to manage it, to contain it, to give the Thread one night of slack in which it might be satisfied.

It has not been satisfied.

The Prophecy Thread grows. Each year, it extends further into the weave, stitching through sections that were never meant to be connected. It links the Needle's rigid order to the Fraying Edge's dissolution. It runs through the Shuttle's pathways without respecting the borders. It passes through the place where the Knot sits, and the Knot, which never responds to anything, trembles.

The dreamwalkers say: when the Prophecy Thread reaches the loom's edge, the pattern will complete.

They say this carefully. They say it with the same tone a healer uses to tell you the diagnosis is not good. Because completing the pattern means the Weaver finishes her work. And finishing means the end. Not fire. Not flood. Not a wolf swallowing the sun. Completion. A world with every thread in place, every knot intentional, every edge smooth. Perfect. Dead. A finished tapestry hung on a wall with no one left to look at it.

There are those who have begun to ask a different question. Not "when will the Thread reach the edge?" They can see it approaching, year by year, a few more inches every Festival. But: "Where is the Weaver?" If the pattern is completing, someone is completing it. If the loom is working, someone is working it. The Hollow still sounds with weaving. The fragments still surface. The pattern still grows.

The scholar with the scrap of original pattern: the scrap that shows the world as the Weaver intended, smooth, orderly, and dead, has begun to wonder if the Prophecy Thread and the original pattern are the same thing. If what's growing in the weave is not a new addition but a correction. If the Weaver is finishing what she started, and what she started was a world without accidents, without gods, without grief, without the beautiful tangled mess of consciousness.

If so, then the final quest is clear: find the Weaver before she finishes. And the final question is not whether to stop her, but whether she wants to be stopped, whether the Weaver is a prisoner of her own pattern, completing it because she can't remember how to stop, weaving because she began weaving and beginning contains ending the way an inhale contains an exhale.

The Festival of Unraveling continues. The knots are untied. The Prophecy Thread grows. Somewhere, the Weaver's hands move in the dark.

And in the morning, when the ropes are reknotted and the looms restrung and the bridges resecured, there is always one thread that was not there before. One connection. One stitch closer to the edge.

One stitch closer to completion.

Next: The final quest begins, and the question that waits at the loom.

Chapter 9: Quest & Apocalypse

Journeys, Endings, and What Survives

I. Opening Manifesto

Every world that begins must end. That's not pessimism: it's architecture. Chapter 1 gave your world a creation: the song, the sacrifice, the accident that made everything possible. This chapter asks the question creation was always leading toward: *How does it stop?* And what lunatic walks toward the ending on purpose? Creation myths promise order and meaning. Apocalypse myths promise the bill will come due. And the quest, the impossible journey, the fool's errand, the road that reshapes everyone who walks it, is the engine that drags your world from one to the other. A world without an end is just a snow globe: pretty, sealed, and nothing at stake.

Here's the secret this chapter is built on, and it's the last major principle in your toolkit:

the Scale Shift. Every quest is a small apocalypse. When the hero leaves home, their old world ends. The village burns, the innocence dies, the understanding of reality that got them this far shatters and never reassembles. And every apocalypse is someone's quest: to survive, to bear witness, to save what can be saved, to choose what's worth remembering when everything else is ash. The Ragnarok that kills the gods is also the quest of Lif and Lifthrasir, two humans hiding in the hollow of the world-tree, surviving on morning dew, waiting for the fire to pass. The flood that drowns the world in Genesis is also Noah's quest: build the boat, choose the animals, endure. The same story scales up and down. Learn to work both ends, and you can build myths that resonate at the personal level *and* the cosmic, simultaneously.

This is the chapter that closes the circle. You've built the world, populated it with gods, given it bloodlines, heroes, tricksters, monsters, relics, sacred places, festivals, curses, and prophecies. Now we ask: how does it end? What journey leads there? And, because no good apocalypse stops at the last fire, what survives?

II. WHAT IS A QUEST? WHAT IS AN APOCALYPSE?

A quest is a journey that transforms everything it touches, the traveler, the landscape, and the world waiting at both ends of the road. Not an errand. Not a fetch-mission. A true mythic quest is a dare the cosmos makes to see what you're willing to lose.

Gilgamesh walks to the end of the world seeking immortality and finds only the walls he built. Odysseus spends ten years trying to get home and arrives to discover that home became a different place while he was gone, and so did he. Inanna, Queen of Heaven, descends to the underworld to confront her sister Ereshkigal, and at each of the seven gates she is stripped of one piece of her divine regalia, crown, beads, breastplate, ring, until she arrives at the throne room naked, powerless, and mortal. She is killed, hung on a hook like a side of meat, and resurrected only because her servant had the foresight to beg for help before the doors closed. The real prize of Inanna's descent isn't power. It's knowledge: she now knows what it feels like to have nothing left, and that knowledge changes every interaction she has with the living world above.

An apocalypse myth tells how the world ends, why, and what, if anything, crawls from the wreckage. It can be cosmic (the sky falls, the gods die, the stars go out) or intimate (a city sinks, a language vanishes, a child forgets her mother's name). Endings reveal a culture's deepest anxieties and its most dangerous hopes. The Hindu concept of pralaya envisions dissolution not as a single catastrophic event but as the universe breathing out, all forms returning to an undifferentiated state at the close of a cosmic cycle lasting 4.32 billion years, before Brahma inhales and creation begins again. Ragnarok gives us gods who know they're doomed and fight anyway, a world consumed by fire and swallowed by the sea, and then, the detail that makes Norse eschatology more than despair, the earth rising again from the water, green and fertile, with fields that sow themselves. The K'iche' Maya Popol Vuh doesn't describe one ending but several: the gods create humans from

mud (failure), from wood (failure), from flesh (failure), destroying each attempt before finally succeeding with maize dough. Each apocalypse is an iteration. Each ending is a draft
.

These two structures, quest and apocalypse, are not separate genres. They're two ends of the same scale. The workshop in this chapter will teach you to build both, and the Scale Shift will show you how to move between them.

III. Part One: The Quest: Five Patterns for the Road

Every mythic quest is a remix of a few fundamental patterns. Here's your palette, not a taxonomy but a set of structural possibilities. Most real quests blend two or more.

1. The Retrieval Quest

Go get the thing. Bring it back. Survive what guards it. Jason sails to Colchis for the Golden Fleece, which is guarded by a dragon that never sleeps and defended by a king who sets impossible tasks: yoking fire-breathing bulls, sowing dragon's teeth, fighting the warriors that sprout from the furrows. In Hindu tradition, the devas and asuras churn the Ocean of Milk to retrieve amrita, the elixir of immortality, a collaborative quest between gods and demons that produces both nectar and poison, and the alliance collapses the moment the prize appears. Chapter 7's Quest Objects live here: the relic that must be recovered, returned, or destroyed.

The Gift: Retrieval quests generate clear stakes, visible progress, and satisfying structure. Everyone understands "go get the thing." The audience knows when the hero succeeds and when they fail.

The Trap: If the thing is more interesting than the journey, you've written a shopping list. The best retrieval quests change the hero's understanding of *why* they want the object; by the time Jason has the Fleece, the price he's paid (Medea's love, which will later cost him everything) has made the Fleece almost irrelevant.

2. The Transformation Quest

The hero must become someone else, or the world must become something new. Inanna descends to the underworld and is stripped bare, killed, and resurrected; she returns as the same goddess with a fundamentally different relationship to power and mortality. In the shamanic traditions of Siberian and Central Asian peoples, the initiate's spirit-journey involves being dismembered, boiled, or devoured by spirits and then reassembled with new bones, often with an additional bone, or one made of iron, marking the transformation as permanent and physical.

The Gift: Transformation quests are engines of character depth. They force the hero to lose the self they started with and earn a new one, and that process, the shedding, the breaking, the reassembly, is where the myth's emotional power lives.

The Trap: Transformation without cost is just a costume change. If your hero descends, suffers, and returns with nothing but cool new abilities, you've missed the point. Inanna comes back from the underworld and immediately sends her husband Dumuzid to take her place among the dead. Transformation has a body count.

3. THE RESTORATION QUEST

Something is broken, the king, the land, the cosmic order, and the quest is to heal it. The Fisher King sits wounded in his castle, his kingdom withering into wasteland because his body and the land are one. In Chretien de Troyes's twelfth-century *Perceval*, the young knight visits the Grail Castle, witnesses the mysterious procession, the bleeding lance, the candelabra, the grail itself, and fails to ask the healing question: *Whom does the Grail serve?* The land continues to rot. The king continues to suffer. The failure is not of courage but of *attention*. In the Popol Vuh, the Hero Twins Hunahpu and Xbalanque descend to Xibalba, the underworld, to avenge their father and restore cosmic order, a restoration quest that requires them to die, be reborn as catfish, return as traveling performers, and trick the Lords of Death into requesting their own dismemberment.

The Gift: Restoration quests connect the hero's personal journey to the fate of the world, the Scale Shift in miniature. Heal the king, heal the land. Your hero's transformation has consequences beyond their own story.

The Trap: Restoration can become nostalgia: the quest to put everything back the way it was. The most powerful restoration quests don't restore the old order; they create something new from the pieces. The Grail doesn't reverse time. It heals forward.

4. THE ESCAPE QUEST

Flee danger, survive the impossible, return from the place that doesn't let people leave. Orpheus descends to the underworld to retrieve Eurydice and almost succeeds; the condition for her release is that he must not look back, and in the last steps before the surface, he turns. In the Hebrew tradition, the Exodus is an escape quest that becomes a foundational myth: the flight from Egypt produces not just freedom but law, identity, and a covenant with the divine. Lot's wife is told not to look back at the destruction of Sodom, a structural echo of Orpheus, and is turned to a pillar of salt when she does. The forbidden glance: the quest's cruelest test.

The Gift: Escape quests generate unbearable tension. The reader knows the destination, knows the danger, and watches the hero navigate the narrowing corridor between survival and catastrophe.

The Trap: Escape quests risk passivity, the hero is running *from* rather than *toward*. The best escape quests complicate this: the escapee discovers that what they're running from has already changed them, or that escape itself requires becoming someone new.

5. THE CHALLENGE QUEST

Prove your worth. Win the contest. Survive the trial that was designed to destroy you. Heracles faces twelve labors, each one impossible, each one escalating in absurdity and danger: from killing the Nemean Lion to cleaning the Augean stables to descending to the underworld to capture Cerberus. In the Mahabharata, the Pandavas are repeatedly subjected to impossible tests, the dice game that costs them their kingdom, the thirteen years of exile, the final war, and the cumulative weight of these challenges doesn't produce triumphant victors but exhausted survivors who have won everything and lost more.

The Gift: Challenge quests are natural frameworks for escalation. Each trial raises the stakes, tests a different quality, and reveals a new dimension of the hero. They also generate beautiful secondary characters: the rival, the judge, the monster that respects the hero's courage even as it tries to kill them.

The Trap: Challenge quests can become episodic, a sequence of tests with no cumulative weight. The labors of Heracles work because they're a punishment, not a game show. Each task costs him something. Make the challenges matter to the soul, not just the scoreboard.

IV. PART TWO: THE APOCALYPSE: SIX WAYS WORLDS END

If the quest is the journey, the apocalypse is the destination nobody wants to reach. Here are six archetypes for endings, the shapes cultures have given to the unthinkable.

1. TOTAL ANNIHILATION

Everything goes. Sky, sea, gods, mortals, wiped to bedrock and beyond. Norse Ragnarok gives us the template: the great winter Fimbulvetr freezes the world for three years, wolves swallow the sun and moon, the Midgard Serpent rises from the sea and poisons the sky, the fire giant Surtr burns everything that remains. The gods die, Odin devoured by the wolf Fenrir, Thor killed by the serpent's venom after striking it dead. And then, astonishingly, the world rises again from the sea, clean and green. Lif and Lifthrasir step out of Hoddmimis holt, the hidden wood in the heart of the world-tree, and begin again. Hindu pralaya operates on the same principle at cosmic scale: the universe dissolves, all forms returning to undifferentiated potential, and then re-manifests. Total Annihilation isn't nothingness. It's a reset so total that even the concept of *ending* is temporary.

The Gift: Total Annihilation gives your world ultimate stakes and, paradoxically, ultimate hope. If everything can end, everything matters. And if the ending contains a seed of renewal, your mythology has a built-in sequel engine.

The Trap: If everything is destroyed, nothing the reader cared about survives, and the emotional investment evaporates. The survivors are the key: Lif and Lifthrasir, the children in the tree. Someone must carry the memory forward, or Total Annihilation is just special effects.

And here the dissolved Afterlife Architect whispers its most important contribution: the dead who are remembered have weight. In the original Afterlife chapter, a soul crossing the river to the land of the dead could only sink, could only complete the crossing, if living descendants remembered their name. The forgotten drifted on the surface forever. Fold that principle into your apocalypse: Total Annihilation tests not just survival but *memory*. What is remembered, endures. What is forgotten was never fully real.

2. DEATH OF THE GODS

The divine order collapses. Mortals inherit a world built for beings greater than themselves, and the architecture is too large, the rules too strange, the leftover power too dangerous. This is Ragnarok's second gift: it's not just the world that ends but the *gods*, and the world that rises afterward is a world where divinity has been replaced by something smaller, more fragile, more human. Greek mythology gives us the succession pattern: Ouranos castrated by Kronos, Kronos defeated by Zeus, each generation of gods overthrowing the last, and the persistent anxiety that another overthrow is always possible. Chapter 2's pantheon built the divine hierarchy. This apocalypse tears it down.

The Gift: Death of the Gods forces your world to confront what happens when the authorities vanish. Who inherits? What rules survive? What was the divine order actually *for*, and do mortals need to reinvent it?

The Trap: The Death of the Gods can feel like a demotion, a less interesting world replacing a more interesting one. Counter this by showing what mortal freedom *costs*. The post-divine world isn't simpler. It's terrifying.

3. FALL OF HUMANITY

People are erased or transformed, but the world goes on without them. The Genesis flood doesn't destroy the earth; it purges it of humanity's corruption and starts the human project over. The Gilgamesh flood narrative (older than Genesis by centuries) does the same: the gods grow tired of humanity's noise and send the waters. In the K'iche' Maya tradition, the wooden people of the second creation are destroyed because they lack consciousness and gratitude, their own possessions turn against them, grinding stones and cooking pots and dogs attacking their ungrateful owners. The world survives. Humanity doesn't deserve it.

The Gift: Fall of Humanity puts the spotlight on what makes people worth keeping, or not. It forces your mythology to articulate what the divine experiment of consciousness was *for*. It also raises the afterlife question naturally: where do the fallen go? Is their oblivion total, or do they persist as memory, warning, haunting?

The Trap: Fall of Humanity can read as divine petulance, gods throwing out a draft because it's inconvenient. Give the erasure *weight*. What was lost that can never be remade? In the Gilgamesh version, the god Ea preserves one family and regrets the flood's totality. Even gods can have second thoughts.

4. BREAKING OF LAW

The fundamental rules of reality, not human law but cosmic law, crack open. Time stops. Dreams die. The boundary between the living and the dead dissolves. In Buddhist cosmology, the cycle of the ages degrades through four eras of declining dharma until the moral fabric of reality has thinned to nothing and the world-system collapses under its own spiritual entropy. This is Chapter 5's trickster energy at cosmic scale, what happens when the rules that hold the cosmos together are violated so completely that reality itself loses coherence. In Gnostic traditions, the material world is already a kind of error, a flawed creation by a deluded demiurge, and the apocalypse is not destruction but *correction*: the dismantling of a false reality to reveal the true one hidden beneath.

The Gift: Breaking of Law produces the strangest, most unsettling apocalypses. When the rules go, anything is possible, and "anything" is terrifying. These endings generate surreal, dreamlike narratives that linger in the reader's mind.

The Trap: Abstract apocalypses risk being *too* abstract, all concept, no consequence. Ground the breaking in physical detail. When dharma fades, what does the street look like? When reality cracks, what falls through?

5. LOSS OF THE ABSTRACT

Not fire. Not flood. Something intangible vanishes, and the world, still standing, is hollowed out. Imagine a world where memory is erased: people wander in peace, unknowing, their history dissolved. Or a world where language simply stops working, words become sounds, stories become noise, and the mythic architecture collapses because no one can tell it anymore. The K'iche' Maya cycle-endings involve the loss of divine connection, the gods destroy their creations not because the world is broken but because the creatures in it can't *worship*, can't remember, can't sustain the relationship between mortal and divine that makes reality meaningful.

This is where afterlife as process meets apocalypse. The dead who are forgotten, truly, irrevocably forgotten, with no descendant to call their name, no festival to mark their passage, no story to carry their weight, those dead dissolve. An apocalypse of forgetting doesn't destroy bodies. It destroys *significance*. Everything remains, and nothing means anything.

The Gift: Loss of the Abstract is the most psychologically devastating apocalypse type and the hardest to counter with heroism. You can fight a monster. You can't fight the absence of meaning. These apocalypses haunt.

The Trap: Loss of the Abstract can feel like a thought experiment rather than a story. Give it a face. Who is the last person to remember? What do they carry, and what happens when they set it down?

6. THE PARTIAL APOCALYPSE

Only a corner of the world falls. Atlantis sinks, but the mainland endures. A forest burns, but the city across the river watches the smoke. Childhood ends, which is to say, a world ends, a real one with its own rules and geography and possibilities, and the adult world that replaces it is not the same world, and the child who lived there is gone. This is the Scale Shift's most intimate application. Every personal catastrophe, the death of a parent, the loss of a homeland, the moment when you realize the person you loved has become someone else, is a partial apocalypse. The world goes on. Your world doesn't.

The Gift: Partial Apocalypse is the most versatile type and the most emotionally immediate. It connects cosmic mythology to lived experience. Your reader has survived a partial apocalypse. They know what it feels like.

The Trap: Partial Apocalypse can feel small, "just" a personal loss, "just" a local disaster. The key is showing the ripple: the city that watches Atlantis sink is never the same city again. The continent that loses a forest breathes different air. The personal is cosmic. That's the whole point.

V. THE SCALE SHIFT: THE CHAPTER'S ORGANIZING PRINCIPLE

Here it is, plainly stated: every quest is a small apocalypse, and every apocalypse is someone's quest.

When Gilgamesh leaves Uruk to seek immortality, his old world, the world where he was king, where his friend Enkidu was alive, where death was something that happened to other people, that world ends. It doesn't matter that the city still stands and the people still go about their business. The world *as Gilgamesh knew it* is over, and the man who walks the road to Utnapishtim is walking through the ruins of everything he understood. That's a personal apocalypse driving a quest.

When the Popol Vuh's gods flood the second creation, the wooden people are destroyed, but the Hero Twins' story is set in motion by that very destruction. The apocalypse creates the conditions for the quest. The twins descend to Xibalba not in spite of the ending but *because* of it. That's a cosmic apocalypse generating a quest.

The Scale Shift is the lens through which you build the workshop that follows. Start with one, a quest or an apocalypse, and see how far you can push the scale in the other direction.

VI. WORKSHOP: BUILDING THE SCALE SHIFT

This is a two-part build. Choose your starting point, a quest that escalates into an apocalypse, or an apocalypse that reduces to a single person's quest, and work through the steps. You'll end up with a myth that operates at both the personal and cosmic scale.

PATH A: QUEST --> APOCALYPSE

Step 1. The Call That Costs a World.

Every quest begins with a departure, and every departure destroys something. What world does your hero leave behind? Not just physically, what understanding, what safety, what version of themselves dies when they step onto the road? In the Erasure showcase below, the archivist's quest begins when she discovers that forgetting has a sound, a low hum that erases names. Her departure isn't walking through a door. It's the moment she realizes the door she came through no longer exists.

Write this now: Name the world your hero loses by accepting the quest. Not the stakes, the world. The one that ends the moment they say yes.

Step 2. The Obstacle That Grows.

The quest's obstacles should escalate not just in difficulty but in *scale*. What begins as a personal challenge, a riddle, a guardian, a physical trial, should reveal that the problem is bigger than the hero thought. The relic they're retrieving is holding something together. The person they're rescuing doesn't want to be saved. The truth they're seeking will, if spoken aloud, end the world. Chapter 7's Pairing Principle lives here: the quest object and its sanctum are co-dependent, and disturbing one disturbs both.

Write this now: Design an obstacle in the middle of your quest that reveals the quest's true stakes are cosmic, not personal.

Step 3. The Moment the Quest Becomes an Apocalypse.

There's a threshold in every Scale Shift narrative where the personal journey tilts into world-ending territory. Identify it. In the Star-Smith's showcase from the original Quest Generator, the smith exiled for forging forbidden weapons discovers that the "star that fell before the world was born" is her own childhood hope, and that recovering it will mean accepting that the world she remembers never existed. That's a personal apocalypse. Now push it: what if recovering the star *actually* dims every other star in the sky? What if the personal truth has cosmic consequences?

Write this now: Identify the tipping point where your quest becomes everyone's problem. What changes, in one sentence, that turns a journey into an ending?

Step 4. What Survives.

The apocalypse has happened, either literally or in the hero's understanding. Now: what's left? The best Scale Shift narratives don't end with destruction. They end with the inventory: what did the apocalypse spare? What does the hero carry out of the wreckage? The Ragnarok survivors carry morning dew and the memory of a world that burned. The flood survivor carries a boatful of animals and a covenant. The hero of your myth carries what?

And here is where the afterlife principle earns its place: the dead who are remembered have weight. What your hero remembers from the destroyed world *persists*. What they forget is truly gone. The act of remembering is itself an act of survival, of carrying the dead forward into whatever comes next. Afterlife is not a destination your characters arrive at. It's a negotiation they conduct with the ruins.

Write this now: List three things that survive your apocalypse, one physical, one abstract, one that exists only because someone remembers it.

PATH B: APOCALYPSE --> QUEST

Work backward. Start with an ending, the world is over, the gods are dead, memory is dissolving, and find the person inside it who refuses to stop moving. Their quest is not to prevent the apocalypse (it's already happened) but to *survive* it, *witness* it, or *choose what it means*. This is the path of Cormac McCarthy's *The Road*, of the last memory-keeper in the Erasure myth, of every survivor who walks out of the ruins carrying something that used to be the world.

VII. WORKED EXAMPLES

SHOWCASE: THE ERASURE (LOSS OF THE ABSTRACT --> RETRIEVAL QUEST)

It begins with names.

Not the names of things, the names of people. A woman in the market reaches for the word for her daughter's face and finds only a blank space where the syllables used to live. She stands there, mouth open, hand extended toward a girl she recognizes by shape and smell and the particular weight of her hand but cannot name.

By evening, it has spread. The archivists notice it first because the archives are their nervous system, and they can feel when something stops working. Scrolls that yesterday held genealogies now hold lists of blank spaces. Tombstones are smooth. Temple walls, which once recorded the names of every priest who served since the founding, are bare stone.

The Council of Names, the governing body that has maintained the Register of the Living and the Register of the Dead for eleven generations, convenes in emergency session. The Register of the Dead, they discover, is empty. Not destroyed. *Empty.* As if no one had ever died. As if death had always been an abstraction.

And the Register of the Living is thinning.

Eska, the youngest archivist, who was given her position not because she was the best record-keeper but because she could hear the archives breathing, could tell by the vibration in the floor which drawer held the document you needed, hears a new sound. A low hum, subsonic, felt in the teeth and the base of the skull. It comes from the east. It comes from the place where the world's edge meets the sea.

She walks toward it. Not because she's brave, but because the sound is *eating names*, and if she doesn't find its source, there will be no one left who knows what a name is.

The journey takes her through a landscape of progressive erasure. First the names vanish. Then the stories, travelers she meets can describe their own lives only in disconnected images, because the connective tissue of narrative has dissolved. Then language itself begins to thin. Verbs lose their tenses. Nouns lose their plurals. Communication becomes a series of gestures and sounds, and Eska realizes with a terror that has no name, because terror is losing its name too, that the hum is not destroying information but *completing* it. It's filling in every gap, answering every question, resolving every ambiguity, and in doing so it is erasing the *need* for stories, because stories exist to make sense of what we don't understand, and when everything is understood, stories die.

The hum, she discovers, emanates from a device, no, a machine *principle*, buried at the world's edge. Something the builders of the world put there at the beginning, a mechanism designed to eventually render the world *fully known*. Not a weapon. A gift. The cosmos finishing its own explanation.

And Eska faces the choice that every Scale Shift narrative demands: let the explanation complete (a world with total knowledge and zero meaning) or break the device and accept that some things must remain unknown, unnamed, unresolved, that the gaps are not errors but *architecture*. That the spaces between names are where people live.

She breaks it. The hum stops. And in the silence that follows, she realizes she has forgotten her own name.

But someone, somewhere, remembers it for her. She can feel the weight of their remembering, like a hand on her shoulder. The dead who are remembered have weight. And the living who are remembered, by the dead, by the future, by the stories that survive the erasure, they have weight too.

The names return. Not all of them. Not quickly. Some are gone forever, the ones nobody remembered, the ones no story carried forward. But the ones that come back come back *changed*, carrying the knowledge of how close they came to silence.

Every year afterward, the archivists hold a new festival: the Naming. One night when every citizen speaks aloud the names of the dead they carry, not from a register but from memory, from love, from debt. The forgotten stay forgotten. The remembered gain weight. And the hum, if you press your ear to the ground at the world's edge, is still there. Quieter. Waiting.

What happened here: The Erasure combines a Loss of the Abstract apocalypse (names and meaning vanishing) with a Retrieval Quest (Eska seeking the source) and a Transformation Quest (she must change her understanding of what knowledge is). The Scale Shift operates throughout: a personal journey (one archivist, walking east) mirrors a cosmic event (the world completing itself into meaninglessness). The afterlife principle, remembered souls have weight, provides both the emotional core and the narrative resolution. The festival at the end connects to Chapter 8's toolkit: the apocalypse generates a living tradition.

CLASSIC MODEL: THE STAR-SMITH'S RETURN

A smith is exiled for forging weapons for a forbidden cause. She is told the only path back to her city is to recover the "star that fell before the world was born." She walks for years, crossing deserts where the sand remembers footsteps that haven't been taken yet, through forests where the trees grow downward into a sky made of soil. Every guide she finds gives her a different direction. Every trail she follows leads to a version of the star that, when she touches it, turns out to be something she lost, a childhood song, a friend's face, the sound of her mother's loom. She never finds the literal star. What she finds, at the end, is that the star was the *hope she carried while walking*. She abandoned the belief that the journey had a destination. She returns to her city empty-handed, and every star in the sky shines brighter, because the act of seeking was itself the light. Her exile is not lifted. But the city, seeing the stars, begins to doubt that the exile was just.

VIII. Quick Menu: Quest & Apocalypse Generator

Roll, choose, or combine. Build strange.

Quest Call: Disaster | Prophecy | Inherited debt | Stolen relic | Forbidden knowledge | Boredom that turns lethal

Quest Goal: Lost object | Healing | Transformation | Escape | Proof of worth | Answer to an unanswerable question

Quest Obstacle: Monster | Riddle | Taboo border | Rival seeker | The hero's own past | Time itself

Quest Ally: Reluctant mentor | Betrayer-who-reforms | Animal guide | Ancestor's ghost | The villain's child | No one

Apocalypse Scope: Total annihilation | Divine collapse | Human erasure | Cosmic law shattered | Abstraction lost | Partial: one city, one forest, one childhood

Apocalypse Cause: Divine judgment | Prophecy fulfilled | Human arrogance | Cosmic accident | Completion | No one knows

Apocalypse Portent: Rivers running backward | Shadows fleeing their owners | Children born already old | Music becoming painful | The dead speaking louder than the living

What Survives: Two people | A single story | A seed | A name | A question | Nothing, and that nothing *means something*

Afterlife Negotiation: The dead earn passage by forgetting | The dead earn passage by being remembered | The dead argue for their place | The dead and living trade debts | There is no afterlife, only the weight of what the living carry

IX. Pitfalls, Traps, and Common Mistakes

The Fetch-Quest Apocalypse. Your quest is about the object, and your apocalypse is about the explosions, and neither one changes anyone's soul. If the journey doesn't transform the traveler and the ending doesn't force a reckoning with meaning, you've built a roller coaster, not a myth.

The Clean Apocalypse. Everything ends, nothing lingers, the ruins are tidy and the survivors are fine. Real myth-endings leave scars: hauntings, ruins that won't stay buried, festivals that commemorate what was lost. The Norse don't just rebuild after Ragnarok.

They find the gods' golden game pieces in the grass and weep.

The Moralizing End. Not every apocalypse is a punishment. Some are random. Some are structural. Some are the cosmos finishing a process it started before anyone was alive to care. The K'iche' Maya destroyed their wooden people not for wickedness but for *ingratitude*, a subtler, stranger failure than simple sin. Let your ending be specific about what went wrong.

The Static Scale. You built a quest but never pushed it toward cosmic stakes, or you built an apocalypse but never found the person inside it. Use the Scale Shift. Always ask: whose personal world is this cosmic event? What cosmic pattern does this personal journey echo?

The Forgotten Afterward. Your apocalypse ends, and you stop writing. But the most resonant endings are the ones that generate *futures*: the festival that remembers, the taboo that persists, the quest that the ending made necessary. Chapter 8's prophecies predicted this chapter's apocalypses. What does your apocalypse predict?

X. Worldbuilding Hooks

Who profits from the myth of the end: priests, kings, doomsday cults, or the people who sell supplies to doomsday cults?

How do ordinary people live with the knowledge that their world will end? Do they deny it, prepare for it, celebrate it, or try to accelerate it?

Are there inherited quests in your world, journeys begun by grandparents that grandchildren must finish? What happens to a family when the quest fails and no one is left to try again?

What do the dead owe the living? What do the living owe the dead? Is this debt formal (law, ritual, ledger) or informal (memory, guilt, love)?

Does your world have a place where apocalypses have already happened, a ruin, a scar, a dead zone, and people still live in its shadow? What grows there?

XI. Annotated Reading List

Primary Myths:

Epic of Gilgamesh: The oldest quest for immortality in human literature, and the most honest: he fails, and the failure is the point. Also contains the oldest flood narrative. Everything in this chapter has roots here.

The Odyssey (Homer): Ten years of trying to get home, and home has become a war zone. The definitive quest-as-transformation narrative, and a reminder that the journey changes the destination.

Popol Vuh (K'iche' Maya): Hero Twins, multiple apocalypses, underworld descents, and creation by divine trial and error. The only mythic text that treats world-ending as an iterative design process.

Egyptian Book of the Dead: Not a book about death but a book about *navigation*: spells, maps, and arguments for surviving the afterlife. The dead as questors, the afterlife as a journey with obstacles, guardians, and a final weighing.

ANALYSIS & CRAFT:

The Hero With a Thousand Faces (Joseph Campbell): The structural map of the hero's journey. Indispensable as a skeleton, dangerous as a prescription. Read it, use what works, break what doesn't. The monomyth is a tool, not a law.

Myths from Mesopotamia (Stephanie Dalley, trans.): Inanna's descent, Gilgamesh's flood, the earliest apocalypses in human memory. Primary sources translated with scholarly care and surprising readability.

MODERN & SPECULATIVE:

A Wizard of Earthsea (Ursula K. Le Guin): A quest for the shadow the hero cast, which turns out to be himself. The most elegant Transformation Quest in modern fantasy, and the book that proves a quest's real destination is self-knowledge.

Zone One (Colson Whitehead): The zombie apocalypse as office work: sweeping the ruins, cataloging the dead, and discovering that civilization's afterlife is mostly paperwork and grief. Devastating, funny, and unlike any other post-apocalyptic novel.

The Road (Cormac McCarthy): A father and son walking through the aftermath of an unnamed catastrophe. The quest after the apocalypse, stripped to its essentials: keep moving, keep the fire, remember that there was something worth surviving for.

The Last Man (Mary Shelley): Written in 1826, the first post-apocalyptic novel. A plague empties the world; one person remains. Shelley invented the genre before it had a name, and her portrait of solitary survival is still the loneliest.

XII. CREATIVE DARE: THE LAST QUEST

Build a myth in which the quest and the apocalypse are the same event, a journey that *is* the ending, a road that, by being walked, unmakes the world. Not a quest that triggers an apocalypse by accident, but a journey where every step *is* a step of the world's dissolution, and the hero knows it, and walks anyway.

Then ask: what do they carry? What do they remember? And who, in the silence after the last step, remembers *them*?

The dead who are remembered have weight. Write the myth that proves it.

THE LOOM, PART 9: THE LAST THREAD

She goes to find the Weaver.

Not because she's been chosen. Not because a prophecy demanded it, though the dreamwalkers have been pointing toward this for longer than anyone alive can remember. She goes because she heard the hum, the same low frequency that Eska heard at the world's edge, the same sound the loom makes when the shuttle is moving too fast for the thread to resist. She goes because the Prophecy Thread has reached the loom's edge, and the pattern is one stitch from completion, and completion means perfection, and perfection means death.

She is the child with one arm woven of grief-thread and one arm of something the Weaver dropped and never named. The hero from Chapter 4, grown now, scarred, carrying the weight of every thread she's mended that came back wrong. She can fix anything. Everything she fixes breaks differently. She has learned to live with that, to love the imperfection of the repaired thing, to see the mended crack as a record, a history, a proof that something survived being broken.

She walks into the Hollow.

She has been here before. Everyone who enters the Hollow hears the weaving, the rhythm of the loom, the whisper of thread through warp, the soft percussive click of the shuttle changing direction. But she hears something else now. Something beneath the rhythm. A sound like breathing, ragged and uneven, and another sound like weeping, and another sound like someone trying to stop and failing, the way you can't stop breathing even when each breath is a wound.

The Weaver is at the loom.

She is smaller than the stories said. Not a goddess, not a cosmic force, not the architect of everything. She is an old woman with thread-cut fingers and a back bent from ten thousand years of leaning forward. Her hands move because they have always moved. The shuttle flies because it has always flown. The pattern grows because the pattern has always grown, and the pattern is almost finished, and the finished pattern is a world with no loose threads, no fraying edges, no knots, no gods that argue, no Shuttle that wanders between borders, no Knot that laughs at the center of everything, no Fraying Edge that pulls the world apart so it can breathe.

A perfect world. A completed world. A dead world.

The hero looks at the Weaver's hands and sees what the dreamwalkers missed, what the scholars with their scrap of original pattern never understood, what the Needle's priests and the Fraying Edge's followers and the Shuttle's wandering scholars all failed to notice because they were looking at the pattern instead of the person making it:

The Weaver is trying to stop.

Her hands shake. Her fingers bleed where the thread has cut them. She is weeping, not from sadness but from exhaustion, the exhaustion of a body that has been doing one thing for so long that the doing has become the body, the way a river becomes its banks, the way a song becomes the singer. She can't stop because she doesn't know where the weaving ends and she begins. She started because silence was unbearable, that first grief, that first thread, and the starting became a pattern and the pattern became a world and the world demanded completion and completion demanded more thread and more thread demanded more weaving and now she is here, at the edge of the last stitch, and she is not finishing the world.

The world is finishing her.

The hero sits beside the Weaver. She doesn't speak, words are the Shuttle's domain, and the Shuttle is somewhere between borders, as always. She doesn't pray, prayers go to the Bright Needle, and the Needle cares about order, and order is what's killing the world right now. She doesn't unravel, that's the Fraying Edge's work, and the Edge has been trying for millennia, and it hasn't been enough.

Instead, she reaches for the thread.

Not to mend it. Not to pull it. To cut it.

She has the tool for this, the unnamed thing her other arm is woven from, the substance the Weaver dropped and never claimed. It was never grief. It was never order or chaos or the wandering between. It was the capacity to stop. The thing the Weaver lost when she began weaving and couldn't find again: the ability to put the shuttle down, to leave the thread unfinished, to accept a world with gaps.

She cuts.

The sound is not dramatic. It is small, a snip, a whisper, the quietest apocalypse in the history of the loom. The Prophecy Thread, one stitch from the edge, goes slack. The pattern, for the first time in ten thousand years, stops growing.

The Weaver's hands go still.

She looks at them, her own hands, trembling, bleeding, free, as if she has never seen them before. As if she has been asleep and the waking is the cruelest, kindest thing that has ever happened. She breathes. Not the ragged breath of someone trying to stop. The breath of someone who has stopped. Who is, for the first time, just a woman sitting at a loom, choosing not to weave.

"It's not finished," the Weaver says.

"No," says the hero.

"It's not perfect."

"No."

"The knots. The fraying. The gods arguing, the monsters eating, the children being born into a mess they didn't ask for."

"Yes."

The Weaver looks at the pattern, the vast, sprawling, contradictory, knotted, fraying, imperfect, living pattern that is the world. She touches the cut end of the Prophecy Thread, and it curls, and it begins, slowly, uncertainly, to fray. The fraying is not destruction but possibility. A loose end is a place where a new thread can be tied.

The Weaver stands. She is unsteady. She has not stood in a very long time.

"I'm going to go," she says.

"Where?"

"I don't know. Somewhere the thread doesn't reach. Somewhere I can hear silence again, not the unbearable silence of the beginning, but the good kind. The kind that comes after a song."

She walks out of the Hollow. The hero watches her go. The loom stands empty, not abandoned, not destroyed, but waiting. The shuttle lies where it fell. The thread trails from the warp, unfinished, uncommitted, open.

The hero sits before the loom.

She does not weave. Not yet. But she places her hands on the frame, and the wood hums beneath her palms, not the consuming hum of completion but a quieter sound, an invitation, the first note of a song that doesn't know where it's going.

She opens her mouth.

What comes out is not the Weaver's song. It is something new, off-key, uncertain, full of mistakes. It does not command the thread. It asks. And the thread, tentatively, skeptically, as if it has been burned before, begins to move.

The loom begins again. The pattern is unfinished. The world is imperfect. The gods still argue. The monsters still eat. The Knot still laughs. The Fraying Edge still pulls. The Shuttle *still wanders, belonging nowhere, needed everywhere.*

And somewhere, the Weaver is walking. Not weaving. Just walking. Listening to the silence between sounds, which is not empty but full of all the songs that haven't been sung yet.

The story continues.

It's your turn.

The Unfinished World

You've been building.

Nine chapters of tools, provocations, examples, and dares, and somewhere in the margins, if you were working alongside me, a world of your own is taking shape. It has a creation myth that contradicts itself. Gods with flaws they can't fix. A family whose founding crime still echoes in the courtroom and the kitchen. A hero who won because it cost them something they'll never get back. A trickster nobody can catch and nobody wants to. Monsters with hungers that reveal more about the world than the world would like. Relics that miss the places they were stolen from. A festival that remembers something the participants have forgotten. A prophecy that nobody wants to fulfil; and that's fulfilling itself anyway.

It isn't finished. Good.

A finished mythology is a dead one. The Greek myths weren't finished when Hesiod wrote them down; they'd been argued over around fires for centuries before that, and they've been rewritten, contested, and reinvented every generation since. The Mande griots don't recite a fixed text; they negotiate it with the audience, shaping Sundiata's story to speak to the room they're standing in. The Kalevala was assembled from oral songs that had been fragmenting and recombining across Finland for longer than anyone could record. No living mythology was ever completed. They were *inhabited*, by tellers, doubters, heretics, and the occasional child who asked a question the priests couldn't answer.

Across this book, we built a mythology from scratch. The Loom, a weaver's grief turned into a world, with gods who argue, families who splinter, a hero born tangled, a trickster who laughs from the center of everything, monsters growing in the dark beneath the pattern, relics surfacing like splinters, and a prophecy threading its way toward a completion that would be the end of everything worth keeping. That mythology is imperfect. It contradicts itself in places. It has gaps I never filled and questions I left unanswered on purpose. It is, in other words, alive; and the things that are alive are the things that can still change.

The hero cut the thread. The Weaver walked away. A new song began. Off-key, uncertain, full of mistakes.

That's the only honest ending for a myth. Not triumph. Not tragedy. A beginning that knows it's imperfect and starts anyway.

I built the Loom to show you what this book's tools look like when they're all running at once, messy, interconnected, and generating more questions than they answer. The creation myth produced a cosmic structure. The pantheon emerged from the creation's flaws. The bloodlines echoed the gods without the gods noticing. The hero carried a thread the pattern didn't recognize. The trickster laughed at the center and refused to be explained. The monsters grew from the scraps. The relics surfaced like splinters. The festival tried to manage the prophecy, and the prophecy grew anyway. The quest led to the apocalypse, and the apocalypse turned out to be completion: perfection as death, the absence of loose threads meaning the absence of life.

None of it came out the way I planned. The Weaver was supposed to be a simpler figure. The Knot was an afterthought that became essential. The hero's choice to cut the thread, rather than mend it, or unravel it, or fight, only made sense when I got there. That's how myths work. You start with an idea and the idea starts arguing with you, and the argument produces something neither of you expected. If your mythology doesn't surprise you, it won't surprise anyone else.

You now have every tool this book can offer. You have archetypes and spectrums and frameworks and principles: the Genesis Engine, the Divine Spectrum, the Mirror Framework, the Hunger Principle, the Pairing Principle, the Scale Shift. You have workshops that walk you through the building, and worked examples that show you what the building can produce. You have reading lists that point toward the traditions where these tools were forged, centuries before anyone thought to name them.

What you do with them is no longer my business. It's yours.

But I'll make one more suggestion, not a workshop prompt, not a creative exercise. A dare.

Write the myth you're most afraid to write.

Not the one that comes easily. Not the one that sounds impressive or fits the genre or makes the worldbuilding internally consistent. The other one. The one that sits at the bottom of your imagination like a stone, the one you've been circling since you started this book, the one that touches something you don't entirely understand and can't quite control. The creation myth that reveals something ugly about what you believe. The god whose flaw is your flaw. The monster whose hunger you recognize. The family whose wound is stitched from your own.

That's the myth your world needs. The one that could shake it, and you, loose from the safe version. The one that, if you wrote it honestly, would change the shape of everything you've built.

Myths have always been dangerous. The first storytellers didn't sit by the fire to entertain. They sat there because the dark was full of questions that couldn't be answered without a story; and the story that answered them wasn't comfortable, or clean, or approved by the authorities. It was the ragged, imperfect, necessary thing that someone with more nerve than sense pushed into the silence and said: *Here. This is what I think it means. Fight me.*

The world isn't finished. Neither is your mythology. Neither, and this matters, are you.

Somewhere, on a loom that might or might not exist, a pattern is still growing. It has gaps. It has knots. It has places where the thread runs out and someone will have to tie a new one on. The Weaver is gone. The gods are arguing. The trickster is laughing. The monsters are eating. And someone, it might as well be you, is sitting before the frame with their hands on the wood, feeling it hum, and opening their mouth to sing a song they haven't learned yet.

It will be off-key. It will be full of mistakes. It will be alive.

The story continues.

Go.

Glossary

A concise, plain-language guide to the book's core concepts, names, and tools.

A

Adopted Line: Ancestry by choice, ritual, or theft: found families, political dynasties, fosterage, and cultures where lineage is earned rather than born. Not a utopian alternative to blood inheritance — another form of family, with all the mess that entails. *See also: Bloodline, Ancestor, Legacy.*

Afterlife: Any realm, process, or state where souls or stories go after death. Can be a journey, judgement, cycle, or oblivion. *See also: Underworld, Psychopomp, Reincarnation.*

Ancestor: A dead forebear who still shapes the living through blessing, curse, guidance, or memory. *See also: Bloodline, Ancestral Curse, Talisman.*

Ancestral Curse: A repeating wound or taboo that travels a family line until it's paid, broken, or transformed. *See also: Taboo, Prophecy.*

Animism: The belief that places, objects, and creatures possess spirit or agency.

Apotheosis: The transformation of a mortal into a divine or divine-adjacent being; becoming a god.

Archetype: A recurring mythic pattern or character type (hero, trickster, world-mother) used as a design template, not a cage. *See also: Motif, Gift/Trap.*

Axis Mundi: The world-axis or cosmic "spine" that connects realms (world tree, sacred mountain, pillar of heaven). *See also: World Tree, Shape of the Cosmos.*

B

Bargain (Mythic): A binding exchange between mortal, spirit, or god; often enforced by taboo or oath.

Bardo: A liminal post-death interval of testing or transition (term from Tibetan traditions); used here generically for "in-between" afterlife journeys. *See also: Liminal, Afterlife.*

Bestiary: A catalog of creatures. In worldbuilding, your living index of monsters, their roles, and ecologies. *See also: Monster, Hunger Principle.*

Binding Oath: A vow with consequences (magical, legal, social) if broken. *See also: Geis, Taboo.*

Bloodline: A family lineage with distinctive marks, gifts, bargains, or burdens that matter to the world. *See also: Ancestor, Legacy, Adopted Line.*

Boon: A gift from gods, spirits, or fate; usually paired with a price.

C

Canon (Internal): The accepted "truths" of your setting. Keep it coherent, but allow living contradictions.

Chaos: Raw, generative disorder; the unshaped stuff before creation or the force that undoes stale order. *See also: Creation Myth, Trickster.*

Chthonic: Of the underworld or deep earth; powers below.

Cosmic Cartography: Mapping the structure of your mythic world: heavens, earth, underworlds, thresholds, and how to cross between them. Now part of the Genesis Engine's treatment of how creation myths produce geography. *See also: Axis Mundi, Threshold, Shape of the Cosmos.*

Cosmology: Your world's "how it all hangs together": origins, layers, laws, and cycles. *See also: Creation Myth.*

Creation Myth: The story of how the world begins (from nothing, egg, dismembered giant, spoken word, etc.). *See also: Cosmology.*

Curse: A targeted harm bound by words, ritual, or story logic; may cling to people, places, or objects. Functions as both magical affliction and social force — a curse is only as powerful as the community that believes in it. *See also: Taboo, Plague.*

Cycle (Mythic): Repeating pattern (ages of the world, rise-fall-rebirth) that shapes history and ritual.

D

Demi-god: A being of mixed divine and mortal origins; liminal in status and obligations.

Descent (Katabasis): A journey down into death, dream, or the underworld to seek knowledge, power, or rescue. *See also: Underworld, Psychopomp.*

Destiny: A foretold role or endpoint that characters must wrestle with, fulfill, or break. *See also: Prophecy.*

Divine Spectrum: The full continuum of supernatural beings, from high gods down to household spirits, ancestral shades, hungry ghosts, and local kami — treated as a single ecology rather than separate catalogs. Gods and kitchen ghosts inhabit the same system; the lines between categories are political, not ontological. *See also: Pantheon, Spirit, Ghost, Deity, Animism.*

Divination: Methods of seeking hidden knowledge from the cosmos (omens, lots, bones, stars).

Dualism: A worldview split along fundamental axes (light/dark, order/chaos) that frames conflicts.

E

Eldritch: Strange, outside ordinary order; useful shorthand for cosmic wrongness without invoking a specific canon.

Enchantment: Imbuing a person, place, or object with power via words, song, craft, or spirit.

Epithet (Divine): A title-name highlighting a deity's aspect ("Zeus Cloud-Gatherer," "Lady of the Lake").

Eschatology: Stories of the world's end(s) and what follows. *See also: Cycle, Scale Shift.*

Ex Nihilo: Creation "from nothing"; one of several creation patterns. *See also: Creation Myth.*

Exile: Social or sacred banishment that creates outsiders and founders. *See also: Founder, Trickster.*

F

Fate: The impersonal weave of events; harder than prophecy, softer than author fiat.

Festival: A cyclical communal event that renews the social-cosmic order through play, inversion, or rite. Festivals do real work: they renegotiate who's in and who's out, feed the gods, and let a culture rehearse its own destruction in a safe container. *See also: Ritual.*

Founder / Founding Myth: The story that legitimizes a city, order, bloodline, or law. *See also: Mandate of Heaven, Sovereignty Myth.*

Fetish Object (Power Object): An object believed to house spirit or force; use the clearer phrase "power-bound object" to avoid confusion. *See also: Relic, Talisman.*

Folk Memory: Cultural memory carried in sayings, taboos, place-names, and ghosts.

G

Geis (Geas): A personal taboo/obligation that grants power but imposes limits.

Genius Loci: The spirit of a place (river, forest, crossroads) with needs and moods. *See also: Animism, Shrine.*

Ghost: The dead persisting as presence: memory-hungry, oath-bound, or justice-seeking. *See also: Undead, Revenant, Divine Spectrum.*

Gift / Trap: The book's analytical engine for evaluating every mythic choice: what does this option open up (the Gift), and what does it commit you to or risk (the Trap)? A design tool, not a moral judgment. Every archetype, every structure, every category in the toolkit has both.

God / Goddess / Deity: A personified power with followers, domains, and contradictions. *See also: Pantheon, Theophany, Patron Deity.*

H

Hero (Mythic): A culture's dangerous dream of itself: not pure, but catalytic; defined by the taboos they cross and the ordeals they survive. *See also: Archetype, Villain, Mirror Framework.*

Hierophany: A manifestation of the sacred in the ordinary (burning bush moments). *See also: Theophany.*

Hubris: Overreach against gods, fate, or order that invites unraveling.

Hunger Principle: The idea that every monster is defined by what it needs and can never fully get. Hunger is the monster's engine — ecological, emotional, metaphysical. A monster without hunger is furniture. *See also: Monster, Bestiary.*

Hybridity: Mixed forms (human-monster, god-mortal) that expose boundaries.

I

Iconography: The visual language of a power or tradition (symbols, colors, animals, tools).

Initiation: A rite that marks and makes a new status (child to adult, novice to adept). *See also: Rite of Passage.*

Invocation: Calling a power by name and aspect to witness, aid, or bind.

J

Judgement Hall: An afterlife scene where a soul is weighed, tested, or measured before passage. *See also: Afterlife, Psychopomp.*

Jinn (as model): A class of spirit with agency and ambiguity; use as a template for free-willed spirits. *See also: Spirit, Divine Spectrum.*

K

Katabasis: See *Descent.*

Karma: Moral cause-effect across lifetimes; use carefully outside traditions that own it.

Key (Threshold Key): An object/rite that opens crossings between realms. *See also: Threshold, Relic.*

L

Legacy: The living effects of ancestry, vows, and past choices on the present. *See also: Bloodline, Adopted Line.*

Legend: A storied event or person near history; looser than myth, tighter than rumor.

Liminal: Betwixt-and-between zones (twilight, crossroads, doorways) where change is possible. *See also: Threshold, Trickster.*

Loom (The): The book's through-line myth, built from scratch across nine installments — one per chapter. Not a model mythology but a live demonstration that myths argue with their makers and resist perfection. *See also: Myth, Mythopoeia.*

Lore: Knowledge carried by a culture (craft, customs, tales) that shapes practice.

Luck (Fortune): Personified chance; often courted by offerings or mocked by tricksters.

M

Magic: A system of rules and ruptures for channeling power through language, symbol, craft, and relationship. *See also: Ritual, Taboo.*

Mandate of Heaven: A divine license to rule that can be lost; use broadly for any sacred legitimacy story. *See also: Founder, Sovereignty Myth.*

Mirror Framework: Building hero and villain as a single process: shared origin, divergent choices, complementary wounds. The villain reveals what the hero can't face; the hero reveals what the villain lost. Neither exists without the other. *See also: Hero, Villain, Archetype.*

Monster: A being that tests boundaries, ecological, moral, or metaphysical, revealing what the world fears or needs. *See also: Bestiary, Undead, Hunger Principle.*

Motif: A recurring image or action (the forbidden door, the storm at sea) that carries meaning. *See also: Archetype.*

Myth: A foundational story a culture lives by. Not "false," but meaning-dense. *See also: Legend, Lore.*

Mythopoeia: Deliberate myth-making in modern works; your job, basically.

N

Nemesis: Retributive force that meets hubris mid-stride.

Numinous: The felt sense of the sacred; awe's texture.

O

Oath: A spoken binding with power, often sworn by name, place, or relic. Breaking it changes the world. *See also: Binding Oath, Geis.*

Omen: A sign read as meaningful about the future; risky if overused, potent if earned.

Oracle: The place or person through which the cosmos answers inconvenient questions. *See also: Divination.*

Origin Story: A specific creation of a people, city, order, or hero. *See also: Founding Myth.*

Otherworld: Any realm adjacent to the ordinary (fae mounds, dream seas, data heavens). *See also: Threshold, Axis Mundi.*

P

Pairing Principle: Every relic implies a sanctum; every sanctum hungers for a relic. Object and place are co-dependent — build one without the other and you've got a prop. The Mirror Framework's cousin, applied to things and the spaces that hold them. *See also: Relic, Sanctum, Mirror Framework.*

Pantheon: A society of deities with relationships, rivalries, and jurisdictions. *See also: Deity, Syncretism, Divine Spectrum.*

Patron Deity: A god tied to a place, craft, family, or cause who grants boons and asks for things in return.

Prophecy: A foretold pattern or warning that pressures choices rather than replacing them. At its most dangerous, prophecy is a living, contested force — communities argue over what it means, and the argument reshapes the world as much as the prophecy itself. *See also: Destiny.*

Psychopomp: A guide of souls between realms (gods, spirits, birds, algorithms). *See also: Afterlife, Underworld.*

Purification: Acts that restore right relation after taboo or corruption (washing, fasting, offerings).

Purgatory: A remedial afterlife state of cleansing or delay; use broadly for "not yet."

Q

Quest: A structured journey with tests, helpers, and costs that changes the seeker and their world. Every quest is a small apocalypse — the hero's old world ends so a new one can form. *See also: Hero, Relic, Scale Shift.*

R

Relic: An object saturated with story (bone, blade, book) that carries power and obligations. *See also: Talisman, Fetish Object, Pairing Principle.*

Reincarnation: Cyclical return of souls in new forms with memory thin or thick. *See also: Afterlife.*

Rite of Passage: Ritual transition between life stages or roles. *See also: Initiation, Festival.*

Ritual: Repeatable, rule-bound actions that reshape relationships between people, powers, and places. *See also: Magic.*

S

Sacrifice: Giving up something precious to seal a bond, pay a price, or open a door. *See also: Ritual, Relic.*

Sacred / Profane: The charged and set-apart vs. the ordinary; the line itself is part of the story.

Sanctum: A set-apart space for power to concentrate (temple, grove, server-shrine). *See also: Shrine, Genius Loci, Pairing Principle.*

Scale Shift: The continuum between personal quest and cosmic apocalypse. Every quest risks becoming an apocalypse if the stakes escalate; every apocalypse contains a personal quest at its core. The shift between scales is a design lever, not a genre boundary. *See also: Quest, Eschatology, Cycle.*

Shaman: A mediator who travels between realms for healing, counsel, or trouble. *See also: Psychopomp.*

Shape of the Cosmos: The large-scale geography a creation myth produces: underworlds, heavens, spirit roads, thresholds, forbidden zones. The act of making determines the architecture of what's made. *See also: Cosmic Cartography, Axis Mundi, Threshold, Otherworld.*

Shrine: A focused site of presence and exchange with a power (from hearth-niche to mountain cavern).

Sovereignty Myth: A story that legitimizes rule through union with land or deity.

Spirit: Non-human agent (ancestor, place-spirit, demon, algorithmic echo) with desires and limits. *See also: Genius Loci, Ghost, Divine Spectrum.*

Syncretism: The blending of deities and traditions into new forms (old gods wearing new clothes).

Symbol: A thing that carries layered meaning across scenes and rituals.

T

Taboo: A culturally charged "do not" that holds a system together; breaking it has real effects. *See also: Geis, Curse.*

Talisman: A carried object that protects, empowers, or marks membership; often ancestral. *See also: Relic.*

Theophany: A god's appearance or arrival; often dangerous. *See also: Hierophany.*

Threshold: A boundary or crossing point where rules change (doorways, borders, eclipse moments). *See also: Liminal, Otherworld.*

Totem: A representative animal/plant/spirit linked to a group's identity and duties.

Trickster: A boundary-breaker who exposes hypocrisy, forces change, and wins by wit. *See also: Liminal, Chaos, Villain.*

Tyrant: A power-hoarder whose rule reveals a system's cracks; the villain archetype of stagnation. *See also: Villain, Sovereignty Myth.*

U

Underworld: Realms of the dead, memory, or shadow; sometimes bleak, sometimes bustling. *See also: Afterlife.*

Undead: Beings who cross the line between life and death (ghosts, revenants, vampires, digital echoes), hungry for what the living can't give. *See also: Ghost, Revenant.*

Unity of Opposites: A design principle: paired forces (life/death, order/chaos) generate story energy.

V

Villain (Mythic Adversary): The story's necessary challenger who embodies a wound in the world or hero. Not "evil for evil's sake." *See also: Tyrant, Trickster, Worldbreaker, Mirror Framework.*

Veneration: Ongoing honoring of gods, ancestors, or places through offerings and memory.

Vision Quest: A deliberate, often risky, encounter with the numinous to gain power, name, or path.

Vow: See *Oath.*

W

World Tree: A vertical connector of realms (roots-underworld, trunk-world, branches-heavens). *See also: Axis Mundi.*

Worldbreaker: A villain archetype who would end or remake the world to resolve a perceived flaw. *See also: Villain, Eschatology, Scale Shift.*

Worship: Practical relationship with powers: gifts, songs, service, and negotiated favors. *See also: Patron Deity.*

X

Xenia (Sacred Hospitality): Reciprocal duties of host and guest; break it and gods notice. Useful for framing social ethics.

Y

Yggdrasil (as model): The Norse world tree; a famous Axis Mundi example. Use as inspiration, not a template. *See also: World Tree.*

Z

Zeitgeist (Mythic): The spirit-weather of an era; the background field your myths breathe.

Acknowledgments

To Janine. Your patience, your honesty, and your willingness to listen to one more explanation made this book possible. Everything I build has your fingerprints on it somewhere. To the readers and supporters of Gods and Monsters: you turned a daily writing habit into a community, and your questions, challenges, and enthusiasm shaped this book in ways you probably don't realize. Every chapter is better because someone in the comments asked the question I hadn't thought to ask myself. And to the tools (analog and digital, ancient and uncomfortably modern) that helped me research, draft, argue with, and refine these ideas over the course of a year. The forge needed more than one pair of hands, and I'm grateful for every one of them. Whatever you build with this toolkit, build it boldly. The old stories were never made alone, and neither was this one.

About the Author

Hannibal Hills is the creator of Gods and Monsters (godsandmonsters.info), one of the largest mythology encyclopedias on the web: a growing collection of over 2,300 entries covering gods, monsters, spirits, and mythical beings from more than 100 cultural traditions worldwide. His daily Substack, Mythology: Gods and Monsters, delivers myth to over 50,000 subscribers.

What started as a personal obsession with hunting down obscure myths grew into a years-long research project spanning every inhabited continent.

He lives in North Carolina, where the local folklore is underrated.

Continue the Journey

This book gave you the tools. The Substack gives you the raw material.

Every day at Gods and Monsters, a new myth lands in your inbox: gods, monsters, spirits, tricksters, and creatures drawn from traditions most mythology sites don't cover. Korean dragon kings. Maltese sea spirits. Ghanaian forest guardians. Basque mountain gods. Over 2,300 entries and growing.

Free subscribers get the daily Myth of the Day, one story, researched and retold, every morning.

Paid subscribers get weekly deep dives: long-form series on mythology-building, cultural analysis, and the craft of making stories that stick.

Join 50,000+ readers who've discovered that the old stories are anything but dead.

godsandmonstersinfo.substack.com

A Favour to Ask

If this book gave you something useful (a framework that clicked, an archetype that unlocked a character, a creative dare that actually dared you), I'd be grateful if you'd take two minutes to leave a short review on Amazon or Goodreads.

Reviews are how independent books find their readers. They don't need to be long or polished. A sentence or two about what worked for you is enough to help another writer, worldbuilder, or game master decide this book is worth their time.

Thank you for reading. Now go build something.